BACKSTORY

ALSO BY WILLIAM L. MYERS, JR.

Remi Bone

Philadelphia Legal Series

A Criminal Defense

An Engineered Injustice

A Killer's Alibi

A Criminal Justice

BACKSTORY

A PSYCHOLOGICAL THRILLER

WILLIAM L. MYERS, JR.

OCEANVIEW PUBLISHING
SARASOTA, FLORIDA

ISBN 978-1-60809-562-9

Published in the United States of America by Oceanview Publishing

Sarasota, Florida

www.oceanviewpub.com

10 9 8 7 6 5 4 3 2

PRINTED IN THE UNITED STATES OF AMERICA

This book is dedicated to Jacky Hunt

*Beloved teacher to generations of
kids at Holy Child School at Rosemont*

Generous friend, great neighbor

Fattener of dogs

Blame it or praise it, there is no denying the wild horse in us.

—VIRGINIA WOOLF, *Jacob's Room*

————

Everyone carries a shadow, and the less it is embodied in the

individual's conscious life, the blacker and denser it gets.

—CARL JUNG, *Psychology and Religion*

BACKSTORY

PROLOGUE

HE PULLS ONTO the dirt and gravel driveway and skids to a stop in front of the garage. The garage door is open, and Helen's car is sitting inside. He races to the driver's-side door. Helen is staring straight ahead through the windshield. She sits perfectly motionless, as though she has no idea he's standing next to her.

He raps on the window. After a moment, Helen slowly turns her head, looks up at him. Her eyes are flat and far away. He stares at her then moves around the back of the car to the passenger's side, opens the door, and climbs in. He shuts the door and they sit in silence.

"I looked everywhere for you," he says. "Called everyone we know."

She doesn't answer, just continues to stare through the windshield.

"Where were you?"

She sighs. "I went to a hotel."

He holds his breath. "Were you . . . alone?"

No answer.

"Helen?"

Another sigh. "No."

A kick in the gut. Still, he presses on. "Who?" The only word he can force out.

She turns to him. "My seducer."

BOOK I

GET OUT

CHAPTER ONE

THE FORCE OF his forehead's impact against the wall sends a shock wave into his jaw and teeth, reverberates into his cervical spine, forces the word "oh" from his mouth. The second blow makes him feel light-headed and brings on a wave of nausea. The third blow dims his consciousness, his sense of self. He becomes dizzy, loses his location in time and space. The nausea spikes and he doubles over, falls to his knees, and throws up. After a time—he doesn't know how long—he gets the sense that he's back on his feet, and moving, wobbling. From far away he hears a woman's voice. He sees a blurry figure approach him but can't make out her face, other than to see her mouth is moving. He hears sounds coming from her mouth and knows that she's talking to him, but he can't understand what she's saying. He feels a hand take hold of his upper arm. And the world goes black.

*   *   *

Get out. Run. Break free.

He hears the words through a fog of pain. He must have the mother of all hangovers because his head is pounding like a jackhammer. His throat burns and his mouth is filled with the sour taste of vomit. He desperately wants a drink. Something strong—a blended whiskey or a single malt scotch. The hair of the dog.

He opens his eyes and comes to in a swirl of activity. He's sitting at a table and there are three people standing over him. One is a large man, easily 6'4", and looking to go three hundred pounds. The second is a middle-aged woman with graying hair pulled into a bun on top of her head. The third person, a fireplug of a man with a thick neck, is wearing a uniform.

"How are you feeling?" says the big guy. He has a bald head, blue eyes, a fat nose. He's wearing an apron over a short-sleeve red shirt and blue jeans.

"I'm all right. Just a bad hangover."

"Hangover? I don't think so." The big bald guy draws closer, leans in toward him. "Here. Use this." He hands over a Ziploc bag full of ice wrapped in a cloth napkin. "I'll take that."

He realizes he's holding a paper napkin to his forehead. He removes it, sees through the haze that it's covered in blood. With his other hand, he touches his forehead, feels the lump. He feels dizzy, confused. "What's going on?"

"Someone smashed your head against a wall, is what." It's the man in the uniform.

"I found you outside," the woman tells him. "You were stumbling around in a daze and had blood all over the front of your forehead. So, I brought you in here and called 911. Deputy Trimble showed up."

"There's blood on the brick wall in the alley," the deputy says. "Can you describe your assailant? Was it someone you knew? Did you get into a fight? Or did they take you by surprise?"

He has no idea how to answer the deputy's questions. He has no memory of getting hurt.

"I don't think you'll need stitches," the large bald man says. "But you'll have a cut and a fat goose egg. Whoever smashed your head against the wall wasn't joking."

"You should see a doctor," the woman says.

They're all talking at him at once and it's too much. He closes his eyes and presses the icepack against his forehead. "I don't remember . . ."

"Then you definitely should seek medical care," the deputy says. "You could have a concussion." He pauses, then says, "You might've been mugged. Do you still have your wallet?"

He reaches around, feels the bulge in his back pocket. "It's still there."

"So, it was just an assault." The deputy thinks for a minute. "Can you think of anyone who'd want to hurt you?"

Before he has a chance to answer, the bald guy jumps in. "Who'd want to hurt Bob? Everyone loves him. And the whole town knows he's gone through so much these past weeks. Seems kinda unthinkable that someone would come after him."

"Well, in my report, I'm going to write this up as a likely assault." The deputy reaches into his pocket and says, "Here's my card. If you can remember anything about who did this to you, call me. Or, you can have Juke here call me."

He watches the deputy walk away and for the first time realizes he's sitting in a bar.

"Listen," says the big guy—Juke, according to the deputy. "You just sit here for a few minutes, take it easy. I'm going to do some things in the back, then I'll come out and take care of you. Take you to the hospital or a doctor if you want. Okay?"

He says sure and watches Juke walk away. His head is still pounding, and though the lump and the worst part of it is in the front, the throbbing circles the whole way around to the back. Is it possible, he wonders, that they're all right—that someone attacked him, drove his head into a brick wall? He tries to remember the assault but can't. Tries to recall what happened afterward but draws a blank on that, too. He closes his eyes and takes some deep breaths, then opens them.

He looks around, sees that it's a small neighborhood bar, the type of place where the walls glisten from decades of beer and sweat and working-class gripes. There are half a dozen tables and the bar itself, which is made of dark wood that matches the walls and the floor. Behind the bar are the usual shelves holding liquor bottles—the cheap stuff at the bottom, good stuff on top. There might be a billiard room in the back, or a space with a big round table for poker or something. He doesn't know.

Has he ever been in this place before? He doesn't remember, though the big guy, Juke, seems to know plenty about him. *He's gone through so much* . . . whatever that means.

He glances toward the back of the bar and spots the woman who said she brought him inside, now sitting at a table by herself. She smiles at him and he smiles back, but she doesn't seem familiar. He tries to search his brain for any instances where they'd crossed paths before, but all he can pull up is blackness. It's like his mind is devoid of all memory, other than what's transpired in the past few minutes. Hell, he doesn't know his own *name*.

Juke said it was *Bob* . . .

"Bob." He repeats the name, to see if it fits, but feels nothing. How can that be? It finally occurs to him that he must be suffering temporary amnesia from the blow to his head. How else to explain why he can't remember anything?

Get out. Run. Break Free.

The words again. A warning. He feels his stomach tighten. He is obviously in danger. But from whom? Whoever assaulted hm, for sure. But if they really wanted to hurt him, why did they stop? Did someone come along and interrupt them, scare them away? Or did he fight them off? He looks down at his hands. His knuckles aren't bruised.

"Hey."

He looks to his right, sees a man in a blue security guard's uniform. His nameplate says Corchado, so that must be the man's name.

"Mind if I join you?" Corchado says, taking a seat. The security guard has brown hair, dull eyes, and a nose that looks like it's been repositioned a time or two. The guard puzzles at the compress he's holding against his head. "What happened to you?"

"They tell me I was attacked."

Corchado stares at him. "What? By who?"

He shakes his head. He doesn't know.

The security guard studies him, then shrugs. After a minute, he wipes his brow. "Man, it's hot outside. I mean, I know it's July, but three straight weeks of ninety-five plus?"

"Probably that global warming." A woman approaches them, smiling. She's young and pretty in her t-shirt and khaki shorts. Bob figures she's the waitress.

"Hi, Dave," the waitress says to Corchado. "Hi, Bob. Are you okay? Juke told me someone hurt you."

"I'll be fine," he says.

"Can I get you anything?"

"A Coors Light for me," Corchado says.

"Make it two," Bob says.

Corchado chuckles. "I don't think so. You've been clean and sober going on ten years now."

Clean and sober? He's an alcoholic? He wonders what made him give it up, and an image comes to his mind of him waking up on a park bench, naked, his chest splattered with vomit, awakened by a poke in the chest from a cop who wasn't happy about it. When *was* that? And what's happened in his life since then? Not knowing the answers is making him feel nervous. That, and the acute sense that he's in danger.

"Just a Coke," he says.

Corchado watches the waitress walk away, then turns back to him. "I'm so sorry about Helen. She was a sweet lady. A gentle soul. You never know why people do it."

Helen? *Helen.*

He is suddenly flooded with grief, and has a hard time catching his breath. He sees himself sitting numbly in the first pew of a church, a coffin in the aisle next to him. Helen was his wife, and she swallowed a bottle of pills, took her own life. This is what Juke meant about him going through so much in the past few weeks. So, Helen's suicide was recent. Is that why he can't remember? Was he suffering traumatic amnesia even before someone banged his head against the wall?

He starts tapping his foot against the floor, tapping his hand against his knee under the table. He feels jittery, the loss of recall starting to stress him out.

Get out. Run. Break free.

"Hey, are you okay?" Corchado leans forward, reaches across the table, wraps his meaty palm around his forearm. The waitress reappears and Corchado asks her to fetch a glass of water to go with the Coke.

"I guess you haven't been getting much sleep," Corchado says.

He searches his mind for memories of Helen, but can retrieve nothing. He can't see her happy, can't see her sad. What was Helen's mental state the last days of her life? The last few weeks? Did she exhibit signs of what was coming? Signs that he failed to see because he was too wrapped up in himself? Or were the signs so subtle no one would have picked up on them? Was it her plan to surprise him? Cripple him with shock. Did his wife hate him?

"Bob? Bob?"

He hears Corchado's voice from far away.

"You want me to drive you home?" Corchado asks.

"No," he answers. "I'm good. I'm parked outside." *Or am I?*

Corchado stands, pats him on the shoulder. "Listen, don't spend too much time alone. It's not good for you. Any time you want, you call me, and I'll come over. Take you out to a movie. Or a ball game. Whatever. Okay?"

He says sure, sure. Corchado leaves and the waitress returns. She hands him a second glass of water and he notices the first glass is empty. He must've drunk it while he was zoned out.

"Are you hungry?" she asks.

"What's your name?"

She laughs. "Good one, Bob."

So, they know each other. But how?

"You know me, always the joker," he says.

She frowns. "Uh, that is *not* how I'd describe you."

He's an asshole then? A serious guy who gets in your face?

"I think I do want something to eat," he says. "How about . . . how about . . ."

"You don't even have to say it. A crying cow."

"Crying cow?"

"Burger with onions," she says. "But you know that."

He wants to tell her he doesn't know shit; instead, something else occurs to him. As she walks away, he reaches for his back pocket, pulls out his wallet. The name on his driver's license is J. Robert Hunter.

He stares at the picture. He has jet-black hair and a strong, square face with dark eyes. The license says he is six feet tall, weighs 185, and is forty-one years old.

He sits back in his chair. "Forty-one." He's not sure how he feels about that. His wild years are long behind him. Behind him, too, is his marriage, it seems, to a woman named Helen. A woman Dave Corchado said was sweet. A gentle soul. He closes his eyes and tries to concentrate on her. A pair of warm blue eyes comes into focus. Smiling eyes. But he can't hold onto them and after a while he opens his own eyes again. When he does, a woman is standing in front of him. She's good-looking. Tall, athletically thin. Long hair. She has the beginnings of crow's feet, meaning she's probably close to his age. There's a bracelet on her left wrist with the initials *K.C.*, and he remembers somehow that her name is Karen but she goes by *Casey*.

She takes a seat at the table without asking and glances around to see if anyone's watching. He spies a wedding ring on her finger.

"I'm sorry I haven't stopped by your house," Casey says. "I should've come around, brought you some food. That's the normal thing to do when . . ."

"When someone dies." He completes her sentence.

"Helen's funeral was beautiful," she says. "The church was full. Everyone loved her."

"She was a sweet and gentle soul."

"Half the pews were filled with children," she says, and he suddenly recalls that his wife was an elementary school teacher. He remembers her curled up on their couch, grading papers, affixing them with blue, red, and gold stars. He can see the papers, the stars, the sofa, Helen's pajamas. But he still can't find her face.

He and Casey sit quietly for a few moments. Then she asks him what his plans are. "Will you go back east?"

He says he doesn't know what he's going to do, wondering what she means by "back east." Did he come here from New York? Washington? The Carolinas?

They sit staring at each other until Casey says, "Damn, it's stifling in here."

He realizes now just how warm it is inside the bar. It must be eighty-five degrees, even with the air-conditioning and ceiling fans he's just now noticing.

A memory sneaks into his mind. He's lying in bed with Helen. It's a hot night and all they have covering them is a sheet. He's in his boxers and nothing more. He's just woken up in the middle of the night, to the sound of Helen crying. She is on her side, facing away from him.

"What's the matter, sweetheart?"

"It's so dark, Bob. Just so dark."

He wraps his arm around her. "Don't worry, I'll protect you."

"Bob?"

He's back at the bar. Casey is leaning across the table again, her hands covering his own. Her voice low, she says, "If you want, I could come over some evening this week. Tom's working nights now."

A picture of Tom forms in his mind. A thick-necked good old boy with narrow-set eyes beneath an overhanging forehead. He wonders how someone as good-looking as Casey ended up with such a Neanderthal.

"It would be just like old times." Casey smiles.

And now he sees the two of them in the back seat of an SUV. Teenagers tearing off each other's clothes. His heart is pounding in his chest. His dick is so hard it hurts. He fumbles with the condom, his hands shaking. This will be his first time. Casey lies back in the seat and spreads her legs and he climbs on top of her. He slides into her and *Christ* it feels so good. Warm and wet and tight. They kiss passionately as they screw, jamming their tongues into each other's mouths. It's over quickly.

"What grade were we in?" he asks.

"I was in ninth. You were a sophomore. Your mom brought you and Jimmy the year before. And you left to go back east in June, after school ended. We had six months. Happiest days of my life." Casey gives him a sad smile.

"Jimmy . . ." he says, realizing that he has, or had, a brother.

"So different from you," she says. "It always surprised me, given that you were twins."

Twins? Identical or fraternal? He searches his memory for snippets of his brother, his mother, but comes up empty. What did they look like? Where are they now? He has no idea.

He refocuses on Casey and finds her staring at him.

"So," she says. "What about my proposal, about getting together?"

He looks away and she removes her hands, sits back. "I'm such an ass," she says. "Of course, you're not ready. It's too soon."

He looks at her, studies her. "And you're married."

Her face tightens. "Don't judge me, Bob. You weren't exactly a saint while Helen was alive."

He sees another image of him and Casey. This time as grownups. They're in an alley. He has her up against a wall. His zipper is open and she's wearing a short dress. She's drunk and so is he—so much for ten years clean and sober.

"I made some mistakes, but I loved my wife," he says, wondering if it's true. Wondering how many times he and Casey got together while he was married to Helen.

Casey jumps up, embarrassed, lifts her handbag. "Please, just . . . forget about this. It didn't happen."

He watches her slink away. She lets the door slam behind her.

His food arrives and he launches into the burger. The meat is red and juicy and some of the blood dribbles down his chin. It's so damned good and he's suddenly ravenous.

He makes quick work of the burger and gets to wondering whether, before he was assaulted, it was his intention to enter the bar. That wouldn't seem to make sense, him being a reformed alcoholic. Unless he's missing something. Which he likely is given that his brain seems to be missing *everything.*

"I saw you were talking to Casey Colleran."

He recognizes the baritone voice as belonging to the big bald man named Juke.

"Sorry it took me a little longer than I thought it would," Juke says. He takes off his apron and sits down at the table. "Be careful of Casey. Rumor is she runs around on Tom. Man, I'd hate for him to catch on. You know what a mean sombitch he is. He'd bust her up bad if he ever caught her stepping out on him."

"Hey, Juke, are we getting any more bottled Coors Light in this week?" It's the waitress.

Juke asks her to bring him something on draft. Then he turns back to Bob. "How's your head? You want to go to the hospital? I'll take you right now."

His head is pounding, but something tells him not to see any doctors. He'd have to admit he can't remember anything, and, for some reason, he gets the strong sense that would expose him to even more danger than he's already in.

"Let me see how I do," he tells Juke. "I'll sleep on it and if it's still bad in the morning, I'll go to the doctor."

Juke sits back and studies him, and he can see the big man is trying to decide whether to push the issue of medical treatment.

Apparently deciding not to, Juke leans forward again, just in time to accept the mug brought by the waitress. The glass is sweating and a thick head of foam extends just above the rim. Bob wants nothing more than to have a beer himself—or maybe a shot of Jameson's—but he remembers what Juke said about him being sober for ten years and contents himself with his Coke.

Juke throws back the glass, then uses his forearm to wipe the extra foam from his mouth. "So, the assault aside, how're you holding up this week?"

He has no idea. "I'm okay."

"You want to go out on Sunday? I got the second Merc running."

The reference to the second Merc tells him Juke has a boat with twin Mercury engines, one of which has been on the fritz. The image of a white-hulled Sportsman Masters with a center console and a pair of three-hundred-horsepower outboard motors pops into his mind. Juke is driving and Bob's seated next to Juke. They are on Pomona Lake, which he remembers is an hour south and east, across I-70 then down US-75. There's no wind, so the water is flat, and they're skating across it. That was two weeks ago, he recalls now. Neither one of them catches anything but they have an okay time anyway . . . until Juke breaks down crying.

"I just can't believe my baby sister is gone," Juke sobs but eventually quiets down as they get to baiting their hooks. "This is the only place I can do it," Juke confides. "Lose control."

Suddenly he remembers why he's in a bar at all. Juke owns the place and Helen was Juke's sister. He comes to Juke's place to be close to someone who misses Helen as much as he does. He comes here to share his pain.

He responds to Juke's invitation to go out on the lake. "No. I think I'm just going to stay home this weekend. Maybe clear out some things."

He sees Juke's eyes moisten and he knows it's because the *things* he's going to clear out are Helen's things. He sees her closet now, the dresses and blouses and slacks all hung neatly, the shoes boxed or displayed in little square cubbies installed by California Closets. Helen was a neatnik, he remembers. Him, not so much—he recalls that now, too, and his mind starts to play movie clips of him and Helen squabbling about the state of his closet, about him leaving dishes in the sink, dropping the Sunday paper on the floor by his chair. He sees Helen standing in front of him, her arms crossed. She's wearing jean shorts and a t-shirt that highlight her petite figure. He still can't see her face, though.

"I have to go home," he says, overtaken by a sudden urge to see the home he shared with Helen. He stands and pats Juke on the shoulder, and as he does so, it hits him that between the two of them—him and Juke—he's always been the alpha. "You take care," he tells Juke, who is crying openly now. So much for the big guy's claim that the only place he loses control is on his boat.

CHAPTER TWO

He lets the door close behind him as he exits "Juke's Place," the name on the sign in front. Overhead, the sun blazes in a cloudless sky. There is no breeze and the stagnant air bakes the cracked asphalt roadway.

He shields his eyes and takes in the street. It's a typical small-town Main Street, down to its name, which he spies on the sign on the corner. Directly across the street from the bar is a men's clothing store featuring suited mannequins in its window. The dummies wear western-style boots.

Next to the men's store is another shop displaying kitchen cabinets in its window, and next to it is a small bookstore, then a hardware store that proudly displays a large American flag. There's also a consignment shop, a women's boutique clothing store, an art gallery, and a pharmacy. The sidewalks look new and are lined with trees, and he remembers something on the news about an ongoing state-wide main-street revitalization project.

All the buildings along the far side of Main Street are two- and three-story red brick structures, clones of the buildings on the same side of the street as Juke's Place. A short distance behind the buildings on the far side of the street, a church tower pokes toward the sky. Closer, and directly behind the hardware store, stands a water tower, a spider supported by four spindly steel legs.

He doesn't know how many streets run parallel to Main, but he suspects not many. It's a small town he lives in, assuming this is his town. For all he knows, he could live two towns over, or on a farm.

He glances up and down the street again and, for the first time, notices a dark gray sedan, a Chrysler 300, with tinted windows parked across the street about a half a block down. He can tell that the engine is running, and he gets the strange feeling that whoever's inside is watching him. He stares at the car, trying to see the driver through the windshield, but the top half is tinted, and he can't make out the driver's face. After a couple seconds, the car starts to pull out of the parking spot. Bob steps off the curb onto the road and watches as the car approaches him. It slows as it gets next to him and the thought crosses his mind that the driver is his assailant, that he'd meant to kill him in the alley and now intends to shoot him dead in the street.

But the car moves past him and, when it does, he exhales. He watches the car continue down Main Street and, more than ever, feels the urgent need to get home. But where? And how?

He reaches into one of the front pockets of his jeans and pulls out a key fob with a Ford symbol. There are no Fords parked on the street, so he looks behind him, toward the bar, and sees a narrow alley. He figures there might be a parking lot behind the bar, and he starts toward the alley. Something stops him though—a pressure in his chest that makes him afraid. But he pushes ahead into the alley. About halfway down, he spots blood on the bricks at a level even with his forehead. The pressure in his chest increases and he turns and strides quickly past it.

In back he finds a parking lot large enough for a couple dozen cars. Only a few are parked there now, but one of them is a white F-150 that's seen better days. He presses the key fob and the truck's headlights flash.

Inside the truck, he doesn't have to adjust the driver's seat or the mirrors. This is his truck, all right. He starts the engine, then sits back in his seat, wondering, where to? He pulls out his driver's license again and sees that his address is 400 Stonehill Drive in Kournfield, Kansas.

"The middle of nowhere." He says the words aloud and that's how he feels—like he's in a void. The Twilight Zone. The Outer Limits.

Glancing again at the driver's license, he wonders where Stonehill Drive is, how to get there. Then he sees the Navigation App on the center console and presses it. Once the Nav screen is up, he presses the destination button and then a button for "home." A map appears and the Nav screen tells him he lives twelve miles away. He leaves town by way of Main Street, which turns into State Road 99 outside of town. He follows it for fifteen miles until the Nav system tells him to turn right onto Stonehill Drive, which turns out to be a country road wide enough for two cars to pass carefully, adjacent to Lake Wabaunsee. After a quarter mile, he approaches a stone and gravel driveway and the Nav system's female voice announces that, "You have arrived."

His house turns out to be a log and stone cabin on a half-acre, sloping, lakefront lot. A detached two-car garage sits next to the house, which has a small front porch beneath an angled canopy. The cabin has a red door with one window to the right and two to the left. Thick trees act as a privacy barrier between the cabin and the neighboring homes to the left and right.

"So, Helen and I were recluses," he says, not sure whether to chuckle or cringe. He doesn't know enough about his life yet to know how to feel about it. Other than his grief for Helen . . .

Something tells him that pain will sharpen once he enters the home he shared with her.

He takes a deep breath to steel himself, then opens the front door into a large living room with a cathedral ceiling and a big bay window looking out onto a wooden deck and the lake below. To the right of the living room are a dining room and a kitchen. The left side of the living room opens to a hallway, which he figures leads to the bedrooms. He considers exploring the rest of the house, but decides to face the reckoning. The living room has a brick fireplace with a wooden mantel. On top of the mantel are framed photographs. He takes a deep breath.

Three hesitant steps take him to the mantel, and there she is—the sweet, gentle soul described by Dave Corchado. A petite blond with kind blue eyes and a shy smile.

The picture opens a door in his mind and he finds himself at Juke's Place. It's early on a Friday night, before the weekend crowd arrives, and the bar is only about half full. Juke is in the back room, counting stock, muttering to himself.

Standing behind the bar, he fills a mug with beer from one of the taps, hands it to a guy who leaves a fiver and returns to a table. The door to the bar opens and a pretty woman with blond hair and blue eyes walks in. She glances around the room, nervously it seems to him, then approaches the bar. She smiles shyly, introduces herself as Helen, Juke's sister. He tells her to take a seat. "I'll pour you something. What do you want? Beer? Wine?"

She shakes her head, thanks him, and asks if he would fetch Juke from the back room. He says sure and excuses himself. Juke turns out to be in the basement and he shouts down the steep wooden steps to him. Juke says he'll be up shortly.

When he returns, Helen is still standing, holding her handbag and looking out of place in the bar. This surprises him. It's her brother's bar, certainly she's been here before.

"Sure you don't want something to drink?"

She shakes her head no again. "I'll only be here for a minute."

He shrugs.

At the end of the bar are two twenty-somethings. Both are wearing jeans and work boots. One has a *Nuke the Whales* t-shirt. The other's shirt is a faded tribute to the Red Hot Chili Peppers. Knuckleheads. He notices them taking turns glancing at Helen.

The whale guy, the tougher looking one, whispers into his friend's ear, then turns to Helen. "Have a seat, sweetheart. I'll buy you a drink."

Helen looks away.

"Come on," the pepper-head presses. "You can make it a double."

"The lady doesn't want to be bothered," Bob tells them.

Both the guys laugh and Whale Boy makes a snide remark under his breath. Bob walks over to them, feeling Helen's eyes following him. He flattens his gaze, puts on his serious face, plants himself in front of the slack-jaws. "Are we going to have a problem?"

Whale Boy smiles and he can see the gears grinding in his head as he tries to decide whether to say something smart.

"There's no problem," Whale Boy says at last. Then, to his friend, "Come on, let's play some pool."

He watches them disappear into the back room, then turns to Helen. "Sorry about that. This place draws a mixed crowd."

Helen seems to study him for a moment, then moves up to the bar, takes a seat. "I think I'll have a drink, after all," she says. "A glass of white wine, please."

Bob's memory leaps ahead to a conversation with Juke sometime after he and Helen started dating. They're in the back, stocking shelves, and Juke turns to him.

"In all the years I've owned this place," Juke says, "the night Helen met you was maybe the second time she actually sat at the bar. I asked her how come she stayed. She told me you made her feel safe."

The memory jars Bob, though he doesn't know why. He turns away from the fireplace, from the pictures of Helen, and moves through the dining room to the kitchen. The tile on the kitchen floor is wearing, but not overly so, and the cabinets could use painting but don't cry out for replacement. He opens the refrigerator and finds it jammed with casserole dishes—undoubtedly brought to him by friends and neighbors in the wake of his wife's death.

The hallway on the other side of the living room leads to two bedrooms furnished in traditional American and a small home office with a metal filing cabinet and metal desk. A set of steps leads to the lower level, which has its own deck and contains a third bedroom with a gas fireplace and its own bath, and, on the other side of the bedroom, a workout room with free weights, a universal gym, a heavy bag, and a speed bag. Three sets of boxing gloves hang by their strings on a rack screwed into the drywall.

He approaches the speed bag, raises his arms and hands and starts in on it, discovering that he is able to command the bag the way boxers do in the movies. He keeps at it until he's sweating freely. Then he moves to the heavy bag and, without thinking, swings his right leg up and around, landing a kick above his shoulder level.

I know how to kickbox?

There's a mirror on the wall opposite the bags and he walks over to it and removes his shirt. He's ripped, not an ounce of fat anywhere and six-pack abs. And there are scars. A long one traversing his abdomen just below his chest that looks like it was made by a slashing knife. A similar scar, though smaller, running vertically. And a round scar the size of a penny three inches to the right of his belly button.

So, he's a tough guy. Tough enough, apparently, to survive a knife fight and a bullet. He wonders where he learned to fight. Wonders what he'd done that ended him up getting cut and shot. Who he'd pissed off. Or was he the one who'd been upset and gone after somebody else? He itches to know the answers, but what he'd love even more is to know why he doesn't know. Why his memory is a jigsaw puzzle with most of the pieces missing. Something tells him the blow to the head isn't to blame for his memory loss.

"Who the hell am I?" He stares into his eyes, and his words cut a small hole in his brain fog, revealing a snippet of memory that starts with him standing in the dark with some other men. He can't tell where they are and he can't see the other men clearly. But he can hear himself talk.

"I brought the money," he says to one of the men. More words are exchanged, but he can't hear them clearly. Then someone points a gun at him and fires.

Back in his workout room, he feels adrenalin surging through his chest.

"Shit."

He paces the room, but his anxiety doesn't lessen, so he decides to work off the excess energy. Loading the long bar with weights, he bench-presses until his chest and arms burn. He does overhead presses, uses the dumbbells to work out his biceps, triceps, does squats and sit-ups. Then it's back to the heavy bag and speed bag. He has a whole routine, it turns out, and he does it by rote.

By the time he's done working out, his wounded head is throbbing, his heart is thumping hard. He goes upstairs to the kitchen, packs more ice into the icepack he'd left on the table. Then he heats up one of the casseroles in the microwave and shovels the food into his mouth until the dish is empty. It's chicken with broccoli and rotini and it tastes so fucking good it's like the first time he's ever eaten chicken casserole.

He takes a long shower, dries off, puts on a pair of boxers, and enters the bedroom he'd shared with Helen. Something opens in his mind, and he sees Helen standing at the altar with him, in her white wedding gown, remembers them dancing at their small reception at Juke's Place. Then he floats next to her along the lazy river encircling the Marriott in Aruba, both of them sipping piña coladas under a cloudless sky.

The memory ends with them standing side by side on the terrace of their hotel room. He's wearing cargo shorts with no shirt. Helen is in a thin yellow skirt. His hand is around Helen's waist as they gaze quietly at a black sky filled with twinkling stars, their tanned skin brushed by a gentle breeze. He turns his head to smell her hair. Then he bends over and lifts her, carries her into their room, Helen giggling the whole way to the bed.

The memory fades and after a few minutes he finds himself in his home office, staring at the laptop on the desk. He opens the lid and powers it up. The home screen appears and asks him for a password.

"Shit."

He sits in front of the screen and thinks. Then he smiles. He types in *Helen* and the laptop boots up. He opens Google and searches *Amnesia*. The first thing that pops up is a definition of amnesia as a memory deficit that can be caused by brain damage, disease, or certain sedatives and hypnotic drugs. He learns there are generally three types of adult amnesia: retrograde, antero-grade, and transient global amnesia—TGA. Retrograde is the inability to pull up existing, previously stored memories. An-terograde amnesia is where memories fail to form in the first place due to trauma. TGA involves confusion or agitation over the course of several hours, seizure-like activity, or a brief block-ing of the blood vessels supplying oxygen to the brain.

He reads for a while and decides at first that he's likely experi-encing some form of retrograde amnesia, which, according to the medical articles, can be caused by trauma to the head. Still, the question persists whether having one's head banged against a wall can cause someone to completely forget who they are.

His doubts take him to a fourth type of amnesia in adults, called dissociative amnesia, caused by severe trauma or stress. Diagnosis is based on history after the other causes of amnesia are ruled out. The worst form of dissociative amnesia is general-ized dissociative amnesia, which involves someone forgetting their identity and life history. It's most common among combat veterans, sexual assault victims, and people under extreme stress or conflict. Onset is usually sudden.

He sits back in his chair. Generalized dissociative amnesia—that's him. He hasn't merely forgotten an event or a select time period in his life: he has completely lost his identify, his life history. So, what in hell was it—what was the trauma—that caused him to lose himself? His mind takes him back to the brief memory of the man pointing a gun at him and firing, and to the acute sense that he remains in danger. Those same words keep repeating in his head: *Get out. Run. Break Free.*

He rises from the desk and walks to the bathroom, stands in front of the mirror. He studies the lump on the front of his head again; its bigger than it was at the bar, and it's starting to turn purple. There's a gash in the center, but it's no longer bleeding, and it doesn't look like it will take any stitches. He removes his shirt to confirm that he has no fresh cuts or scars, let alone a fresh bullet hole. He sighs and returns to the bedroom he shared with Helen. This time, when he walks in, he sees Helen sitting in the dark in a straight-backed chair in the corner of the room. The blinds are closed and the drapes are drawn on both windows. He pulls up a second chair and sits behind her. Helen doesn't acknowledge him, and, for a while, he doesn't say anything, just watches her, watches over her. Then, he leans forward, places his right hand on her shoulder, and talks quietly into her ear.

The memory fades and he's left staring at their empty bed. His bottom lip starts to quiver, and his chest fills with grief. He walks to Helen's closet, pulls out a blouse, then opens her bureau and takes a pair of blue jeans. He arranges the clothes on the bed as though she were lying in them, then lies down beside them.

CHAPTER THREE

WHEN HE AWAKENS the next morning, Saturday, his eyes sting with salt and he lumbers to the bathroom sink to splash water on them. When he dries off, he studies his forehead. It has a melon on it with a red wound running vertically down the middle.

The most painful part of his body, though, isn't his head, but his heart, which is heavy with grief. His wife has been gone for three weeks now and he surely has been grieving her all that time, but his grief feels as sharp as if he'd just found out Helen was dead. Is that normal? He doesn't know; he's never lost someone before.

Or has he?

He balls his fists. "Jesus Christ." How can he not know whether he's ever had to face the death of someone he loved? "What the hell happened to me?"

He returns to the bedroom, throws on a button-down shirt and some jeans, then heads to the kitchen and makes himself some coffee. Hungry but in no mood to fix breakfast, he walks to the small home office and sits at the desk. Maybe if he looks through his and Helen's records, he can figure out who he is, and what happened to cause him to lose his memory. In the bottom drawer, he finds some hanging files and begins reading through them. He learns that he and Helen bought their cabin seven years ago. The F-150 he bought new about two and a half years ago. Apparently, they also own a Ford Focus, which he expects he'll find sitting in the garage because he can't imagine himself selling Helen's car so soon after her death. Helen's death certificate shows she was thirty-six when she died and their marriage certificate tells him they were hitched nine years ago when Helen was twenty-seven and he was thirty-two. He finds no records showing that either of them had been wedded before, but a memory injects itself into his mind of Helen telling him that she had in fact been married right out of college, but that it fell apart after a year when she caught her husband cheating on her. A related memory comes to him of Juke telling him that Helen's first husband was a piece of shit and that Juke had clobbered him, broken his nose, when he found out what the prick had done to his little sister.

He comes across other records—credit card bills, car inspection reports, receipts from restaurants and stores. But nothing giving him any real insight into who he is.

He gets antsy and leaves the office, walks outside to the deck off the living room and stares out at the lake. At the edge of the property, there's a dock leading to a boathouse. Does he own a boat? Is it a motorboat like Juke's or does he sail? Or does he canoe? Kayak?

The air is hot and still and he spots an American flag hanging limply on a pole in his backyard. He fixes on it for a while, then raises his eyes to the sky. There are no clouds and he can see the sky stretching forever in all directions. Yet he feels there is more empty space inside him than above.

He leaves the house from the lower level, walks to the boathouse. Inside is a twelve-foot, flat-bottom boat, hanging from chains. The white paint on the wood hull is faded, chipped, and peeling and he gets the sense it hasn't been used in a long time. Hanging from wood dowels on the wall are two orange vests. He glances at the boat again, his eyes blinded by sunlight reflected from the water.

It's a pleasant early afternoon in May and he and Helen are out on the small lake. They are sitting on the two center seats of the boat, facing each other, a picnic lunch set out between them. There is a mild breeze and the water laps gently against the hull. Helen's long blond hair shimmers in the sunlight. He must have just said something funny, because Helen is laughing. Her smile is wide, her eyes are filled with light. He throws his head back and laughs, closing his eyes as he does so. When he opens them again, Helen's hair is shorter, duller, her face drawn, her eyes lifeless. The temperature is in the eighties, but she sits hunched over, as though to protect herself from cold air.

"This was a bad idea," she says, almost inaudibly. "Please take me back. Take me back."

The juxtaposition of the two memories jars him and he leaves the boathouse. He returns to the house and spends a couple hours in the workout room, lifting weights, jumping rope, focusing his concentration with the speed bag, exhausting himself on the heavy bag. A few more recollections dribble into his brain like the first drops of a rainstorm. He sees himself and Helen sharing meals on the back deck. He sees them cuddled together on the sofa, watching movies on Netflix, sees himself playing baseball with a bunch of guys while Helen and some other wives sit on the benches and cheer them on.

But how is he feeling inside? That's the other big question. Even when he is able to locate memories, he can't seem to locate how he *felt* about anything. Was he happy, contented, on the couch with Helen, on the lake with her, or was he a captured cat itching for freedom? He can see the look on his face, but not what's behind it.

That night, he sits at the small picnic table on the upper deck, eating a casserole, when his brain offers up a troubling memory. He and a second guy are shoving a third man along, next to some railroad tracks. They stop and a fourth man approaches. The faces of the three men with him are out of focus, but the eyes of the fourth man are crystal clear. They are predator's eyes. Reptilian.

He and the reptile talk to the third man, who is weeping, pleading for his life. After a few minutes, Bob pulls out a gun, shoots the pleading man in the knee. The scene falls out of focus for a minute, and when it sharpens again, the pleading man is lying dead on the ground. The man with the reptile eyes turns to him and says, "Now you're all in."

An idea comes to him and he walks into the house, through the living room, down the hall to the bedroom. He stares at the bed for a minute, then reaches between the mattress and box spring. Feeling around, his hands find a hard object and he pulls it out. It's a gun. Not a revolver, but an automatic. He ejects the clip, then the bullet that's in the chamber. Holding the gun, he finds that it feels familiar in his hand. More than familiar—it feels good. He inhales the gun's smell, the oil, and powder, and remembers that he's always liked that smell. He inserts the clip, chambers a bullet. Turning the weapon in his hand, memories flash into his mind of him pointing this same gun at targets in a firing range. Another image slips into his mind, too, of him pointing another gun down a dark alley, toward a fleeing shadow, and pulling the trigger. He feels the recoil and the memory ends. He tries to recall the memory, see how it played out, but is unable to do so, and this frustrates him. Surely shooting at someone would be a significant event, something he would remember. How is it that his recall stops before the climax? Did he in fact shoot someone down? Was this so traumatic that his brain has suppressed it? He asks the last question but he already knows the answer, from his other memory of shooting the man on the railroad tracks. Shooting people wasn't traumatic for him; it was a normal part of his life.

He has the sudden urge to return to the workout room, pump a few slugs into the heavy bag. But he dismisses the idea. A neighbor might hear the shots and call the police. If they did, there'd be questions. Like, why was he firing a gun in his house? Is he sure it's a good idea to have a gun right now, the cops would ask, given that he'd just lost his wife? They'd suggest he give the weapon to a friend to hold for him until he's not so upset.

This last idea rubs him the wrong way. He would never give up his gun. Never leave himself so vulnerable.

Vulnerable to what? To whom?

That night, he finds himself sitting on the couch watching *Saturday Night Live* when a memory slithers between his ears. It is late at night and Helen is long asleep. He slips out of bed, tiptoes down the steps to the workout room, and walks out onto the lower deck. He carries his cellphone and, once he's outside, punches in a number.

"It's me," he says. He listens as the person on the other end talks. Then—and this is the strange part—he says, "I assume I'm still dead." He nods. "Good. Thanks, Richie. You'll let me know if that changes?" He smiles, sadly, it seems. "Good," he says again, then he hangs up and walks inside.

Back on the couch watching *SNL*, he sits up, gently presses the lump on his forehead, which is finally shrinking. Who is

Richie? And what in the hell did that mean, about him being dead? He thinks on this, then reaches to the coffee table and picks up his cellphone. He doesn't know why he hasn't thought of it before, but it hits him that he should look at his texts and emails, reconstruct who he's been in touch with. He presses the messages icon and finds a text from Juke asking if he's okay. But that's it. There are no texts from anyone else. Opening his email app, he finds only a few junk emails and an email from the funeral home with a bill attached. So, he's not a guy who uses his phone for anything other than calling. He leans forward to place the cellphone back on the table, then changes his mind and pulls up his telephone contacts list. To his surprise, the phone demands a password to access the list.

"What the . . ." He punches in Helen's name but it's rejected. The same thing happens when he types in "Bob." Why would he be so secretive about his contacts?

His mind skips back to the scene where he's standing with men in the dark and one of them aims a pistol at him and fires. This time, he hears himself yelling, panicked, "I brought the money! The suitcase is in the car. We're even." But the guy shoots him anyway.

*   *   *

When he wakes up Sunday, he feels a breeze blowing through the bedroom window. Through the window, he sees clouds starting to form and he realizes that the prolonged heat wave must have broken overnight. He glances toward the night table, sees the pistol lying next to his wallet. Did Helen know he kept a gun under their mattress? Did he ever discuss with her his reasons for doing so? He sits up, takes the gun and stuffs it back between the mattress and box spring, then heads for the bathroom.

An hour later, after wolfing down some fried eggs and a short stack of pancakes, he's inside the boathouse. He finds a pair of splintery wooden oars lying on the floor. They are covered in dust and cobwebs and he takes a few minutes cleaning them off before loading them into the boat. He tosses an orange life vest into the boat, too, and stands for a few minutes before a pair of fishing rods supported horizontally on the wall by dowel rods hammered into a beam. A tackle box sits below the rods and he considers loading the box and a rod onto the boat. He decides not to because his plan isn't to fish for dinner, but for memories. Yesterday, two scenes of Helen and him out on the boat popped into his mind; he figures that if he goes out on the lake, he might be rewarded with more memories.

He studies the chains from which the rowboat is suspended for a few minutes, then starts lowering the boat into the water. Once it's floating, he leaves the boathouse, walks down to the boat, unhooks it from the chains, and climbs in. Lake Wabaunsee is a small, man-made lake, and it takes him no time to row out to the middle. He drops anchor and sits quietly, scanning the shoreline, hoping those lost memories will bubble up from the lakebed and find their way to his brain. Half an hour passes and nothing happens. Frustrated, he raises the anchor and begins rowing furiously around the lake. He rows until his arms burn and his back and shoulders ache. Then he pulls in the oars and drifts for a while. Overhead, the clouds darken and a light rain begins to fall. In a matter of minutes, the wind picks up and the rain grows heavier.

He's angry with his brain for playing this game with him—doling out snippets, flashes, of memory, like a miser handing out pennies. He feels like Oliver Twist, barely surviving on thin gruel, and a twice-weekly onion. Obviously, his mind—or some part of it—has decided that it's better for him to know part but not all of his history. Why? What's the harm in learning who he is?

The rain is so heavy now that he cannot see the shore, making him as lost outside as his mind feels inside. The deluge feels like a cold blanket dropped onto his head, robbing him of air, making him feel claustrophobic.

Get out. Run. Break free.

Those words again. Those fucking words. Obviously coming from him, yet not in his own voice, but a deeper one, and quieter, like a low growl.

He feels a rush of adrenalin and puts the oars back into the water and rows hard, having no idea what direction he's headed in, no idea what is behind him.

Get out. Run. Break free.

CHAPTER FOUR

MONDAY MORNING ARRIVES and he's about to return to the desk in the home office, see if he can find some more papers to look through, see what else he can learn, when the phone rings.

"Hey, Bob. It's Matt. I heard you were coming back to work this week and thought you might want a ride."

Work. He hadn't even thought about it. What does he do for a living? Obviously, he no longer works as a bartender for Juke. When did that end? And why?

As soon as he asks the bar question, a memory assaults his mind: It's of a big fight he had with Helen when he came home from work one night and she smelled booze on his breath. Helen went ballistic. She'd always said it wasn't a good idea for him to be working in a bar, not with him being an alcoholic. There was too much temptation. Well now she was putting her foot down. He was going to find another job and that's all there was to it.

He remembers going onto the internet, submitting applications. But where did he land? The question raises a vision of him inside a vast factory, surrounded by giant machines. He's dressed in jeans and a blue shirt with a United Steelworkers emblem. Beyond that, he draws a blank.

He accepts a ride with Matt, who says he'll be there in fifteen minutes. After they hang up, he searches his drawers and closets for work clothes that might give a clue as to what he does at the factory. He can't find any obvious answers, though, so he pulls out a pair of jeans and a blue work shirt, then walks to the bathroom to wash his face, brush his teeth. He sees Helen in the mirror with him, brushing her hair as he stands behind her and works some kind of product into his hair to hold it down.

"I've got to keep it under control," he tells her. He looks closely at his face and notices a dark glint in his eyes, the devil in his eyes.

Recalling it now, he senses he was really talking to himself, not Helen. And the remark about keeping it under control wasn't about his hair.

A horn sounds through the bathroom window and he looks out to see a blue Subaru station wagon idling in the driveway behind his truck. That must be Matt.

When he gets to the car, the front passenger door opens and a short, heavyset man in his early fifties gets out.

"Jesus, what happened to you?" the short man asks, his eyes aimed at his forehead.

"Fell down the steps. It's healing now. Not a big deal."

Bob sees doubt in his eyes. Doubt and compassion.

"Okay," he says. "You can take my seat, ride up front."

"How're you holding up?" Matt asks as he climbs into the vehicle.

He gives a vague answer, then faces the windshield, knowing he's going to have to memorize the route to wherever his job is.

"How have things been at work?" he asks.

"Same old same old," Matt answers.

"Same bullshit, different day," says the short man in the back seat.

"Rumor is Dick's leaving and they're going to bump someone up to replace him," says Matt. "There's a pool on who it'll be. Want in?"

Something tells him to try being funny, so he says, "A Jackson says it's me."

"You don't kiss enough ass," Matt says.

So, he's not one to coddle up to the bosses. Is he a rebel? A troublemaker? He sees himself in the bathroom mirror again—the glint in his eye, his unruly hair. He thinks of the gun hidden in his bed.

They cruise up 99 North to I-70/40 East toward Topeka. He spends the time staring out the windshield while he tries to remember where he works . . . what the hell he does for a living. The clouds and rain of the day before are well past, and the air is hot again, and stagnant. Overhead, a few thin clouds hang motionless in the blue-white sky.

They continue along I-70 for thirty minutes, take exit 358 to 75 North, exit onto US-24 east toward Lawrence. After a few minutes, he spots an exit sign for the NW Goodyear Road exit, and they make their way along the access road and take a right into a big parking lot across a wide lawn from a building so big it looks like it should be measured in acres rather than square feet. They exit the car, pass through a fence, toward a long blue canopy that announces the place as Goodyear-Topeka. In a flash, he remembers that the plant manufactures medium-sized truck and earthmover tires.

Just behind the entrance door, they pass through a security station.

"Bob!"

He focuses on the security guard, who turns out to be Dave Corchado, which explains how he knows the man. Dave says hello to everyone, then leans into Bob and quietly asks him to meet up at lunchtime. "Not in the cafeteria, though," Corchado says. "Out front, in the south lot."

He can't decipher the look on Corchado's face other than he's being serious.

"Sure," he agrees, then turns to find Matt waiting for him.

"I thought maybe you forgot your way around this place." Matt laughs, not realizing that his joke is no joke—that Bob has no idea where in the plant he works.

Matt turns and starts walking, and he follows behind, taking in the building's interior. It's a vast space—cinderblock walls painted blue on the bottom half, white on the top, blue and white floor-to-ceiling steel girder pillars, cement floor, suspended fluorescent light tubes below exposed ceilings. He and Matt pass men and women working machines used to create tires. He's glad to find that he recognizes the machines and their functions—from mixing, extruding, and calendaring to tire building and, finally, testing.

Matt leads him past one grouping of men and machine, then another, and another, until they reach a set of offices in the middle of a large work area, each office with enough room for a metal desk and some filing cabinets. In the center of one of the desks sits a large arrangement of colorful flowers in a glass vase.

Matt nods at the flowers. "Everyone's been thinking about you," he says. "You need any help with anything, let us know. The whole team's here for you."

He thanks Matt and watches him walk to the next office over. Then he enters what must be his own office and sits behind the desk. A wireless keyboard sits in the center of the desk, which is cluttered with papers, a calculator, a coffee mug, a couple pens, a yellow marker. On the left corner of the desk is the computer monitor that goes with the keyboard. On the right corner of the desk is a framed photograph of Helen. He can see that the photo was taken on their upper deck, on a sunny day. Staring at Helen's wide smile, he wonders how a guy who drags another man down to the railroad tracks and shoots him could be married to a sweet woman like her.

He glances around the office and through the window to the plant outside, and his history here comes to him in a flash. He started out as a maintenance mechanic, and his job was to maintain these machines—troubleshoot, calibrate, install, repair, and conduct preventive maintenance. He used blueprints, sketches, maintenance manuals, and manufacturer's specs. At some point, he was promoted to maintenance specialist, and his job now is to oversee the mechanics working under him.

As if in harmony with his recollection, a small group of men gathers outside his office. He figures these are the men he supervises, and he rises and moves to meet them. One by one, concern in their eyes, they express their condolences and welcome him back. If there's anything they can do, they tell him, just ask. In the meantime, they've already worked out their job assignments among themselves. One of them hands him some papers, listing the various job tasks they need to take care of today.

"We figured we'd give you some time to catch up," the guy tells him.

He thanks them all, then returns to his desk. He glances again at the photo of smiling Helen and tries to remember the day. But what his mind brings up instead is the image of Helen sitting in the dark in the corner of their bedroom. His heartbeat quickens and he feels nervous. *Deep breaths*, he tells himself. *Inhale. Hold for ten. Exhale.* The exercise doesn't help him relax, so he leaves his office, walks around. He approaches a man working to fix a carcass drum. The man seems frustrated.

"Mind if I take a shot at it?" Bob asks, gently pulling a tool from the man's hand. He spends the next few minutes working on the drum. Then, satisfied with the results, he steps back and returns the tool to the mechanic, who thanks him.

For the next couple hours, he walks around his area of the plant, watching his men work. He finds that he has an easy way with them. He trades jokes, talks about the Royals and the Chiefs. Asks about their families, though as to that, he can't remember any specifics, so he couches his questions in general terms. *How're things at home?* And, if he spots a wedding ring, *How's your wife doing?* One guy he does this with is a tough-looking guy with short hair and tats on both of his arms, and the man looks at him crossly.

"I don't think Ed would be happy with you calling him my wife," the man says.

He apologizes and the man turns away.

It gets on toward noon and Matt walks up to him, asks if he wants to join him for lunch. He's about to say sure when he remembers Dave Corchado asking to meet in the parking lot. He begs off and walks outside, finding Corchado waiting at the end of the blue canopy. They walk into the lot, where Dave leads him to a pickup truck and they climb inside. They are soaked in sweat from the heat and Corchado starts the truck to turn on the air-conditioning.

"Don't tell me there's no such thing as global warming," Corchado says. "I know its July, but a twenty-day heat wave? Give me a break." He removes a handkerchief from his pocket and wipes his forehead. "I thought that storm yesterday meant we were done with this."

He waits until Corchado returns the handkerchief to his pocket. "Why did you need to talk to me? And why so private?"

Corchado looks around to make sure they are not overheard, an action that seems ridiculous given that they are inside his running truck. "Are you in some kind of trouble? Any reason someone might be after you?"

This takes him aback. "Not that I know of. Why?"

Corchado looks around again. "Well, I was at the beer distributor yesterday and some guy comes up to me and says it was terrible, what happened to your wife. You know, like he was a good friend of yours and Helen's. But then he starts asking me questions about you."

"About me? What kind of questions?"

"Weird questions. Like what kind of guy do I think you are? Have I ever seen you do something that tells me you have a dark side?"

"A dark side?"

"Yeah. Then . . ." Corchado hesitates.

"What?"

Corchado takes a deep breath. "He asked one question that seemed really strange. Offensive. I hate to even repeat it."

He stares and Corchado takes another deep breath. "He asked whether I thought it was possible that Helen didn't really, you know . . . do it herself."

Anger sweeps over him. His heart starts to race. "What the hell?"

"Yeah, that's what I thought. I told him what happened with Helen was none of his fucking business and to get lost. And he did."

His mind leaps to the gray Chrysler 300 that was lingering outside Juke's Place on the day he was assaulted. He wonders if the same guy did it all—attacked him, hung around afterward, grilled Corchado for information at the beer place. "This guy, did he say who he was?"

Corchado shakes his head. "I should have asked. I should have made him show me some ID after a question like that. I feel like a jerk."

He locks eyes with Corchado. "This guy shows up again, find out who he is. Then tell him to come to the source."

"I will."

They return to the shop, where he grabs a quick lunch with Corchado in the lunchroom. He learns from Corchado that he's the captain of the company baseball team and that he and Matt run the company's annual Toys-for-Tots drive at Christmas. Corchado nods toward a woman sitting at a table nearby.

"She still hitting on you?" Corchado whispers.

"Hitting on me?"

"Why you acting like this is news?" Corchado asks. "You're the one who showed me the boob pictures she texted you."

He wonders if the photos are still on his cellphone. Not that he'll spend any time trying to find out. He can't even imagine thinking about another woman.

When he returns to his office, he turns on his computer, punching in Helen's name as the password. There are hundreds of unopened internal company emails, many of them appearing to be condolence messages. He skims the emails, hoping that reading the senders' names will trigger memories. Only a handful do so, and the memories consist only of brief scenes of things that took place at the plant. From a few of the emails, he learns that Goodyear is pressuring the state for tax concessions to help fund an expansion of the plant. At the same time, the company's contract with the United Steelworkers is set to expire in a month, and, with each side digging in its heels, there is talk of a strike. He wonders how interested, how involved, he would normally be in this type of company news. That he has no idea frustrates him, so he turns off the computer and spends the rest of the day walking the plant, talking to his men, helping out. The whole time he does it, he feels like he's an outside observer, hovering just below the ceiling, watching some guy named Bob.

*   *   *

The next day he drives himself to work, parks in the lot in front of the building, says hello to Corchado as he passes through security. He meets with his men outside his office, letting them tell him what they think are the most pressing issues, then going along with the tasks they've already assigned themselves. He spends the next hour receiving his marching orders from his own boss, who tells him that he expects Bob to pick up the slack the following day, take charge of his men again. He promises he will, though his heart isn't in it. Isn't in working at all, really.

He takes lunch with Matt and some other guys—his regular crowd, he comes to learn—ignoring the glances he's getting from the woman Matt said was hitting on him. After lunch, it's two hours digging into his emails and a thick stack of papers his boss handed him, then two hours on the floor.

After work, he stops at the grocery store and picks up a steak, with plans to grill it on his deck. At home, he lets the steak marinate. Then, when the grill is hot, he lays it on the grill.

"I think you're going to like this," he tells Helen, three or four years earlier as he stands by the grill, brushing lemon butter onto a piece of salmon. "I mixed some white wine into the lemon butter."

He's doing his best to engage Helen, who sits listlessly by the table. In response, she offers up only an occasional word or two, or says nothing at all. When the salmon is finished, he takes it and the asparagus he'd been grilling to the table and serves Helen and himself. She doesn't move to lift her fork. She doesn't reach for her wine.

"I'm worried, babe," he says. "It's happening again."

Helen sighs. Then, after a long wait. "It's not that bad this time."

"I don't know," he says. "It's been two days, and it's following the usual pattern—you can't sleep at night, you're fatigued during the day. I'm afraid you're going to stop eating again, have to take another week off work."

She doesn't answer.

The memory fades and he opens the grill, flips the steak briefly, then lifts it onto his plate. He has a potato baking in foil and he places that onto his plate as well, and takes the plate to the table. He sits for a while and his mind takes him back to the day he grilled the salmon for Helen, then skips abruptly to a scene of him driving down a two-lane country road to a grouping of two-story, steel-sided industrial buildings. He pulls behind one of the buildings onto a cracked cement parking lot. Beneath an American flag is a steel door announcing the place as a boxing gym. He opens the door, walks inside.

"Hey, Walt," he says to a heavy guy who appears to be in his late sixties sitting at the reception desk. "Anyone here you think might want to go a few rounds?"

A rough-looking guy standing nearby approaches, introduces himself as Griggs. They shake hands and Griggs says, "I'd be happy to kick your ass."

"Here we go," Walt says.

He spars three rounds with Griggs, though the big man is essentially finished by the end of two. Afterward, Griggs doesn't want to shake his hand but forces himself to anyway.

When he returns home, he finds Helen standing by the sink, peeling potatoes for dinner. She looks up at him. "How was batting practice?"

The steak now cold on his plate, he mulls the memory. So, he spent that afternoon at the boxing gym but lied to Helen, told her he was somewhere swinging a bat. Why did he lie? And what else was he hiding from her?

CHAPTER FIVE

It's Thursday, almost two weeks since his head injury, and the days are blending together. He gets up, goes to work, returns home, works out with his weights and bags, sits alone or walks the house trying to drum up memories. He'd hoped, even expected that his memory would return all at once, but all he's found are dribs and drabs. Scenes of him and Helen sharing meals, going for walks, sitting in a movie theater. Memories of him playing baseball with the guys at work, going fishing with Juke. But even those recollections have been superficial—a snippet of conversation, a brief flash of emotion. Nothing giving him deep insight into himself, or his history.

As the days crawled by, he experienced spikes of grief and searing flashes of pain over Helen's death that brought him to his knees. Most of the time, though, he's dragged himself around in a state of lingering melancholy.

In addition to the emotions associated with the loss of his wife, he's been beset by the sense that he is under threat. It's because of this that he's kept his amnesia a secret, put off going to a doctor to have his brain examined for evidence of injury from the assault outside Juke's bar.

Last week, he finally decided to get help. On Wednesday, he'd been sitting on his sofa watching mindless television—some show featuring naked people bickering on an island—and was suddenly terrified by the vast holes in his memory. The fear was so intense he decided to seek medical help the next day. In the home office he found records from Kournfield Family Practice and set up an appointment for that Friday. He met with the doctor, confessed his amnesia, and requested some type of medical testing of his brain. The doctor set him up for a CT scan, which was conducted Monday, and now, three days later, he's back in his primary-care doc's office to review the results.

Sitting in the waiting room, a memory flashes of Juke bringing him here shortly after Helen's death.

"Everyone here was heartbroken to learn about Helen," the doctor told him in the examination room. "She was such a kind person. Caring."

Standing behind him, Juke chimed in. "He's not doing so good, Doc. He's . . . well, he keeps breaking down. Falling apart. I can't get him to eat. He's losing weight."

The doctor shook his head. "Well, that's understandable. Something like this . . ."

The physician was talking to Juke now, like doctors talk to the parents of young children, but Bob didn't care. He didn't care about anything.

"I'm going to write a prescription," the doctor told Juke. "It will dull some of the pain. Help him function. His appetite should improve."

But he didn't want to function. Didn't want to enjoy food again. The thought of resuming life seemed like a betrayal of Helen. His sweet wife was dead, so what right did he have to go on living?

He and Juke left the doctor's office and Juke drove him to the pharmacy, where his friend picked up the prescription before taking him home. He promised Juke he'd take the pills but threw the bottle away as soon as Juke left.

"Mr. Hunter?"

He looks up and sees a nurse standing at the door that leads from the reception area to the exam rooms. She leads him to the end of the hallway, motions for him to enter the doctor's personal office, where he finds the white-haired physician waiting for him. The office is a cluttered, homey space. Framed photographs of the doctor and his family are on display in the bookshelf behind him, along with fat medical books. A full body skeleton hangs from a stand in one corner. The desk is littered with files, pens, a coffee mug, a glass jar filled with paper clips.

The physician stands to shake his hand, then they both take seats across the desk from one another.

"Well, Bob, we have good news, and bad news, is the way to put it, I suppose." The doctor motions to a manila file sitting on his desk. "The CT scan results are negative for any type of brain injury. No bleeding, no swelling. That's the good news. The bad news is that this leaves us with no explanation for the amnesia."

"Are there other tests that can be done?"

The doctor hesitates. "Well, I guess, technically, you could have an MRI, though that's more expensive. And your company insurance can be a chore . . ."

"Seriously?"

"Now, Bob, I'm not saying no." The doctor raises his hands defensively. "I'll just have to jump through some hoops is all."

"Then jump."

The physician chuckles uncomfortably. "In the meantime, I'm going to write you another prescription, to help you relax—"

"I don't need to relax, Doc. I don't need pills. What I need is to know what's going on with my fucking head!"

The older man leans back in his chair, shock on his face. *"What?"*

The doctor pauses. "I've been your doctor for, what, ten years now? I've seen you around town, too. In restaurants, the barbershop. I've watched you at baseball games—my son plays with you on the Goodyear team." He pauses. "In all the years I've known you, all the situations I've seen you in, I don't believe I've ever heard you curse once."

They stare at each other.

"Have you noticed any changes in your personality since you were assaulted?"

He wants to shake the man, ask, *How should I know what my personality is? I don't remember anything about me!*

"This is going to sound like an odd question," the doctor says, "but do you get the feeling that people are after you?"

"What? You think I'm paranoid? Delusional?" He crosses his arms. "Is that a sign of a head injury?"

"I'm going to make sure you get that MRI." The doc smiles and stands, signaling the meeting is over.

He leaves the office fretting about the free-floating anxiety he's been feeling, the sense that he's in danger. It's late when he leaves, after dark. His original intent was to stop by Juke's Place, see his brother-in-law. But the lack of sunlight and his disquiet cause him to decide to go straight home. By the time he reaches his house, he's feeling nauseated and he decides to lie down for a few minutes on the sofa. He removes his shoes, closes his eyes, and wraps his arms around his chest.

*   *   *

He wakes to the feeling of someone's hand on his forehead. "Very hot. Bad fever."

He opens his eyes. It's the cleaning lady. Bob is eight or nine years old, home from school with a virus. He'd vomited his dinner, spaghetti, the night before and this morning he woke up dizzy and nauseated with an elevated temperature. He's on the sofa because when he's sick, he doesn't like to be locked up in his room alone. At a doctor's visit herself now, his mother left him in the care of the cleaning lady. She's a large woman with dyed blond hair, an émigré to the U.S. from some Eastern Bloc country. She asks him if he wants some soup, but the idea of eating makes him want to puke again and he says no and pulls the blanket over his head.

The cleaning lady has the TV on, tuned to a televangelist show. Dressed in a tan, double-breasted suit, the preacher struts back and forth on the stage, waiving a bible and going on and on about guilt and sin. "Let your conscience be your key," the reverend says. "Don't focus on whether something feels good in your body, but whether it feels good in your *soul*."

After a while, he falls asleep, and the entertainer follows him into his dreams, shouting after him. "Let your conscience be your key!"

It's close to ten p.m. when Bob wakes up, an adult again. He hears the doctor asking whether he thinks someone is after him, then sees the wacky preacher from his childhood prancing around the stage. He searches the childhood memory for meaning. Why would that particular recollection surface now? Does it mean something?

He forces himself off the sofa, walks to the kitchen. There's a plastic container of soup in the refrigerator and he pours it into a bowl, heats it up in the microwave. When it's done, he carries the bowl to the kitchen table. A loaf of bread sits on the table. He takes out two slices and butters them, to go with the soup. For some reason, the doctor's visit and the preacher memory have his pulse up and he isn't hungry. But he knows he must eat and forces down the meal.

When he's done, he sits for a long while at the table. He looks around the kitchen, hoping to free up a memory but none show up. He thinks about the sense of danger that delayed him seeing a doctor and wonders what he's really afraid of. After a while, a disturbing thought makes its way into his head: What if the real reason he didn't go to the doctor is that he doesn't *want* to remember?

He shoots from his chair. "This is nuts." He grabs his empty bowl and water glass, rinses them roughly in the sink, then tosses them into the dishwasher, closing the door a little too hard.

"This is bullshit." Of course he wants to remember. He *needs* to remember. The past is the key to the present, and the present is the key to the future.

Let your conscience be your key.

CHAPTER SIX

FRIDAY AFTERNOON. A tall, gray-haired man approaches his office about an hour before quitting time.

"How are you doing, Bob?" Then, before he can answer, "Let's go to my office and talk."

He figures he's about to be fired. He's probably been screwing up at his job these past two weeks—missing things because he doesn't remember his job as well as he'd thought. And isn't the end of day Friday when they normally let people go? He wonders whether the boss man will call Corchado or some other security guard to escort him out of the building.

The man's office, though larger than his own workspace, is small and fitted with cheap laminate furniture—a desk, two chairs, a small bookcase. On the wall, mass-produced prints. Overhead, fluorescent lighting.

The nameplate on the desk identifies the boss as Charles Martin Jr., a name that's been mentioned by his coworkers at lunch in less than reverent tones. Martin tells him to have a seat.

"You may have heard that Dick Burt has decided to retire," Martin begins. "And that we're looking for someone to move up, take his place as Production Manager I."

An uneasy feeling bubbles up inside Bob's stomach. He knows where this is headed.

"Your name has survived the cuts, and right now you're at the top of a very short list." Martin pauses to see how he reacts. "Are you interested in moving up in middle management, really sinking your teeth into it? Production Manager's a big job. You'd be formulating policies."

Maybe he's an ass-kisser after all. He doesn't think so, but he can't be sure. "Would you mind sharing with me why I'm being considered?" he asks.

"Well, that's a fair question." Martin smiles. "Do you remember when you came here? I do. You knew nothing about making tires. You couldn't have picked out a transfer ring from a carcass drum to save your life. The only reason you were granted an interview here, let alone were hired, is that some bigwig owed a big favor to your brother-in-law. But hired you were, and once you were here, you caught on faster than anyone expected. People were so impressed that four years after you were hired, you were promoted to specialist. You're smart, and you have drive. And you're a natural leader, as demonstrated by the fact that you're the captain of our baseball team, and you even run our Christmas charity."

Martin pauses, probably waiting for Bob to say something. But he keeps quiet, and Martin continues.

"The only thing that's keeping me from formally offering you the position is I have no idea what your work history really is. Your résumé includes the job you held at Juke's bar down in Kournfield and lists a bunch of other bars you said you tended in the Big Apple. I called information to reach some of those bars, but there are no numbers for them. Now, I know a thing or two about bar and restaurant turnover, so the fact that those places are out of business doesn't particularly bother me."

The Big Apple. Manhattan. So that's the "back east" Casey was talking about. His mother had brought him and his brother, Jimmy, here when they were in high school and, presumably, took them back to New York.

Martin shifts in his seat, leans forward. "We ran a criminal background check on you in New York State and didn't find anything. But those checks aren't worth crap, in my experience. "So, I have to ask . . . do you? Have a criminal record, I mean?"

He smiles. "Well, not that I know of." Sure, he shot some guy on the railroad tracks, and he knows how to kickbox and keeps a gun in his bed. And he has bullet and knife scars. But that doesn't mean he was ever *convicted* of anything.

"I didn't think so." Martin chuckles again. Then he slides a piece of folded paper across the desk, nods for Bob to open it. "Quite a raise, eh?"

He has no clue because he doesn't know what he's making now. He hasn't bothered to look at his bank account and today will be his first paycheck since returning to work.

"I'll say."

"This could be a stepping-stone to a bright future at Goodyear. On the other hand, it's a lot more responsibility, more pressure. You want some time to think about it?"

The notion that his future will be built on the manufacturing of tires strikes a chord of fear in him. He takes a deep breath and says, "Yeah, a couple days would be nice. Can we meet again on Monday?"

Martin starts to say *sure*, then stops himself. "If you really think it's something you might *want*"—he emphasizes the word . . . "then, yes, I'll give you until Monday."

"Of course, I'm interested. Who wouldn't be? I just want the two days to take an inventory of myself and make sure I'm the right man for the job."

"Now, *that's* what I was hoping to hear," Martin says.

They stand and shake hands. He clocks out, leaves the building, and walks to his truck. He has no idea if he wants to move up in middle management. He hasn't thought about it. Or maybe he has—how the hell would he know? But there are certain things that must be said in certain situations. When someone offers you a job and asks if you might want it, the answer is yes.

He turns out of the company parking lot, makes his way from the Goodyear access road to Route 24 then I-70, accelerating hard down the interstate, his goal being to get as far away as fast as he can. "Get out. Run." He says the words aloud this time. "Break free."

The speedometer inches up. Eighty. Ninety. The plant is miles behind him now, but his heart is hammering in his chest. He glances in the rearview, sees the dark eyes looking back at him.

What in hell am I running from?

*   *   *

At home that night, he tosses and turns in bed, his mind unable to let go of the question: What is he afraid of? The doctor promised to set up an MRI, but he hasn't heard back from the physician's office about it.

"Fuck." He climbs out of bed, throws on some jeans and a polo shirt and walks out to the deck, picking up a bottle of water along the way. The heat has tapered off some, but it's still in the mid-eighties at one o'clock in the morning. There's some cloud cover and every now and then lightning flashes in the sky. The clouds are not rain clouds, though. It's not going to rain any time soon, and the lightning is only heat lightning.

He closes his eyes and when he opens them, he's sitting at the kitchen table with Helen. They are having breakfast and he's just refreshed their coffees and brought over a dish of scrambled eggs and sausages for them to share.

Helen cuts a small piece off one of the sausages and carefully slides it onto her tongue. He watches her chew, waits for her to finish. She looks over at him.

"What?" she asks.

He waits a beat, then, "What does it feel like?" he asks. "Physically? These depressions you get. I mean, I've read a lot of articles on it, online, and I have a general sense of how people feel with depression. But I don't know what it feels like to you. Maybe if I did, I could help you through it better."

Helen thinks on this for a long time. "What does it feel like?" She repeats his question. "It . . . it starts out like a fog sweeping over me. A fog of sadness. I can feel it in my head, my shoulders, my chest, arms and hands, abdomen, hips and legs—every part of my body. The sadness deepens into despair, then darkens to an overwhelming feeling of hopelessness. After a while, the fog gains weight, mass. It creates its own gravity that weighs me down, paralyzes me—every limb and digit. Then it crushes me, crumples me like a piece of paper until all that's left of me is dread." Helen takes a deep breath, forces down some eggs. "Lots of people with it retreat to their beds, hide under the blankets."

"But you sit in the chair, in the corner," he says.

She nods. "The solidness of the chair comforts me. I'm afraid that if I laid in bed, I'd sink into the mattress and disappear."

They sit in silence for a long while, slowly finishing their meals, lost in their thoughts. Then Helen turns to him.

"It helps," she says. "When you sit behind me. Talk to me. Tell me funny stories about the plant. Your baseball games. Everything."

"I wasn't sure," he says. "You seem so far away when you get like that. Sometimes . . . sometimes it feels to me like someone else is talking to you, too."

Her eyes flare, but only for an instant. Then they flatten and she looks away.

"Thank you for sharing that with me," he says. Then he smiles, reaches across the table, gently places his right hand over her left. He does this to reassure her. But on the inside, his heart is racing.

Get out. Run. Break free.

CHAPTER SEVEN

SATURDAY AFTERNOON FINDS him back at Juke's Place. The bar is busy. The bar seats are filled with guys getting a head start on their weekend bender. A middle-aged couple sits at a table, nursing mixed drinks and grudges. At another table, a younger couple eats quietly, a sleeping baby in a stroller next to them. In the corner are four codgers who've probably been drinking here since before Juke owned the place.

Juke himself is sitting across the table from him, complaining. "The starboard Merc gave out again, and this time the port motor failed, too."

He listens but doesn't say anything. Juke's been bitching since he sat down, and he wonders whether the man has always been this negative, or whether Helen's death has embittered her older brother. His mind is sprinkled with memories of Juke going both ways. He sees Juke smiling at the turkey giveaway that he runs out of the bar every Thanksgiving, and he sees Juke mumbling and cursing alone for hours in the bar's back room. He sees Juke talking trash about the government, his customers, even his friends, and he sees him running outside to help an old lady with a walker cross the street. It's as though the jury's out on Juke, trying to decide whether he's a good man, content and generous, or a bad man, nasty and small inside.

Juke finishes his rant and Bob tells him about the job offer. "Does that sound like something I'd want? Based on what you know about me?"

Juke frowns. "How the hell should I know what you want?"

"Have I ever talked about moving up in management?"

"You don't remember?"

He wants to blurt out that he doesn't remember anything, but he only shakes his head. "No, I'm just . . . just not right in the head yet, is all."

"Hey, I get it. Boy, do I. Ever since Helen's death, I haven't been right. With our parents gone, she's the only family I had left."

Bob's mind flashes back to a memory of Juke and him in the bar after closing time. He and Helen had just announced their engagement. Juke sits across one of the tables, a mug of beer in his hand.

"You're the best thing that ever happened to my sister," Juke says. "She's finally come out of her shell. I never thought she'd be herself again. And her depression . . . You've been a godsend."

Recalling it now makes his heart race, and he has to force himself to sit still.

Then the baby in the stroller across the room starts to cry and a whole series of memories floods his brain. Helen with her reproductive schedule, telling him it's time to have sex again. Helen insisting she has to be on her back with her legs raised high in the air, ordering him to perform even when he's too tired or stressed. After three years of marriage without Helen getting pregnant, she was baby-crazy, going to this doctor and that, looking for ways to increase her fertility; making Bob go to doctors, too, for sperm counts. Special diets for her, pills for both of them. Their sex always, and only, according to the schedule, like it was carved on a tablet brought down by Moses.

It ruined one of the most important parts of their marriage. Not that sex was everything to him. That was never the case with Helen; he'd loved her like—

"Oh my God."

Juke's eyes flash with worry. "What's the matter?"

I loved her so much . . .

In that moment, his love for Helen drives itself into the center of his heart. Tears begin streaming down both sides of his face, and even though he's in public and people are staring at him, he doesn't care.

"Hey, hey." It's Juke. "Talk to me, man." Then, to everyone around them: "What are you looking at? The man just lost his wife, for fuck's sake."

Bob excuses himself, goes to the men's room and splashes his face with water. He stands in front of the mirror, searches his eyes. How is it possible that the magnitude of his feelings for Helen is only hitting him now?

"Was I a coward with her?" he asks his mirror image. *Was she married to a man who always kept himself half in and half out of the marriage?* His eyes start to moisten again, but he rubs them dry.

There's a knock at the door and Juke pokes his head in. "Just how big of an emotional shit are you taking in here?"

The remark strikes him as hilarious and he laughs so hard his gut hurts. Juke joins in and they laugh together.

"Fuck-a-doodle-do," Juke says, and they laugh even harder.

They end up side by side in front of the mirror, hands on the sinks, supporting themselves.

"Oh, man." Juke looks over at him. "You had me scared there. I was thinking of calling the cuckoo cart, have them rush here with a straitjacket."

"It's okay. I'm all right now. It just hits me sometimes."

"Hits us both," Juke says.

They stand quietly for a moment, then Bob looks at Juke. "Can I ask you something?"

"Sure, anything."

"When I first came here, what did I say about myself?"

Juke gives him a confused look. "Uh . . . you said you knew your way around a bar. You could mix any drink. Hold your own against somebody who was acting up. And you told me you were an alcoholic, but that you were clean and sober going on a year. Said you'd lived here for a short time in high school, but your mother took you and your brother back east. My own parents didn't bring me and Helen here until after you'd come and gone, so I didn't have any memories of you."

"Did I tell you anything about why I came back?"

Juke thinks on this. "You said you'd gotten yourself into some trouble back east, that it wasn't safe for you back there, but you didn't elaborate. Why're you asking me this now?"

He shrugs. "A guy bashed my head against the wall, for starters. Then a security guard from work told me some guy approached him with questions about me . . ."

"And you're thinking someone from back east is coming after you? After all these years?"

It seems unlikely that some guy harboring a grudge would wait ten years before acting on it. But maybe there's a reason his assailant had held back. Maybe he just got out of prison. Maybe he promised someone he wouldn't come after Bob, but now that someone is dead.

"Seems like a stretch," Juke says.

"You're probably right. I'm just being paranoid."

But he doesn't think so.

Emotionally spent, he heads home and watches a ball game on TV, then goes to bed. He also begs out of a Sunday on the lake with Juke. He knows he's being selfish, especially given how supportive his brother-in-law has been, but he can't risk a second emotional typhoon in as many days.

CHAPTER EIGHT

CLOSING HIS EYES, he falls quickly to sleep and his head fills with dreams and shadows. Faces come out of the mist, stare at him, smile at him, frown at him, then break apart and disappear. He is dropped into half-formed scenes—standing on a beach next to a woman with long blond hair; volcanic sex with a woman with blazing green eyes; sitting on the bed of a sick young girl, holding her hand; handcuffed in a police car watching a house burn, watching the EMTs bring out a body bag.

Memories? Inventions? He can't tell. Each seems as real—and as unreal—as the next.

Then, the darkness falls still. There is no movement, no sound, only emptiness. He floats in the space between sleep and waking, aware that he's on his bed, but feeling as though he is somewhere else, some*one* else.

A gentle "Hey" sounds in his ear.

He hears her voice and opens his eyes and there she is sitting on his bed next to him: Helen. Her body is only a shadow, but her face is fully in focus, and lit. She says his name and her warm blue eyes fill with love. He tries to sit up, embrace her, but cannot.

"Lie still," Helen says. She takes one of his hands in both of her own. Like her face, Helen's hands are in sharp focus. Her fingers are thin, her nails painted pink.

"I always loved your hands," he says.

"They look so small in yours," she says.

He tries again to sit up, but cannot move.

"You're having a hard time, aren't you?"

"I miss you," he says. Then, "Why did you do it?"

She smiles sadly. "Let's not talk about unpleasant things."

"You broke my heart."

"You need to get out, sweetheart. Run."

Get out. Run. Break free . . . Has it been Helen who's whispering the words in his head? He thinks no, the voice is lower, more like a growl.

"It's nice you're spending some time with Juke. That you've tried returning to work," she says. "But you're getting bogged down. Trapped."

He opens his mouth, but before he can say anything, Helen leans over. She kisses his hand and lays it down beside him. "I have to go now. And so do you. Leave this place and don't come back."

Fear surges in the pit of his stomach. "I'm afraid if I leave here, I'll never see you again, that I'll leave all my memories of us behind, before I even find most of them."

Helen smiles. "You'll see me again, I promise."

"No. I'll lose you forever."

A dark light flashes in Helen's eyes. "You're not going to lose me. You'll find me. But not until you're ready. Not until it's time."

"I'm ready now."

She shakes her head. "No, you're not." She stands, moves away from him. "I have to go now. And so do you. How does that song go? Hit the road, Jack, don't you come back no more, no more, no more, no more."

He smiles. "My name's not Jack."

"Close enough."

Helen disappears into the shadows and he struggles in vain for a third time to rise from the bed. When she is gone completely, his throat tightens and his eyes fill. After a while, he falls into a deep sleep. The darkness of his room grows darker, and takes on a form that starts to move. He is twelve years old, on the verge of the hormonal onslaught of adolescence. His twin brother, Jimmy, stands to his left. His mother is to his right. They are at the zoo, watching a panther pace from one end of its cage to another. The creature's silky fur is black as polished coal. Its teeth are whiter than piano keys. Menace glows in its yellow eyes.

"Why does he keep walking back and forth?" Jimmy asks their mother.

"He's looking for a way out," their mother answers.

"What happens if he gets out?" Jimmy asks.

After a minute, their mother answers. "If he gets out, *watch out.*"

He hears the exchange between his brother and mother, but he doesn't take his eyes off the panther. He's hoping the big cat will pause for a moment, catch his eye, make a connection with him.

The predator moves by him once, twice. On the third pass, it pauses. They lock eyes and he sees through the menace to what lies behind it—rage. Fury at being restrained. Imprisoned.

"Why does he want out?" asks Jimmy.

He turns to his brother and his chest fills with anger at such a stupid question. He and Jimmy are going to get into a big fight tonight. He knows because he's going to start it.

*   *   *

Sunday morning, he wakes up and makes his way down the hall toward the kitchen, to make himself some coffee. On the way, he passes through the living room, where he notices right away that the alarm is off. He knows he turned it on the night before.

"That's strange." He reaches for the front door and finds it unlocked. Someone opened the door and deactivated the alarm by punching in the code. But who besides him and Helen had a key to their house? Who knew their alarm code? Adrenalin rushes into his system as he races around the house looking to see whether anything has been taken. He searches the rooms one by one, until he gets to the home office. And that's where he sees it; not something missing, but something left—a key. A small silver key, sitting on the desk. He lifts it, inspects it, tries to figure out what it might be for. The key is smaller than the key to the front door. He holds it up to the light, looking for any markings that might indicate what the key is for, but can find none.

He lowers the key to the desktop. There is no doubt in his mind now that he is being stalked. Someone bashed his head in, asked Corchado about him. And now the stalker has broken into his house, planted a key. So, what's their agenda?

The whole thing is unnerving and he spends an hour pacing the house, trying to calm down. He pours himself coffee, but lets it get cold. Fries eggs, but doesn't eat them. He can't seem to get settled.

Then he looks out of one of the living room windows and sees the Chrysler 300 parked in the street, directly across from his house. He races outside, marches up the driveway. The car pulls away and starts down the street, picking up speed as it goes. He walks into the middle of the street and watches the car disappear around a corner.

He stares down the street even after he can no longer see the car. Then he turns around, walks toward the cabin, stopping at the mailbox. He never retrieved the mail the day before and the box is stuffed with junk mail, credit-card bills, utility bills, and, folded in half, a mustard-colored envelope that says it's from the county coroner's office. He stares at the envelope, almost afraid to touch it.

"Fuck." He must have asked for a copy of the autopsy report. But why? He already knows Helen died of a deliberate drug overdose.

He returns to the house, drops the mail onto the coffee table. Lowering himself onto the sofa, he stares at the coroner's envelope. After a long time, he leans forward, lifts the envelope and opens it, hoping to God it doesn't contain any photographs. He breathes a sigh of relief when he finds only the typed report. But he quickly sickens as he scans the clinical details relating to his wife's remains—her height, weight, eye color, hair color.

Then he gets to the part where the medical examiner relates the weight and condition of the various organs. Nauseated, he is about to close the report and toss it onto the coffee table, when his eye catches what the examiner wrote about Helen's uterus and he leaps off the couch and screams.

"No . . . *No.*"

She was pregnant. Six weeks. His wife killed herself while carrying their child.

He crumples the report in his hand, circles the living room shouting, cursing. This can't be real. Can't be happening. He feels like he's in hell. Like he literally died and went to hell.

Helen not only took her own life but that of their child, as well. Killed the baby she had wanted for so long.

Grasping for some straw to hang his sanity on, he realizes that Helen could not have known she was pregnant. As depressed and hopeless as Helen could get, she would never have ended her life if she knew she'd be killing their baby, too.

He sprints for the kitchen, grabs his keys, runs outside, climbs into his truck and drives to the one person he knows can save him from his darkest fear. Speeding the whole way up 99 to Kournfield, he arrives at the man's house in thirteen minutes, narrowly avoiding knocking down the mailbox on his sharp turn into the driveway. The front door opens even before he reaches it.

"Bob?" The man, Helen's OB-GYN, has his arms held out to stop him. "Calm down, now."

"Tell me she didn't know! *Tell me.*"

But the look in the doctor's eyes says it all.

Bob doubles over. "Oh God."

"Hey? Bob? Stand up and come inside."

But he cannot stand. Cannot move.

The doctor's wife appears in the doorway. "Bob, please, let us help you."

But there is no help. Not for this. Not for this.

"Helen was very ill," the doctor says. "You know that. The depression. The pills. The days sitting in the dark with the curtains drawn. It wasn't her fault, what happened."

But it didn't just *happen*. Helen made a choice, then she acted on it, destroying herself, destroying their child.

His mind kicks him back to that awful day. Him coming home from work to find her on their marriage bed, convulsing because she's swallowed so many pills—enough to kill her, but not quickly. He picks her up, carries her to the living room, to the phone, crying out, "Helen! Helen! What did you do? Stay with me! Stay with me!" Then the excruciating moment when he tears himself from her to call 911.

He struggles to control his voice enough that the emergency operator will be able to understand him, giving the address and shouting "Pills! Pills! My wife swallowed a bunch of pills!"

"What kind of pills, sir?"

"I . . . I . . . fuck, they're in the bedroom!"

"I've already dispatched someone, sir. Try to remain calm."

"What should I do?"

"Try to remain calm, sir."

"CPR? Should I do CPR? Breathe into her mouth?"

"Is she awake, sir? Can you get her to walk around?"

"She's convulsing, for chrissake!"

"I apologize, sir . . ."

And on and on and on for hours, days, weeks, years, until the ambulance arrives and the EMTs go to work—a final, agonizing, drawn-out, and futile attempt to save Helen's life.

And when all is finally lost and some of the neighbors appear with Juke, he flies into a rage and orders them out of his house. Once they are gone, he returns to the bedroom, picks up the empty bottle, and flings it against the wall. He flops down on the bed and it is then that he sees it on the nightstand—a photograph of him and Helen removed from the frame and torn down the middle, separating them—Helen's suicide note, telling him that she was tearing herself away from him. He gathers the two pieces, holds them to his chest, and drops down a dark hole. In the days that follow, he haunts the earth, a zombie going through the motions, helping Juke make the funeral arrangements, sitting in the church, listening to the preacher utter words that may as well be in Swahili, standing in the receiving line at the reception at Juke's Place, roaming his house and property for days on end like an old blind dog trying to find its way home from far away.

Back now in front of the doctor's house, he hears the OB-GYN calling after him as he stumbles from their front step down the driveway to his truck. And all the way home, all he can think about is Helen's convulsing body. And his gun. The gun he keeps hidden in the bed with the clip full of hollow point bullets big enough to bring down a bear.

Big enough to end his pain.

CHAPTER NINE

HE STORMS INTO the house, flies through the living room then down the hall to the bedroom and retrieves the automatic from between the mattress and box spring. Then he sits on the bed and falls into a dark reverie. His wife is gone, dead by her own hand, having taken their unborn child with her. The child she'd once wanted with all her heart. Helen, the elementary school teacher who loved children, now a *killer* of one.

He shakes his head. It just doesn't make sense.

And then it bursts through—the memory—like the summer sun punching through a rain cloud. It begins on the morning of Helen's death. She cooks him a big breakfast and tells him that when he gets back from work, she has a big surprise for him. He clears the plates while Helen walks onto the upper deck, and when he's done, he follows her outside, finds her leaning over the railing, gazing out at the lake. She turns to face him and, when she does, the light shines on her face, makes her blue eyes sparkle.

"It's all so beautiful," she says. And she's *smiling*!

His memory leaps to later that day. He's in the truck, driving home, thinking about how he hadn't seen a joyous look on Helen's face in a long time. Which is why he left work at exactly three o'clock without hanging around, shooting the shit with

Matt or Corchado or the others. He drives down the stone and gravel driveway, parks in front of the house, and races into the house, eager to find out what it is that's made Helen so happy.

He calls out her name as soon as he opens the front door, hoping, almost expecting, that Helen will run to his arms or at least appear with that same smile. But she doesn't appear, doesn't even answer him, so he calls her name again. Again, all he receives is silence, and he thinks maybe she's out back on the deck, so he runs outside. But she isn't there. He goes back inside the house, calls her name as he walks down the hallway, a tide of worry rising inside him. Then he enters their bedroom and finds her, racked by violent spasms, foam frothing from her mouth, empty plastic pill bottles on the bed beside her. The horrible drama plays out with the ambulance and Juke and the neighbors all showing up, restraining him, comforting him until he orders them out. Then Helen's body is covered and carted away.

Remembering it now, he shoots from the bed, tosses down the gun, and makes his way to the kitchen, every nerve in his body electrified. Opening the refrigerator, he finds the remaining casserole dishes brought by his friends and neighbors in the days following Helen's death. He removes them one by one and there it is, jammed against the back wall—*the rack of lamb, the mint jelly*. The meal Helen always served when she wanted to celebrate something. So, yes, she knew about the baby . . . in fact, she was *rejoicing*. Her pregnancy, he now realizes, was her big surprise. At long last, they were going to be a family.

Helen's pregnancy. The trouble he'd made for himself back east—so much trouble that he kept a gun in their bed, so serious he'd told Juke he could never go back. And now, some guy assaults him, asks around about him, even breaks into his house. The import of all this hits him like a lightning bolt.

Helen didn't kill herself. She was murdered.

Some monster forced her to choke down the pills. Then the killer tore their photo in half to symbolize how he'd ripped the couple apart, forever separating him from Helen. That's the only way it all makes sense.

His mind leaps to the key. The key left by the stranger who broke into his house. The stranger who either had a key to the front door or knew how to pick a lock and disable an alarm system. A bad guy. A professional. The type of guy the bad guys back east—whoever they were—would send to hurt him, hurt him in the worst way possible: by killing the woman he loved. Then, afterward, leave him a key that means something to him.

"Mother*fucker.*"

He races to the office, lifts the key from the desk. What *does* it mean? What is the message the killer is sending him?

His mind is spinning out of control. His heart a hammer pounding in his chest.

"Stop it. Slow down."

He says the words, then forces himself to sit and think. Forces himself to slow his breathing, slow his heart. *Inhale. Hold for ten. Exhale.*

"Okay," he says. "All right." A key is to open something. The first question is open *what*? The second question is *where* is the *what* located? His initial thought is that the key is to open something back east. But what if it isn't? What if the key opens something inside this house—something he brought with him when he'd moved here ten years ago? Yes, yes. That's it, that's the answer. The key is for something in this house, something that will provide him with answers, serve as a message between him and the killer, a message he can use to figure out who the killer is, and where.

He takes a deep breath and then another. Then he stands and makes a mental map of his home. He will proceed methodically, search every room, every corner, every nook and cranny, until he finds what the key unlocks. He'll start at the bottom and work his way up.

* * *

Three hours later, soaked with sweat, covered with dirt and dust and cobwebs, he holds it in his hands: a metal strongbox. He found it in a crawl space under the roof, accessed by a trap door in the ceiling of a bedroom closet. He went into the closet, separated the hanging clothes, looked up, and there it was. And as soon as he saw the door, a memory arose of him staying home from work one day, pretending to be sick, then, after Helen left for work, digging the box up from where he'd buried it in the backyard and sneaking it into the crawl space.

He takes the box to the home office, sets it on the desk, and stares at it. It's just a gray metal box, a foot square by four inches deep. Yet, he knows it holds his secrets. Secrets he intended to hide from his wife. Parts of his life back east that he wanted to keep forever separate from his life with Helen.

He picks up the key, inserts it into the lock, and turns it. When he lifts the lid, the first thing he sees is a badge. The words "Police Department—Philadelphia" hang above two women flanking a shield with the scales of justice above it. The badge number is on the bottom.

So, back east was Philadelphia, not New York.

He lays down the badge and lifts a photograph. The face looking back at him has wide-set dark eyes, dark hair, and a square jawline. It's his face. In the photo, he's wearing a uniform with peaked cap. The picture is one of those official police academy photos they publish in the newspaper when an officer is killed in the line of duty. His mind brings up the memories of the guy pointing a gun at him and firing, and him calling the man named Richie and asking if he was still dead. So he was a cop, but he hadn't died in the line of duty, though maybe people thought he had.

He lowers the photograph and removes the other items in the strongbox one by one. First, he takes out a revolver. It's a .38 special. He looks it over and finds the serial number has been filed off. He lays the revolver down and removes three stacks of vacuum-sealed hundred-dollar bills, each stack holding $10,000.

What the hell was he into back east that he had all this money? That he needed yet another gun?

The next thing he removes is an expired Pennsylvania driver's license with a Philadelphia address. The name on the license is Jackson R. Hunter, whereas his Kansas license identifies him as J. Robert Hunter. His first name is Jackson, then.

The last thing he finds in the strongbox is another key. He recognizes it as a vintage key, though to what model of vehicle he can't tell.

He scans the contents of the strongbox, taking them in one by one. What is the message Helen's killer intended the contents to send him? For that matter, how is it the killer had the key to *his* strongbox?

He mulls these questions until his head hurts. Then he gets it. The killer is telling him to come back to Philadelphia. Telling him that's where the killer will be waiting for him, where the thing between them, whatever it is, will be settled. *Come and get me*, the killer is telling him. Taunting him. He picks up the revolver. "Don't worry, motherfucker. I'm on my way. I'm coming."

He stands in time to hear the large truck approach the house on the gravel driveway. He looks out the window and sees it's a brown UPS truck. Lowering the gun, he walks to the front door to accept the package. It's a large cardboard box, six feet by four feet by six inches thick. Helen must have ordered something before her death that only arrived now. But what could it be? He waits until the delivery truck pulls away then takes the box into the house. He lowers it onto the floor and pulls hard at the edges, ripping out the staples. He opens the box and moans.

It's a crib.

CHAPTER TEN

THREE DAYS LATER, his house listed for sale, Helen's car sold, most of his furnishings and clothes cleared out and donated to charity, he's in the truck pulling out of his driveway. On the back seat of the club-cab are his suitcase and a backpack holding the thirty grand, his automatic, the .38, and a framed photograph of Helen.

He pulls out of the driveway and heads for town. He's already called Mr. Martin at work, told him thanks but no thanks for the promotion. He isn't the right man for it. He got ahold of Matt, too, told him he was going back east and asked Matt to let everyone else know, especially the guys on the baseball team. He'd have told them himself, except he can't remember any of their names. Or their faces, or anything about them.

His next stop is Juke's Place.

"Hey, Bob. Have a seat," Juke says. "I'll make you some coffee."

He shakes his head. "I'm hitting the road."

"The road to where?"

"Back east."

Juke nods cautiously. "How long?"

He shrugs.

Juke pulls a rag from his back pocket, rubs the bar top a few times. "You sure that's smart? Going back there?"

"Probably not, but I have to." He's already decided he's not going to tell Juke that he thinks Helen was murdered, probably to get even for something he did back in Philadelphia. His brother-in-law is suffering enough already. And if he shared his suspicions with Juke, Juke would insist on coming along, and he can't have that. Bob alone brought this on Helen and he has to fight this war by himself. And he has no doubt that's what it will turn out to be—a war.

They stare at each other, then Juke walks around the bar, locks him in a bear hug. When Juke pulls away, he sees tears in the big man's eyes.

"No need for that," Bob says. "We'll be seeing each other again."

Juke shakes his head. "Nah, I don't think so. Whatever happens back east, I don't expect you'll be coming back this way."

He knows Juke is right. That's why he decided to sell his house and unload his belongings. He made a place for himself in Kournfield, a life. But it never fit him, not really. He was from somewhere else, *of* somewhere else. And it's time to go back, come what may.

He slaps Juke on the shoulder and turns away before his brother-in-law can see the tears in his own eyes. He walks outside to his truck, climbs inside, and drives away, smiling as he wonders how long it'll take Juke to discover the brick of hundreds he slipped into Juke's apron as they hugged.

BOOK II

RUN

CHAPTER ELEVEN

HE OPENS HIS eyes. "Oh shit!"

He turns the wheel hard to swing back onto the roadway.

God, he's tired. He's been on the road for three days, a full day of which he spent in a roadside motel near Columbia, Missouri, puking his guts out. Now, he's on I-76 East, passing a sign that says 24 miles to Valley Forge. His eyes are bleary, his ass hurts from sitting in the driver's seat so long, and his right leg is getting a cramp.

Beyond the narrow tunnel caused by his headlights, it is pitch black, and only rarely does another car or truck pass him going in the opposite direction. He opens the windows to help keep him awake.

He continues for a while, planning to drive the whole way to Philadelphia. But he's caught himself drifting to the left, drifting to the right, speeding up and slowing as his exhaustion pulls him down to sleep, so he decides to get off the highway at the Valley Forge exit. He'll find a hotel, collapse onto a bed, and sink into a delicious sleep.

He leans over to change the radio station and sees flashing lights in his rearview mirror. He glances at the speedometer and finds he's doing ninety miles an hour.

"Shit."

He slows down, slides onto the berm, and stops. The trooper pulls up behind him. In his side-view mirror, he watches the trooper approaching, flashlight in his left hand, the right hand resting on his sidearm, ready for action because everyone knows traffic stops are the most dangerous things police officers do.

He lowers his window and squints as the flashlight hits his eyes. He knows enough to keep his hands on the wheel until the trooper asks him for his license and registration. He tells the cop his wallet is in his back pocket, asks for permission to reach around and get it. The trooper says okay but do it slowly. He retrieves the wallet, slides out the driver's license, and hands it to the trooper, who gives him permission to open the glove compartment for the registration.

He puts his hands back on the steering wheel as the trooper studies the registration and the license. The trooper shines the light into his face again. Then he shines it into the truck cab, fixing it on one spot. He looks down and sees the trooper has fixed on his Philly police badge, which is sitting on the center console. He remembers now that he left the badge there when he started out.

"You want to hand me that?" the trooper says. When he does, the cop compares the badge to the driver's license. "A Philly cop badge but your license is from Kansas."

"Injured on duty. Had to leave the force. I moved to Kansas to be with my family." He's surprised at the ease with which the lies roll off his tongue.

"I'll overlook the speeding because you're a member of the club, or were. But there are some guys out here who wouldn't be as lenient."

He watches the trooper return to his patrol car, then starts up the truck and pulls away. A short time later, he pulls into the parking lot of the Radisson Tower at the Valley Forge Casino and Resort. He parks and enters the round, fifteen-story building to find an atrium overlooking a lobby with a large water fountain. He approaches the desk clerk, a woman in her twenties with a name tag that identifies her as *Emelia*. She looks him over then smiles and asks how she can help him. He asks for a room, says he doesn't have a reservation, which doesn't seem to concern her. Emelia pecks at a keyboard and asks him for a credit card.

He hands her a hundred-dollar bill instead. "I don't carry plastic."

"How many nights?" she asks.

"Probably just one."

"Business?" she asks.

"Monkey," he answers, and they both laugh.

"Will you be going over to the casino?" she asks.

"No. I never liked to gamble."

Is that true? he wonders.

She hands him a paper to sign then gives him an electronic key the size and shape of a credit card. "Have a nice night."

As soon as he gets into the room, he tosses his wallet, cellphone, and badge on the bed stand, lays his suitcase and backpack on the bed, and heads straight for the bathroom. He had to take a piss the whole time he was stopped by the cop and he stands before the toilet for a long time. When he's done, he zips up, turns around, and sees the dark face staring back at him in the mirror above the sink. He takes a step, leans into the mirror to study the new scar on his forehead. Fading, but still red, it's a two-inch vertical line precisely in the middle of his forehead, seeming to split him in half.

As if on split screens, two memories pop up at once. In one, he and Helen are standing by the stove in their kitchen, laughing and dancing, bumping their hips together, each holding a saucepan over a burner, him drinking a Coke, Helen a glass of wine. In the other memory, he's in the front passenger seat of a car, which is off the side of a two-lane road. It's night and it must be moonless and starless because there is virtually no light. He and the car's driver are beating the hell out of each other. He can't see the driver's face because of the darkness, but he can tell the driver is a woman.

"What the hell?"

The memory of him and the woman in the car upsets him. He closes his eyes, tries to find her face in the shadows, but can't. What he is able to access, though, is the fury he feels as they struggle. Fury, and something else. Another type of energy. An alertness, a feeling of power. A *high* . . .

His heart begins to pound in his chest and he leaves the bathroom, paces the bedroom. As he does so, another memory from the car comes to him. It's the woman's voice.

"Fuck you, Jackson!" she says as she slaps at him, scratches him, pulls his hair.

Jackson? He thinks on this, then lifts his cellphone, looks up Casey Colleran, and dials.

"So, you're taking me up on my offer?" she says, a singsong lilt in her voice.

"This is serious. I have a question. What did I go by back in high school?"

"What did you go by?"

"What did people call me?"

A pause. "Everyone called you Jackson. That's your name. Your first name. And I have to tell you, the *Bob* thing never really sounded right to me. But it's what you wanted to be called when you came back ten years ago, so I went along with it. Everyone did. Why are you asking me?" She pauses again. "I suppose you're not calling to get together."

"Not tonight." He hangs up. *Not ever.*

He tosses the phone onto the bed and resumes pacing the room, no longer exhausted but supercharged with adrenalin. After a few minutes, he forces himself to sit on the bed, take deep breaths. His angst eases, but he's not the least bit sleepy now. He'll go stir crazy if he stays in the little hotel room, so he decides the casino isn't such a bad idea after all.

When he gets to the casino floor, he is assaulted by the noise. Electronic ditties, the sounds of dropping coins, flashing lights announcing winners. It's Saturday night and the place is hopping.

He finds a blackjack table with an empty seat and watches a couple of hands to make sure none of the other players are doing stupid things. Nothing mucks up your chances more than playing alongside stooges who don't understand the game.

How does he know that?

He takes the empty seat and a waitress approaches and asks him if he wants a drink. He orders a Coke and she says, "You don't like alcohol?"

The memory of him waking up naked on a bench after a bender flashes through his mind, along with a couple of scenes of him in high revel at some bar or club. "I love alcohol," he says. "It just doesn't love me back."

The waitress smiles, says she'll return with his drink.

He plays a few hands, turns a hundred dollars in chips into five hundred, then a thousand. The dealer, a sexy redhead, slides him a sly smile. "Nice play."

And that's when it hits him: he loves to gamble, always has. And he's damned good at it. Memories of him and some other guys traveling to Atlantic City to hit the Borgata pop up inside his brain like daisies in a field. He made that same trip down the expressway two or three times a month with that crew. But who *were* those guys? He has no clue.

In another memory, he sees himself in the casino with a woman. She stands behind him as he sits at the table, put her hands on his shoulders. He glances down, sees her long fingers, painted nails. She leans into him, nibbles his ear, whispers things, naughty things, telling him how hot it makes her to watch him win all that money, tells him the things she's going to do to him when they get back to their room. The things she's going to let him do to her. He gets hard and starts losing, has to leave the table.

He remembers the smell of the woman's perfume, the sound of her smoky voice. What he can't seem to bring up is her eyes, her lips, her face.

Then his minds jumps, and he's sitting on a ratty, plaid couch in a ratty living room. A woman sits beside him but he can't see her in his memory, because he's focusing on three lines of white powder on the surface of a glass-topped coffee table. He leans down, puts a straw in his nose, and snorts two of the lines.

"Hey, save some for me." The voice of the woman sitting next to him. He ignores her, focusing instead on the intense euphoria that envelops him. He sits back on the sofa, and turns his head toward the woman. But the memory ends before he can glimpse her face.

Someone taps his shoulder and he turns to see the waitress handing him his Coke. He thanks her, hands her a $10 chip for the free drink. He plays a bunch more hands, and the dealer starts flirting openly with him. Is she trying to distract him? Get him to make mistakes, start losing? He doesn't think so, but she's a good-looking woman, certainly doesn't have to go out of her way to find a date. Maybe she's self-destructive, one of those troubled women always looking to get themselves into more trouble. Or maybe she has a daddy fixation; he's a good deal older than she looks to be.

He flirts back and keeps winning. Eventually, another dealer approaches the table to replace the redhead. The new dealer is a man with gray hair, dead eyes, and a pockmarked face. There will be no sly smiles from this one. The player to his right must not like the male dealer, because he gets up right away, takes his chips from the table. After a couple of hands, a twenty-something fills the empty seat and it's clear from the outset that the boy has no idea what he's doing. He suffers the fool for three hands, then calls it quits and heads to the craps table. An hour later, he's up five thousand and cashes in his chips. On the way out, a pit chief offers to comp him a room for the night, but he knows that game and politely declines.

He leaves the casino, ready now for some serious sleep.

*   *   *

The next morning, he wakes to the sound of a toilet flushing. The door to the bathroom opens and the redhead slides into bed with him. It's the dealer from the night before. He ran into her at the entrance to the hallway connecting the casino to the hotel tower. She served up the same sly smile she dealt at the blackjack table, told him about a bar nearby. He agreed to go with her and they had a few drinks, traded small talk.

"I like a man with big hands," she said at the bar.

He looked down at his large hands, the thick fingers of a tough guy. The mitts of Jackson, the Philly cop. And that's who he really was, right? Before he was Bob, living in middle America, married to a sweet, gentle woman named Helen.

She emptied her drink, looked up at him. "You want to bring me back to your place?"

He was exhausted, physically and emotionally spent. But there are expected answers to certain questions, and when an attractive woman asks if you want to take her home, you say yes. Hell, yes. So, he'd spent a good part of the night screwing a twenty-six-year-old redhead named Darcey.

Now, in the sunlight, sitting with her back against the headboard, Darcey pulls a cigarette from a small purse next to her on the nightstand. She lights it with a green plastic lighter, takes a long drag. Then she holds out the smoke for him. "So, what's on your agenda for today?"

He is about to decline the cigarette when something tells him to try it. He accepts the smoke and takes a drag almost as long as Darcey's. *Jesus Christ, that's good.* A dozen memories of him lighting up seep into his brain, reaching back to the time he and Jimmy stole a pack of Pall Malls from their mother and took it to an alley near their house. Jimmy had a Zippo lighter and they used it to light up two cigarettes, which they coughed their way through over the next few minutes. When they were done, they each lit up again. By the time he was halfway through the second smoke, he felt dizzier and more nauseated than he could ever remember. He threw the butt to the ground, crushed it with his sneaker, vowed never to smoke again. And he didn't, until the next day, when he and Jimmy returned to the alley.

"Hey, you with me?" Darcey asks.

"Huh? Yeah, I was just . . ."

"I asked what you're going to do today?"

He doesn't hesitate. "I'm going to begin the search for the man who murdered my wife."

That gets her attention. Darcey's eyes practically bulge out of her head. She starts to say something two or three times, but stops herself. Eventually, she is able to push out, "I'm so sorry."

If there'd been a chance that he and the redhead were going to roll around another time or two before he headed off to the city, his declaration puts a quick end to it. Darcey finishes her cigarette, throws on her clothes, and leaves. She does write down her number before she goes, but he knows he won't call her and doubts she wants him to, big hands or not.

Once she's gone, he takes a shower thinking that a little more than three weeks ago he was turning down Casey Colleran because it was too soon after Helen's death. Now, here he is having sex with a woman he never met before. What's going on with him? He thinks on it until another question arrives as he steps out of the shower: Him who? Small Town Bob? Or Big City Jackson? He walks up to the mirror again, stares at the red line dividing him in half.

CHAPTER TWELVE

AFTER HE SET off for Philadelphia, he realized that once he got there, he'd need a starting point—someone to meet up with and open doors for him. He recalled the memory he'd had of a call with a guy named "Richie," who told him he was *still dead.* So, he pulled out his cellphone and pulled up his contacts list. He'd failed to gain access to the list using "Bob" and "Helen" as passwords. This time, though, he typed in "Jackson," and got through, finding the name Richard Francis next to a number with a 215 area code. He considered calling Richie from Kournfield, telling him he was on his way back east, but decided not to, because for all he knows Richie is connected to the guy who killed Helen. It seems unlikely because the call from Richie that he remembers made it seem like Richie was on his side, acting as his eyes and ears back in Philly, letting him know there were people there who thought he was dead. But as little as he can remember about his time in Kournfield, he recalls even less about his life in Philadelphia. All he knows at this point is that he was a cop, that he knows a guy named Richie, and that he has a brother, Jimmy, who may or may not be living there. His only option is to use those few facts as a springboard to reconstruct the man named Jackson Hunter.

Now, as he drives down I-276 East, he's close enough to Philly that it feels safer calling Richie; even if Richie is connected with the guy who killed Helen, there won't be time for Richie to make plans before he arrives. He reaches for his cellphone, punches in Richie's number, and listens over his truck speakers as the phone rings.

"It's been a week, Jackson," Richie says. "Not a month."

Richie's knowing it's him before he speaks tells Jackson that his own phone number is listed in Richie's contacts list, and Richie's comment about it having been only a week since they'd spoken, not a month, tells him that he and Richie have a standing phone date every thirty days or so. But why?

"I'm on my way there."

"What?"

"I want to meet."

"Are you out of your mind?"

"Someone came out to where I've been living, started asking around about me. Attacked me."

"Shit."

"Someone killed my wife."

Dead silence from the other end.

"Richie?"

"You can't come back here. Ever. Everyone thinks you're dead, remember?"

"Everyone." He repeats the word.

"Starting with Donny."

He says nothing, hoping Richie will volunteer more info.

After a long silence, Richie says, "I don't even like saying that bastard's name. You know he's the chief inspector of detectives now? Word is he's being considered for deputy commish."

Again, he says nothing.

"He'll kill you if he finds out you're alive."

"Not a forgiving soul," he says to Richie, keeping his voice neutral so Richie will interpret it however he wants.

Richie gives him a mirthless laugh. "He wouldn't forgive a guy for stealing five bucks from him, let alone a million-two. I'm serious, Jackson. You can't come back here."

"I'm on 276, almost at the exit for 309 South."

He hears a choking sound on the other end of the line.

"Oh, man." Resignation in Richie's voice. "What are you driving?"

"An F-150."

"All right, listen. I've moved my garage to a new place." He gives an address on Old Bustleton Avenue. "I'll have one of the bay doors open. Pull inside and I'll close the door behind you. Wait until the door's fully down before you get out of your truck."

He hangs up but not before hearing Richie on the other end mutter, "Fuck me."

From the conversation, he gathers two things. First, he stole over a million dollars from a cop named Donny. Second, Donny's a dangerous man.

Twenty minutes later, he brings the truck to a stop in Richie's garage and hears the door rattle down behind him. He steps out of the truck and Richie is standing there, arms crossed. The mechanic is a hefty guy, over six feet and going an easy two-fifty. He has thinning brown hair, and jowls.

He smiles at Richie. "You look like you've seen a ghost."

Richie extends his hand but doesn't smile back. "This is a bad idea, man." He nods to the other side of the garage and leads him, limping, toward a small office.

He takes in the place as they walk. The garage has six bays with lifts and lots of light pouring in through big windows and skylights. The smell is of oil and grease and gasoline—a smell he's always liked, he suddenly remembers. There are red metal toolboxes and hoses and stations for electronic testing. Only one thing is missing.

"There's no one here," he says.

"I sent everyone home."

"Before noon?"

Richie ignores him, closes the door behind them after they enter the office. There's a cracked leather couch pushed up against a wall and he takes one end of it.

"You want some coffee?" Richie asks, nodding to an automatic drip machine crusted with dirt.

Jackson declines and watches as Richie pulls a dirty glass decanter from the machine and empties it into a faded porcelain mug. He senses motion near Richie's desk, watches as a ragged brown calico saunters into the center of the room. The cat appraises him, then sits and starts licking itself.

"I didn't figure you as a cat guy."

Richie shrugs, drops onto the other end of the sofa, sips his coffee. "I wasn't, until I moved my business here. I think this place is some kind of underground railroad for rats. So I went to Animal Control, told them to give me whatever cat was next in the line for the rainbow bridge."

He studies the cat. "What do you feed it?"

Richie stares at him. "Ain't you been listening?"

They sit in silence for a while. Then Richie looks at him. "You said someone killed your wife?"

"It looked like Helen took a bunch of pills. But it didn't make sense because she'd just found out she was pregnant. She told me she had a big surprise for me when I got home from work, and she made my favorite dinner. She . . . bought a crib." He starts to choke up, but stops himself.

Richie nods but looks away.

"You think I'm grasping for straws. That I've convinced myself my wife's death was a murder, not a suicide. But Helen's death was only the first thing. A couple weeks ago, someone snuck up on me and bashed my head against a brick wall. Someone, maybe the same guy, asked a coworker a lot of questions about me. Then someone broke into my house." He tells Richie the stalker left him a key that turned out to fit a strongbox he'd hidden in a crawl space. A strongbox filled with money, his police photo and badge, and a revolver.

"He was leaving me a message that he's from here, from Philadelphia, like me, and that I have to come back here to settle this."

Richie shakes his head. "It doesn't make sense. First off, how would he have the key to the boxful of money you hid? How would he even know about the strongbox? And why kill your wife and not you? I can't see Donny doing that. Sure, it would hurt you to lose your wife, but that wouldn't satisfy him. He'd want you dead."

"And if he kills me now that I'm back here, he gets his wish. Plus, he's tormented me in the meantime." Jackson thinks for a minute. "You say it doesn't sound like something Donny would do. What if it wasn't Donny? Can you think of anyone else who has a score to settle with me?"

Richie looks at him strangely. "Are you shitting me?"

From the way Richie says it, he gathers there are plenty of people who'd want to see him suffer. "All right. I hear you."

Richie leans toward him on the sofa. "Forget for a minute the danger you've placed yourself into by coming back here. Think about everyone else. Me, for starters."

"You?"

"When you left ten years ago, Donny had his boys work me over pretty good . . . before that video showing you getting shot in Florida came to him. He figured maybe I'd know where you'd disappeared to with his money." Richie pauses. "You look like this is news to you, but you already know it."

At the mention of Florida, he remembers what went down there. The recollection begins with him being forcefully pulled by two beefy guys from the back seat of a dark sedan. They'd driven far from Miami to the middle of some swamp. The air was fetid and so humid he was soaked through his shirt almost as soon as they'd forced him from the car. Two other guys, one holding a gun and the other looking like he was in charge, were waiting in the bog.

"I brought the money," he told the boss. One of the stooges punched him in the gut, doubled him over. When he straightened back up, he saw that the other stooge was holding up a small camcorder. "You're *videotaping* this?"

The boss smiled. "Performance art."

"Look, I brought the money!" He was yelling by this point. "You have the suitcase in the car. We're even."

"The money does not make us even," the boss said.

"But you *agreed*—"

The flash from the shooter's gun barrel is the last thing he remembers.

"Why would Donny think you'd know where I'd—" Even before he completes the sentence, a memory pushes its way into his brain. He's in a car, wearing a patrolman's uniform, sitting next to a younger, thinner Richie. A call comes in that someone reported suspicious activity in an electronics store three blocks away. Richie responds into the mic that they're nearby and will take the call. They pull up in front of the building and hear something in an alley abutting the right side of the store. They walk to the alley, drawing their weapons, but before they have a chance to take in the scene, he sees a flash of light. Richie grunts and falls to the ground. He returns fire and hits someone, who drops and starts screaming. At the same time, a second shadow turns and runs down the alley. He races after the perp and, as soon as he clears the alley, finds the guy waiting for him. The perp fires and the slug hits him on his lower right side and the next thing he knows he's on his knees. The perp aims the gun at his head, but it jams and the guy runs away. Jackson scrambles to his feet and pursues the perp, catches up to him, and shoots him during a struggle, killing him.

He's lucky because it turns out his wound was a through-and-through, no organ damage. He's in and out of the hospital in three days and makes a full recovery.

Richie isn't so fortunate. The bullet that hits him splinters his knee and ends his cop career only two years after it began. For the next three years, Richie is in and out of drug and alcohol rehab. Then one morning, he finds Richie on a park bench, naked and covered with vomit . . . *That was* Richie, *not him.* He takes Richie to a friend's hunting cabin in the Poconos and handcuffs him to the bed. He stays with Riche through the hellish nights of DTs, Richie shrieking that he's covered with bugs, begging him to shoot him, put him out of his misery.

When the worst of the withdrawals are over, he tells Richie, "You do this again and I *will* shoot you. And I'll bring your body to your ma's house and hold her while she cries and rips out her hair. Is that what you want? Make your decision."

Six months later, he and Richie co-invest in a small garage with two bays. Richie eventually buys him out and grows his business to the point that he has five employees. Everyone who knows them from the force says Jackson saved Richie's life, twice.

So, yeah, it makes sense for Donny to think that Richie might know where his ex-partner went with Donny's million—and beat the shit out of Richie to find out. But he's pretty sure he never told Richie about Florida, so Richie only found out when everyone else did—when the boys from Miami sent Donny the video showing them shooting him and rolling his body into the swamp—and the news spread down the grapevine. The last part, being put in the swamp, Jackson doesn't remember—he only heard about that from Richie, when he called Richie a year later and told him he was still alive.

All of this—the whole memory—appears fully formed in his mind.

"I'm sorry they roughed you up," he tells Richie. "I didn't see that coming." Or did he?

"That's why I'm telling you this now. You need to understand what'll happen if you suddenly return from the dead. Donny will make a list, and it will have my name on it. And your brother's."

"Jimmy."

"He's got a wife to think about now. And a son."

"A son?"

"Nine years old, I believe."

He still remembers nothing about his brother. Was Jimmy married when he left? Apparently not, based on the way Richie put it. His brother certainly couldn't have had a son then; Jackson left town ten years ago and the boy's nine. "Where's Jimmy living now?"

"I was afraid you'd ask me that."

Richie stares at him, probably hoping he'll reconsider, withdraw the question.

He doesn't and Richie rises from the couch, walks behind his desk, reaches for a notepad. He scribbles something on the top page, tears it off, and holds it out.

He walks over and takes the paper.

"It's a little borough just outside of Lancaster," Richie says, talking about a small city about an hour and a half west of Philadelphia. They stand for a minute and Richie says, "I'm surprised you haven't mentioned the car. I suppose you'll want to take it."

His mind flashes to the key he found in the strongbox; he pulls it out and shows it to Richie.

"Come on." Richie leads him out back to a stand-alone building with two garage doors, windows painted black. Behind the building is a stone railroad trestle sprayed with graffiti painted over the top of graffiti. Only one message hasn't been desecrated: *JRgonegetU!*

Richie unlocks a side door, reaches in, and turns on the light. Following Richie inside, he sees a car covered in a tarp, and a memory materializes of the two of them standing in Richie's first garage, the one they bought together.

Richie took him to the farthest bay from the garage doors and lifted the cover to reveal the rusted wreck of an automobile. A convertible. The front hood sat on top of upside-down seats, along with the windshield. No steering wheel.

"The hell is that?" he asked Richie.

"That, good buddy, is a 1974 Jaguar E-Type XKE Series III V12 Roadster. Manual 4-speed transmission. 254-horsepower engine. Top speed of 217 miles per hour."

"Looks like a pile of junk."

Richie looked over at him. "Not for long."

The memory fades and he's back in the present, Richie still standing next to him. Richie whips off the tarp and the gleaming black sportscar takes his breath away.

Richie laughs. "After you died, I was going to keep it for myself. Hell, I did keep it for myself. I even drove it to your memorial service."

A curtain inside him parts to a small, outdoor memorial service. He sees Richie there. Also present is a man who looks just like him—his twin, Jimmy. A woman with strawberry-blond hair on Jimmy's left, an attractive woman looking to be in her fifties on the right. A few uniformed cops and some suits. He'd been long settled in the Midwest by then, but had returned when Richie called to say he'd been declared dead by the courts, and that his family was holding a small ceremony. He'd watched the memorial service from a distance, through field glasses.

The memorial scene triggers another memory. His mother has two of her friends over to their house on a Sunday morning. He's nine or ten years old. He passes the two women in the living room, waiting for his mother, who is in the kitchen making them coffee. He glances at the women, then goes upstairs. At the top of the steps, he pauses to listen in on their conversation.

"Which one was that?" one of the women asks.

"Not the good one. The good one is more polite."

The second woman's words cut loose a bunch of memories; running down an alley when he was a kid after breaking a bunch of garage door windows; fighting a classmate in junior high; sitting in detention in high school; stumbling drunk as a skunk through the back door of their house one night during summer break from college. He gets to wondering where his brother, Jimmy, was in all this. Jimmy, who, from the woman's comment, was the "good" one.

Richie nods at the car. "I take her out once a week, at night. Race her up and down I-95 and 476, clear her head, and mine." He looks down at the car. "She's all yours now."

"No. I'm not ready yet."

"You? Not ready? That's a good one. I guess wherever you've been living has smoothed some of your edges."

They stand quietly for a while, then Richie turns to him. "You really need to think about this, Jackson. Being alive will likely end up getting you killed."

"I have thought about it. Someone murdered my wife. Maybe it was Donny. Maybe someone else. Either way, I have to find them and make them pay."

"Make them pay." Richie nods his head slowly. "Seems you haven't changed that much after all."

CHAPTER THIRTEEN

HE LEAVES RICHIE'S garage with the intent of driving straight to his brother's house in Lancaster County, but spots a diner a few blocks away and decides to stop. It's almost noon and he's hungry. He also wants to chew on his conversation with his old partner, the questions it answered, the questions it raised.

The waitress approaches and takes his order for a Philly cheesesteak, fries, and a Coke. He catches her staring at him and he wonders whether she knows him from his previous life in the City of Brotherly Love. She walks away, and he pulls out his cellphone and roots around Google until he finds Donald G. Franco, chief inspector of the detective unit. The face belongs to a man in his early fifties. He has salt-and-pepper hair shaved close to the head, pale skin, thin lips, and reptilian eyes that seem to look through you. It's the man on the railroad tracks when Jackson shot the guy in the knee—the guy who ended up dead—prompting Donny to say, "Now you're all in."

Somehow, he managed to steal a million bucks from Donny. Did he work a con of some sort or steal it outright? Either way, Donny hates him and, according to Richie, he's the kind of guy who's willing to kill.

He shifts gears to the guys in Miami. Who were they and what was the deal he reached with them that included Donny's million? His memory of the swamp tells him he was using the money to make up for something he'd done to piss off the Miami guys. So why did they welch on the deal and kill him?

And the biggest question of all—how the hell is he still around if they shot him and dumped his body in a swamp?

The waitress returns with his food and he immediately lifts the cheesesteak and takes a big bite. Its unique flavor and texture take him back to Pat's Steaks in South Philly, when he and some other uniforms were guarding an actor in town making a movie who wanted to experience a real Philly cheesesteak. Some of the cops wanted to take the actor to Gino's, but Jackson persuaded the guy that Pat's was the genuine article. The actor bought sandwiches for himself, all the cops, and the crowd who'd gathered round.

He opens his eyes, sees a young Hispanic guy in a white apron and hat standing by the swinging door to the kitchen, staring at him. The cook quickly averts his eyes and disappears through the door.

He glances at the waitress, sees that she's watched the whole thing. "That guy, the cook. Why was he looking at me?"

The waitress's eyes go wide and some of the color drains from her face. "Oh, he wasn't looking at you. He just stands there sometimes in the doorway is all."

"Get him."

Her mouth opens.

He flattens his eyes and she turns and walks to the kitchen. A minute later, the cook comes out, his hat in his hand. He gulps hard as he approaches the table. The man, thin and appearing to be in his twenties, walks with a pronounced limp.

"Have a seat," he tells the cook, who cautiously slides into the booth opposite him. "Do we know each other?"

The cook looks down. "Not for a long time. A really long time." He looks up then. "I've been out of the business since, well, you know. I *swear.*"

Jackson keeps his face blank, waiting.

"I didn't know anything about what happened," the cook continues. "I was just a kid back then. It was my *brother's* fault."

He looks panicked now and Jackson decides to let him off the hook, though he can't remember what the hook is. "Don't worry about it. I've been out of the business myself for a long time, too."

The cook exhales so loudly that some of the other diners look over at him.

He nods for the cook to go and the guy stands up, and hovers, hat in hand again. "I heard—I heard you were—"

"Dead." He completes the sentence. "I was. But it didn't stick."

He watches the cook limp away, wondering who he must have been in his past life to make the man want to serve up his own brother. Wondering what the cook meant when he said he'd been out of the business since, "well, you know."

*   *   *

Two hours later, he's parked on the edge of a lot bordering the backyard of a small asbestos-shingled Cape Cod near Lancaster, Pennsylvania. In the yard, a good-looking woman is playing with a kid. Jackson recognizes the woman as the blond next to Jimmy at his funeral. The woman and boy are squirting water pistols at each other and laughing. Water pistols—there's something he hasn't seen in years.

The address is the one Richie gave him, where his brother lives. The woman must be Jimmy's wife, the boy his son. Jackson's happy his brother has a family. He wonders how happy Jimmy will be to see him, learn he's not dead after all.

He exits the car and walks across the lot toward the backyard. When he gets close, the woman notices him and he can tell she's straining to make sense of what she's seeing. All at once, her face contorts in a combination of shock and terror. She stumbles backward so abruptly that she actually falls to the ground. Then she jumps up, grabs the boy by the hand, and pulls him inside.

He's about three steps into the yard when Jimmy races out the back door and down the steps. It feels strange to see his own face looking back at him.

Jimmy plants himself three feet in front of him, steel in his eyes. If Jackson was expecting a reunion of hugs and tears, he's not going to get it.

"You fucker," Jimmy seethes. "Alive all this time and letting everyone think you were dead. Me and Pam. And Mom."

So, his mother's alive. Good. "I wanted to keep you all safe."

"Safe? Tell that to my broken ribs. My bruised kidney."

"Donny Franco?"

"Who else? You had to know he'd come after me. Try to beat it out of me . . . where you'd gone with his money." Jimmy pauses. "So the rumor about you getting whacked was bullshit."

"It didn't feel like bullshit at the time." As far as he can remember.

"Is it true? The part about you stealing a million bucks from Donny Franco?"

"Who told you that?"

"Donny did, when his thugs were beating the crap out of me."

He opens his mouth, but before he can apologize, Jimmy continues.

"You want to tell me why you did that?"

He wishes he could. But he has no idea. Another missing piece of the puzzle.

"Some things are best left unsaid." Over Jimmy's shoulder, a curtain moves and Pam—Jackson assumes this is the Pam Jimmy mentioned—looks out at him.

Jimmy glances toward the window, then back at him. "Keep your eyes off my wife."

All at once, the memories explode like fireworks. Scene after scene of him and Pam having sex. Sex in cars. Sex in bedrooms, hotel rooms, on beds, floors, in the shower. Sex from the back, the front, the top, the bottom.

Oh, hell. He was nailing his own brother's wife . . . Is that the reason Jimmy hates him?

What kind of prick was I?

Jimmy takes a step closer. "You must know that by showing up here, you're putting the rest of us in danger. Donny will sic his goons on me again. And now that I'm married and have a kid . . ." Jimmy's voice trails off but the fire in his eyes remains. "Why are you here? What do you want?"

"Someone killed my wife and left clues leading me back here."

The news seems to rattle his brother. "I'm . . . sorry to hear . . ." Jimmy stares at him, some of the anger melting from his face. "Where have you been all this time?"

"The Midwest. I settled down."

Jimmy laughs. "You? Settled down? I don't believe it."

"It was different out there. *I* was different, it seems."

Jimmy thinks on this. "So, which version of you came back from *out there*? The different you, or the old you I know?"

He looks down, kicks at the ground. "I'm not sure yet." He sighs. "Can I ask you something? How bad was I, before I left?"

Jimmy closes his eyes, and he can tell his brother is taking a mental inventory before answering. His brother opens his eyes again, and the fire is back.

"Let's put it this way," Jimmy says. "You were bad enough that even though you're my brother and even though I thought you were dead and I haven't seen you in ten years, I'm not going to invite you into my home for dinner or even a glass of tap water."

With that, Jimmy turns and walks up the back steps. On the landing, he turns. "Go back to whatever rock you've been hiding under before someone stupid enough to love you gets hurt, or worse." Jimmy walks inside. The screen door slams behind him.

He walks back to his truck, uses the Google app on his cell to look up Jimmy's house number, and leaves a message with his cellphone number. He tells Jimmy to call him, but he knows that's not going to happen.

* * *

That night, lying in bed in a Comfort Inn east of Lancaster— because he'd decided to think things through a little more before heading back to Philadelphia—he fights off more memories of him and Pam going at it . . . in a small apartment, in the tiny bathroom of an airplane. No wonder she fled from him in the backyard.

He forces himself to lie back down and his mind drifts to the redhead, the dealer at the casino, and he wishes he weren't alone. He's feeling a restlessness here, back east, that he doesn't remember feeling in Kournfield. But that doesn't tell him anything because he can't remember much about himself in the Midwest.

All he knows is that ten thousand years ago on the other side of the world, he was an ordinary man—Bob—who loved a woman named Helen. They had friends and jobs and a little house.

He decides he needs some fresh air, so he goes outside, hoping to clear his head. As soon as he gets out of the door, he spots the dark gray car, the Chrysler 300 with the tinted windows from Kournfield. He strides toward the car and the headlights illuminate and the car starts pulling away.

"Hey! Hey!" He chases the car, shouting. The sedan picks up speed and races out of the lot but not before he notes that the car has no license plate.

There is little doubt in his mind now that Helen's killer is from the east, meaning he's one of Donny Franco's guys, which means Donny has decided to get even with him after all. Chewing on this, though, he spots some flaws in his logic. Donny would want his money back, and he'd be more likely to get it by kidnapping Helen and threatening to kill her unless Jackson turned over the cash. And even if, for some reason, Donny just wanted revenge and was content to forego the money, he wouldn't kill Helen with pills; he'd use a method that was a lot messier, a method that involved blood.

And how did Donny find out he was still alive? That he'd been living in Kansas? As far as he knows, Richie is the only person who knew the Miami guys had somehow failed in their attempt to kill him—which itself makes no sense, because he remembers the gun going off at point-blank range. And Donny evidently received a video showing the Miami guys rolling him into a swamp.

Richie. His former partner, a man whose life he saved. Did Richie rat him out to Donny Franco? Why would he do that?

He walks to the front of the hotel, by the lobby, and sits on a bench. He's jumping to conclusions and he knows it and he doesn't like that he's questioning the loyalty of his former partner. So, he takes a deep breath and pulls out his cellphone and punches in Richie's number.

"It's me," he says when Richie picks up.

"Where are you?"

"I saw my brother."

"How'd that go."

"Not well."

"What'd you expect?" Richie pauses. "Was Pam there?"

"Until she saw me. Then she bolted."

"Can you blame her?"

He takes a deep breath. "Listen. I was thinking about Donny, trying to figure out how he knows I'm still alive." He pauses. "You and me go back a long time. So I'm not going to beat around the bush—"

"Really? Beating around the bush seems like exactly what you're doing. So I'll beat you to the punch. You want to know if I'm the one that ratted you out to Donny, told him you were still alive. And the answer is no. And the other answer is *fuck you* for even thinking it."

"Ouch. But thanks."

There is dead air between them until he tells Richie, "I'm going to have to face Donny sooner or later. I want to know all the angles before that happens. I want to know everything that came between me and him, made me do what I did."

"There are only two angles, Jackson. The money and . . ."

"And what?"

"Do I really have to say it?"

"Say it."

"*Her.*"

In a flash, his mind races back to the memory of being in the car with the woman whose face he can't see. He's speeding down a snaking country road late at night. This time he doesn't see her hands, only the back of her head, on his lap. The road-head and coke have his heart racing faster than the Jag. He knows it's crazy, mixing the drugs, the sex, and the speed, but that's the way they live now. Her and him.

She finishes him off, lifts her head, licks her lips. The rest of her face is hiding in the darkness of the moonless night, but a sliver of light illuminates her lips, full and pouty. He stuffs himself back in his pants and the dashboard light shines on the tattoo on the inside of her wrist—a skull and crossbones.

They got the tattoos together—he remembers that now.

Sitting on the bench outside the hotel, he glances down at his arm and there it is, on the underside of his forearm, the Jolly Roger.

"Her." He speaks the word aloud.

A sigh on the other end of the call, then Richie says, "She was the beginning of the end for you, Jackson . . . no, wait, that's wrong. She was the beginning *and* the end."

He doesn't disagree. He doesn't know enough to disagree, or to agree for that matter. Because other than her lips, her hands, the tattoo, the blowjob, nothing of the woman has made its way into his memory.

"Say her name," he tells Richie.

A long pause at the other end. "Vanessa."

"Vanessa." He repeats her name and something comes over him. It's the feeling you get when a storm approaches, the hair on the back of the neck, on your arms, rising from the electrical charge in the air.

"Where is she, Richie?"

"No. It won't be me that sends you to her door."

"The address."

"I'd chain you to the fucking bed, like you did for me, to keep you away from her."

"Don't make me come there, Richie."

"You saved me from my addiction. Don't ask me to feed you to yours."

The line goes dead. He lays the cellphone on the bench beside him, studies the skull and crossbones on his arm. In the days of pirates, the Jolly Roger meant the pirate crew flying it would take no prisoners. Pillage and death awaited every sorry soul aboard a vessel attacked by a ship flying the black flag—the same emblem, it seems, that he and Vanessa adopted to symbolize their relationship.

Tomorrow, he will wake up and find *her*. Vanessa. She was the end of him once, Richie said, and maybe she will be so again. But she could be a stepping-stone to Donny, someone with inside information on him, a weakness in Donny's armor.

He's about to stand when his cellphone rings. He's hoping it's Richie, having changed his mind about giving him Vanessa's address. He punches the button. "Hello."

"You're alive." A woman's voice.

Before he can answer, she continues. "Your brother called me. It would've been nice if you had called me yourself . . . *ten years ago*. I gave you life, after all."

"Mom." He wonders how she has his cell number, but then figures Jimmy must have given it to her.

A dozen fresh memories crystallize in his brain. Her serving meals to him and Jimmy, taking them shopping for school clothes, watching TV with them at night, cheering them on at high-school football games. Ordinary memories of an ordinary childhood.

"I'm sorry, Mom," he says. "It was a shitty thing to do—"

"Shitty? A son not calling his mother for two weeks or a month, that's shitty. What you did to me—letting me think you were dead, murdered—goes way beyond that. But what could I expect, given what you'd become?"

What I'd become . . .

"I'd like to see you," she says.

"Yes. Of course. Where are you?"

"The Governor's Residence, in Harrisburg."

"The Governor's Residence?"

"You don't know? That Howard's governor? Where have you been all this time?"

"Kournfield."

"Why on earth did you go back there? No, don't tell me. We'll talk about everything tomorrow. I'll put you on the approved list with security. Eleven o'clock."

They hang up and suddenly he can see his mother clearly. She's a good-looking woman—long, dark hair, olive skin, hazel eyes. She's tall and thin and carries herself elegantly. Her name pops into his head—Evelyn. A sophisticated name. It fits her.

The memory takes place when he and Jimmy are in tenth grade. Evelyn lowers herself onto a wing chair across the coffee table from her sons and gets right down to business.

"We're going to be leaving the area for a while."

He and Jimmy glance at each other, then back at her.

"What does that mean?" Jimmy asks.

"We're moving. Out of state."

"*What?*" He and Jimmy jump up at the same time and the scene that follows is ugly, his memory of it ending where he storms out of the house, slamming the door behind him.

Another memory pops into his mind of him in the passenger seat of their family car, his mother driving, Jimmy in the back.

"This will be an adventure," his mother says.

"I can't believe you let him run us out of town," he says.

"This wasn't Howard's idea; it was mine. There are things going on you don't understand."

"We understand plenty, Mom. With Dad out of the picture for so long, you decided to find someone else. But instead of a single guy, you ended up with a someone who's married—your boss, Howard. And now that Howard's running for district attorney, you have to get out of Dodge before the press finds out."

"Don't talk to me like that. I'm your mother. And how dare you listen in on my private conversations?"

"It's not a private conversation if it happens in our living room." This from Jimmy, stewing in the back seat.

On the bench outside his hotel, Jackson searches his brain, trying to recall what his adjustment was like after they moved to Kansas. He remembers him and Jimmy deriding their new town, calling it Cornponeville. At the same time, a scene flashes into his mind of getting into a fight with a new schoolmate, the other guy ending up on the ground after Jackson lands a solid kick to his head. Looking back on it now, he realizes he must have learned to kickbox when he was a kid.

He lifts himself from the bench and walks back to his hotel room, wondering what it will be like seeing his mother after all these years. Wondering what she's like now. Wondering what she was like *then*, when they were living in Kournfield . . . and when they came back to Philly.

CHAPTER FOURTEEN

HE PARKS HIS truck in the lot on Second and Mackey Streets and walks the few blocks to the Governor's Residence, a three-story, brick neo-Georgian-style mansion. Once inside, he gives his name to a security guard, who escorts him upstairs to the private residence, and into a conservatively opulent living room. The guard tells him to have a seat, but he chooses to remain standing and walks to a window, takes in the view of the Susquehanna River.

He doesn't hear his mother enter but feels her behind him and turns around. In her sixties now, she is still an attractive woman, the olive skin still mostly smooth, her figure trim. She is dressed in a white blouse over dark slacks.

She smiles at him—a guarded smile, he can tell—and they walk toward each other and embrace. At first, she gives him what he senses is a politician's hug, arms loose around him, hands on the shoulder blades, ready for a quick pat. But then she steps into him, squeezes him—a mother's embrace for a long-lost son. He reciprocates and they hold each other for a long time.

She releases him and steps back, and he watches the warmth drain from her eyes.

"I'm so angry at you," she says.

"I know, I know, I deserve it. Not letting you know I was alive."

"Oh, Jackson. If that were all of it . . ." Her voice trails off. She signals him to sit and they lower themselves onto facing arm chairs.

"I wasn't a good man."

"It broke my heart seeing what you became," she says. "Watching you turn your back on your brother, your wife."

"My wife?"

"That poor girl idolized you since you were kids. You knew that. How you could treat her so callously is beyond me. Thank God Jimmy was there to pick up the pieces."

"Jimmy? *Pam?*" His brother is married to his ex-wife? He takes some deep breaths to gather his thoughts and a video starts playing of him standing at the altar as Pam's father walks her down the aisle. Pam is radiant in her white gown, and he can't believe this is the same skinny girl he and Jimmy used to play with as kids. He smiles until another memory sprouts up of him stumbling into the house one morning as Pam confronts him, eyes red and swollen.

"Where the hell have you been?" she seethes. "As if I don't *know.*" She throws something at him. A shoe? A book?

He slinks around the house, takes a shower, gets dressed and leaves, Pam crying the whole time in their bedroom. Then, driving to the station, he gets a call on his cellphone and it's Jimmy yelling at him for being such a prick to Pam. How could he do that? She grew up with them.

"Oh, don't act so surprised," says his mother. "Who did you think Pam would turn to when you performed your disappearing act? Jimmy was good to her even when she gave him the cold shoulder, even when she married you."

He keeps his eyes on the floor, knowing he deserves whatever his mother is dishing out.

"They're happy now. Both of them. And they have a son. Randy. So, don't you dare ruin things for them."

He looks up at her, wanting to say he'd never do that. But he apparently already had, once.

A butler appears with coffee service, lays the silver tray on the coffee table. Evelyn signals the man to leave, pours a cup for him and for herself. He accepts the coffee and drinks it, enjoying how the cream takes the bitterness from the coffee.

"Jimmy told me you were married," Evelyn says. "And that your wife died."

"She didn't die. She was murdered."

Evelyn pauses. "And you came east thinking the killer is here?"

He nods.

"So now what?"

He looks at her.

"What happens if you find the person who did it?"

"I haven't thought that far ahead."

"Apparently, you haven't thought ahead at all. If you had, you'd never have brought yourself anywhere close to Donny Franco." She puts down her cup. "I could ask what you were thinking, stealing from that man, but I'd first have to ask what on earth drove you to join up with him in the first place. There've been whispers about Donny since the day he joined the force. The only reason he didn't go down was that half of his family's with Internal Affairs."

She shakes her head, stands, and crosses her arms. "I still cannot believe my own son was a crooked cop. And not just one of them, the worst of them."

"The worst?"

"Don't you dare pretend. Your reputation preceded you. But I expect that was the point."

So, he was a crooked cop surrounding himself with other crooked cops. But crooked in what way? The *worst*? How? He can see that his mother's patience is wearing thin, that she's not going to want to get into it with him. So he switches gears.

"I'm going to confront Donny Franco about my wife's death. Before that, though, I need to find out as much information as I can, get all my ducks in line." He pauses. "I need to find Vanessa."

His mother cringes. "Don't say that name in my presence. It's disrespectful to Pam, who is still my daughter-in-law."

He waits.

"No," she says. "I'm not going to help you find her."

"But you know where she is." It's a guess on his part, but his gut tells him it's a good one.

She looks away, then back at him. "Your wife in Kournfield, what was her name?"

"Helen."

"Were you good to her? Was she good to you?"

"We were great together." Based on what he's learned so far. "Helen was a good woman. And I was a good man, with her."

"I wish I had met her. She must've been a miracle worker or a saint if she made you into a good man." She closes her eyes. "Jesus, why did you come back here? Why stir up the demons that corrupted your soul?"

There is a small writing desk in the room and Evelyn walks over to it. She scratches something on a piece of stationery with the state seal at the top, then hands him the sheet.

"Things would probably work out better for you if I screamed and the security guards ran in here and shot you dead," she says with a shrug.

He accepts the paper, folds it, stuffs it into the pocket of his jeans. They hug again and when his mother turns and leaves the room, he spots a tear on her face, and his mind takes him back to what Jimmy said about "anyone stupid enough to love you."

In his car, he pulls out the sheet his mother gave him. Written on it are two lines.

Symphony House

Don't!

CHAPTER FIFTEEN

Symphony House is a luxe condominium building on South Broad Street, rechristened Avenue of the Arts to make it sound more cosmopolitan. A block down, across Broad, is the Double-Tree Hotel. He checks in, drops his belongings in his room, and walks to Symphony House. He enters the building and the receptionist keeps her eyes locked on him as he approaches the desk. She's pretty, eye candy for the wealthy tenants, he figures.

She smiles at him. "May I help you?"

"I'm here to see Vanessa."

"Vanessa?"

"You know who I mean." If Vanessa's what he thinks she is, she's the type who leaves an impression.

"We have several Vanessas who live here," the desk clerk says, a sparkle in her eye that tells him she knows exactly whom he's referring to.

He smiles. "I'm looking for the one who leaves a trail of broken hearts behind her."

The woman smiles back. "Is yours one of them?"

"Tell her Jackson Hunter is here."

She gets that the game is over and pouts. She makes the call and when she gets to the part where she says his name, she waits.

"Miss Reif?"

So, Vanessa is a Miss not a Mrs. He thought maybe the mention of her last name would shake something loose, but it doesn't. All he can retrieve are the lips, the hands, the tattoo, the back of her head.

The desk clerk listens then hangs up the phone. "She says I can let you up in twenty minutes."

Vanessa, it seems, wants time to ready herself. To primp. He likes that.

He leaves the building, spots two uniforms down the street guarding a seemingly stalled car at the entrance to a large parking garage. One's tall, the other short. Mutt and Jeff.

He meanders up to them. "I used to be on the force," he says, breaking the ice.

Mutt asks when and what district.

"It was back in the day," he answers. "I was with Donny Franco's crew."

The smiles on the young patrolmen's faces disappear. They glance at each other, and he can see they're silently warning each other to be careful.

"So, what do you have here?" He nods at the car.

"C&C," Jeff replies. "Corpse in a car."

He bends down, looks through the window, sees the driver slumped over, eyes open. "Damn."

"We're getting them all the time now," Mutt explains. "Some guy gets into his self-driving car, punches in an address, and away he goes. Along the way, his time runs out. Sometimes another driver will see what's happened, call it in, and Dispatch will have us tail the car, handle whoever's waiting for the guy. Other times, the car delivers the stiff and . . . *surprise!*"

"Isn't technology great," says Jeff.

"You know anything about this guy?" he asks, and just then a woman runs out of a hotel, races toward the car, screaming.

"We will soon enough," Mutt says, steeling himself for the hysterics.

Jackson turns away, walks back to Symphony House.

The pretty receptionist points to the elevators. "She's in 505."

His heart speeds up and he takes some deep breaths. His police partner and his mother both told him not to see *her*, this woman who turned out to be his undoing, his beginning and his end. He'll soon know why.

He knocks on the door and, after a minute, hears heels on a hardwood floor, the click of the lock, the chain being slid off. The door opens and suddenly it's thirteen years ago.

He's on patrol in North Philadelphia with Ken Fellner, the partner he had after Richie. A call comes in about a domestic dispute and Ken accepts it. Five minutes later, they pull up to a two-story row house on Sheffield Avenue. A frayed American flag hangs limply below a second-floor window. A pair of white plastic chairs sit on the postage-stamp lawn, which is divided by a cracked cement walkway. They climb the steps to the front door, eavesdrop on the shouting on the other side. Ken knocks hard on the door and they both shout, "Police!"

"You bitch." A man's voice.

"*I* didn't call them. Asshole!" The wife.

The door is unlocked, and they open it, walk inside, separate the lovebirds, a ragged middle-aged couple. Ken escorts the husband into the kitchen; Jackson sits the wife down on the worn sofa.

"Has he hit you?" he asks the wife, scanning for bruises.

"Just let him try," she says.

"Do you feel you're in physical danger?"

"Someone lights a match to his breath, this whole house will go up."

And on it goes, until he and Ken are satisfied there's little chance of imminent physical injury and neither Prince Charming nor Cinderella wants to press charges, which tells him that it was one of the neighbors who called 911, hoping to get a few minutes' peace from all the yelling.

Then it happens. He and Ken are on their way out when nineteen-year-old Vanessa makes her appearance from a back bedroom. And just like that, it's game over. Everything he was, everything he is now, is swept away. A single word escapes his mouth.

"Fuck."

Ken pulls him out of the house, waits for him to buckle up in the car. "What the hell was *that* about?"

They drive around for a while, pull into a chicken place for a bite. Ken orders their food, brings it to the table. He picks at the soggy thighs, tries a plastic spoonful of the watery mashed potatoes.

"Forget about her," Ken says.

He looks at Ken—father of four, married twenty years. Overweight, drooping jowls. His polar opposite in just about every way. But right now, at this minute—and he knows this is the only time he will ever feel this way—he would consider trading places because he knows—he knows in his very bones—what's coming.

"I am so screwed."

That night, he makes love to Pam—the girl he grew up with, the girl who has loved him since they were both in braces, the woman he has come to love, honor, and even cherish most of the time—and he feels like he's fucking cardboard. Because he's known from the instant he saw that other woman's face—and,

Jesus, he doesn't even know her name yet—that she's his china white. The drug compared to which everything else will feel flat and flavorless.

That night, Pam holds him in their bed, not knowing that the man she loves is dying beside her, the clock ticking down on the last hours, the last minutes, of everything that had been good in him.

Now, thirteen years later, standing in her hallway, he's staring into her emerald green eyes. They are flat, and he can tell she's studying him, evaluating him, making her calculations. He stares back at her, doing the same, wondering just how dangerous she still is.

Vanessa steps back to invite him into the apartment and he takes in the rest of her. She is tall, 5'9" or 5'10", and thin. Luxurious auburn hair. Full lips. An oval face of porcelain skin. She was nineteen when he first laid eyes on her, nineteen to his twenty-eight, which means she's thirty-two now.

She goes to turn, but he reaches out, grabs her by the wrist—not roughly but not gently, either. He rolls up her silk sleeve and there it is—the tattoo. She nods toward his arm, and he rolls up his own sleeve to show her he still has his, too. Pirates they were, and still are.

She smiles when she sees the skull and crossbones, then leads him down the hall into her living room. It's a comfortable space, coolly elegant, with a white cloth sofa and chairs, marble-top coffee table, floor-to-ceiling drapes framing the windows, which face south and west and wash the room with light.

He walks to one of the windows, gazes out at South Philadelphia—blocks and blocks of row houses stretching the whole way to the stadiums. Behind him, Vanessa leaves the room, then returns from the kitchen with a wineglass in one hand, a tumbler in the other. He accepts the tumbler and they clink glasses. The liquor is fire in his throat, and he likes it.

They face off at the window, neither wanting to move. Neither wanting to talk, because they both know that when they do, the past will rise up behind them again. They will be prisoners of the present, chained by the mistakes and pain of every day they've lived until now.

He watches her take a long, deep breath.

"Back from the dead," she says. Then she slaps him in the face. He takes it and she slaps him again, and again it fails to get a rise out of him, and she gets angry. "Seems you're more dead than back."

"I'm only dead for you," he says.

A flicker in her eyes tells him she thinks that's funny, as in ridiculous. Impossible.

She turns from him, walks to the sofa, her motions languid, feline.

His mind flashes back to the memory of the ratty plaid couch in the ratty room where he snorted coke next to a woman whose face his memory didn't share with him. He doesn't need to see her face to know it wasn't Vanessa. The woman next to him on the ratty couch gave off a different kind of energy, a lesser energy—a rattier energy?—than Vanessa's. Clearly someone he dated before Vanessa.

He takes another sip of the whisky, glances out the window, then takes a seat on the other end of the sofa. They study each other for a long time.

"Penny for your thoughts," she says.

And the memories flood his brain.

CHAPTER SIXTEEN

IT'S THE NIGHT after he met Vanessa, and he's hanging out after work with some fellow patrolmen at a cop bar in North Philly. The other guys are talking Phillies and Eagles and what shits their corporals and sergeants are, but he's standing there in a daze. All that day he's been fixated on *her*, trying to figure out a way of seeing her again without knocking on her parents' door. He doesn't know where she works or goes to school. He doesn't know anything about her, other than that he must be with her, and he knows that she knows it, too. He saw it in the look she gave him.

It's his turn to buy and he walks up to the bar, thinking one last drink and then he'll go home. He glances out the window and there she is, staring in at him. In a flash, he's outside, facing her on the street.

"How'd you know I'd be here?" he asks.

"Most popular cop bar in the Northeast."

He stares at her.

"I got tired of waiting," she says.

"Not even twenty-four hours."

"Seemed like forever."

He grabs her by the arm, pulls her into an alley beside the bar, throws her against the wall. They kiss each other so hard he thinks his lips will bleed.

"Take me," she says.

"No, somewhere nice. Not here."

"Here," she says. She fumbles with his zipper, pulls him out. She climbs onto him, wraps her legs around his waist, and he sees she's wearing no panties under her short skirt.

"Take me," she repeats. And he does.

"Harder," she says. And he complies.

An hour later they're in the back seat of his car, naked from the waist down. She pulls a joint from her handbag, lights it up, and they pass it back and forth.

He stares at her. "Where did you come from?"

She laughs. "Catholic school."

*   *   *

"What? A penny's not enough?" asks Vanessa from across the couch.

"You don't want to know what I'm thinking about."

She leans forward. "Me, obviously. We had good times."

"Bad times, too," he says, and he's pulled into another memory. It's the second or third year he's been mixed up with Vanessa and he's lost weight from the partying, the stress. His face is gaunt, his muscles ropy. He stumbles home late one night, reeking of booze and sweat and salty sex. He opens the front door and his face explodes. Jimmy's punch sends him flying backward, onto the porch. A second later, Jimmy's on top of him, pummeling him. Jimmy's a good fighter, damned good. But he's better and he manages to get Jimmy off, and they go at it standing up—punching and kicking. Behind them, Pam is screaming, begging them to stop. Some of the neighbors come outside and they shout, too, but no one wants to get between these snarling beasts.

Finally, he has Jimmy on the ground, one hand around his brother's throat, the other in the air, a hammer ready to drop.

"You shit," Jimmy seethes. "You fuck. You're killing her. You're breaking her heart."

"That's none of your business," he says, but he knows it's not true because Pam has been a part of Jimmy's life as long as she's been in his. He hovers over his brother, not sure what to do, when the squad cars arrive and the uniforms pour out, pull him off Jimmy, throw him to the ground. Cuff him.

"You're making a big mistake," Jackson tells the patrolmen. "You know who I am? Who I work for?"

The memory skips to a different scene. He walks into Donny's office and Donny tells him to sit down and close the door, and he does as he's told. Across the desk, Donny stares at him with alligator's eyes.

"So, you get into a fight with your brother," Donny begins, his voice all gravel and sandpaper and smoke. "A fight so bad it spills into the street, where everybody can see. So bad the neighbors call the cops and you get hauled in and I have to kiss some lieutenant's ass to get you out of trouble."

He averts his eyes.

"Look at me," Donny says. Then he sits back in his chair, puts his hands on his lap, and slowly shakes his head. "I'm starting to have my doubts about you."

The memory ends, a projector running out of film, and he's back with Vanessa.

"Actually, I'm thinking about Donny. That's why I came here. Donny must've found out where I was living, because he sent someone out there to get even with me. Well, he got even, and now I'm going to get even back. I just want to know as much as I can about what happened between me and Donny. For starters, what happened that made me steal from him?"

"How would *I* know that? It's not like you shared your plans. You disappeared. You left me." She glares at him. "You want to tell me why? You want to give me an answer to *that* question?"

He shakes his head and another memory drives itself into his brain.

"Slow the fuck down!" His hands are pushing against the dashboard, his right foot pressing against the brake pedal that isn't there because Vanessa's driving. They left the loft party, both of them high as kites on cocaine and booze, and she beat him to the Jag, and jumped into the driver's seat. She said she wanted to drive for once, and he was so fucked up he let her.

They ended up on some back road and now she's driving like Andretti, if Andretti were drunk and high on coke.

"I said slow down!" He shouts at her again, but all it does is make her laugh and drive faster. Finally, they come to a curve so sharp even she can see they aren't going to make it, and she slams on the brakes, but the car slides off the road, doing 360s before it comes to a rough stop. He curses her out, smacks her in the head, and she slaps him back and scratches his face and they slap and punch at each other until they aren't fighting anymore but ripping off each other's clothes.

"Take me, Jackson. Harder, harder." Her mantra.

And when they're done and he's panting in his seat, loving her and hating her guts, he knows that something has to give. Their relationship—the fucking, the fighting, the booze and drugs and late nights—is both making him feel alive and killing him inch by inch. He decides he's finished, but in the same instant, he realizes he'll never be able to leave her, never be able to turn away from his twisted new life.

Back in Vanessa's apartment, he remembers all these thoughts going through his head, and he wonders what finally gave him the courage to leave.

"You had a million bucks, more than a million," Vanessa says. "You knew I'd follow you anywhere. But you never asked me to. You just took Donny's money and—"

"Died," he cuts in. "Got myself shot and kicked into a swamp by the guys in Miami."

"But you didn't stay dead. They made some kind of mistake and you came back. But you didn't come back for *me*. I was left here alone with a broken heart and a million questions."

"A broken heart. That's a laugh."

"I was sick in love with you, Jackson. From the second I saw you in my parents' house, tall and strong in your uniform. A man in control. There's a guy who can take me places—that's what I told myself. A man who can show me things. And I saw in your eyes the same thing that looked back at me every time I looked at myself in the mirror ever since I was a little girl."

"What *thing* is that?"

"There's no name for it. It just is. A thing that waits inside your bones, ready to wake up and pounce, and all it needs to break free is to find another one of its kind in someone else."

He wills himself to the present, studies Vanessa.

"Remember the poem?" she asks.

"Poem?"

"The one we wrote together." She pauses. *"If we by chance should come to meet on some forbidden night . . ."*

He sits up and recites without hesitation: *"Should circum-stance defeat the plan to keep us disunite . . ."*

"In wild, rampageous dance we'll greet . . ."

They finish it together: *"And set the world alight."*

He lowers his head, whispers, "Jesus. What did we do?"

"Don't you remember? We did it *all.*"

He holds her stare, and something stirs inside him.

A knock comes at the door.

"That must be someone from the front desk," she says. "Other-wise, they'd have called up. I don't want to deal. Can you get it?"

He walks to the door and opens it. Two large men are standing on the other side, and he knows right away what's happening.

A memory surfaces from the first year of their relationship, before the mania and drugs and booze started to take their toll on him. They are in the kitchen of the two-story row house he rents for her in South Philadelphia. It's a warm night in June and the windows are open to let in air. A slight breeze carries the street sounds into the house—people walking down the street engaged in quiet conversation, the occasional beeping car horn, a loud television in the living room of a house nearby. Every evening, an old man sits on his steps across the streets and lights up, and he and Vanessa can hear him coughing, smell the smoke from his cigarette.

Vanessa is dressed in blue jean shorts and a wife-beater t-shirt, and he can see her nipples pushing out the fabric. Her auburn hair is tied on top of her head, but a few strands are stuck to her sweaty neck. She reaches across the table to dish herself some more spaghetti and meatballs, a move he finds sexy, like every other move she makes.

He dishes himself some spaghetti, then stands and walks to the refrigerator, pulls out another beer. The bare wood floor creaks under his weight. He likes that, likes that the floor actually sags a little, that the walls aren't perfectly square. He likes that the house is a hundred years old and still has the original windows, the wood framing for which has probably been painted and stripped scores of times. In the winters, he can smell the oil from the basement furnace. In the summers, he can smell all the odors that have seeped into the walls and floors and ceilings over the decades.

The house feels real to him. And he feels more alive here than anywhere he's ever been. Part of that, of course, is Vanessa. She awakens, electrifies, every sense in him. He seems to have the same effect on her.

"Look at us," Vanessa says. She reaches across the table, covers his hand with hers.

"What?"

"Sitting still." She smiles.

"It won't last," he says.

She gets that look in her eyes. "Not if I can help it."

After the meal that night in the row house, he and Vanessa led each other upstairs. Instead of their normal clawing, rapacious fuck-fest, though, they made love. It was gentle, sweet, its rarity now giving the memory enough power to punch through his amnesia.

With the two goons hovering in Vanessa's doorway, he turns to her. The coldness in Vanessa's eyes now is so different from the heat he saw during their relationship. He also notes the contrast between the South Philly row house and Vanessa's hermetically sealed condo, closed off to the sounds and smells of the outside world, with wall-to-wall carpeting over concrete flooring that seems unaware of their presence.

It hits him that Vanessa's furious, fiery passion has frozen over. "What happened to you?" he asks her.

"You left me." She stares at him for a long moment, then over his shoulder at the apartment door.

He turns around. "Come on in," he tells Donny Franco's goons. "The sooner we get this over with, the better."

CHAPTER SEVENTEEN

Donny's boys take him to the garage, where a third hench-man, a driver, is waiting. They search him for weapons then shove him into the back of a dark sedan. No one says anything until they pull onto Broad Street. Then the guy in the back seat with him looks him up and down.

"So, you're the legend we've all heard so much about? You don't look that tough to me. Hey, Ted," he says to the guy riding shotgun. "Does he look tough to you?"

"Shut up, Andy," Ted says without turning around. "Just keep your eyes on him."

"Don't worry. He makes a move, I'm ready for him."

He envisions Ted rolling his eyes at Andy. He looks over at Andy, takes his measure. Andy appears to be in his late twenties, early thirties. He's a big boy, for sure, can probably hold his own in a street brawl. But he doubts Andy has ever faced off against someone who really knows how to fight. Ted is older, early fif-ties, and of the three guys in the car, he's clearly the one in charge. The driver is morbidly obese, wouldn't be much good in a fight. He figures Andy and Ted are detectives and the driver is some-body's cousin.

"When did you join the force?" he asks Ted.

"No talking," Ted replies.

"You're probably coming up on your twenty, looking forward to a nice, cushy retirement."

"I said 'no talking.'"

"I wonder how much you've stashed away, working for Donny."

"Not a million-two, that's for sure," Andy pipes in.

Ted turns around. His face is red. "Andy, will you shut the fuck up?"

Jackson looks from Ted to Andy and chuckles.

"You think this is funny?" Andy says. "We can pull the car over right now."

"I swear to God," Ted mumbles, turning around.

The driver takes them behind 30th Street Station. The rail yard is a jumble of tracks and ballast and catenary poles, with dirt and gravel roadways just wide enough for trucks to drive down. The rail yard is bordered on one side by a giant stone wall painted with graffiti. *KRACKKILLS121,* and *POP* and *OBI,* and *MARIK* and *YAZ,* in bright oranges and yellows and blues. And, in black letters on a white background, *JRgonegetU!*—the same message he saw at Richie's garage.

Ted tells the driver to park the car; they sit there until it gets dark and Ted's cellphone rings.

"Yeah, we have him," Ted says into the phone. "Sure, yeah, right." Ted hands the phone to the driver, who says, "I remember where it is," then passes the phone back to Ted.

They make their way to I-95 and take it south across the state line into Delaware. A series of country roads leads them to a gravel service road running parallel to four sets of railroad tracks, and a memory flashes of him and another cop taking a guy to another set of tracks, the line that leads from Philly to Harrisburg.

Their prisoner whimpers in the car and cries outright when they pull up to the tracks and make him get out. Donny meets them there and when they're all gathered, a locomotive headlight appears in the distance. The man looks up at Jackson.

"You know who I am?" Jackson asks.

The man looks down and sobs. "You the man. You *JR*." He sniffles and starts begging. "Please don't do this. I already learned my lesson."

Donny turns to him. "What are you waiting for? Shoot him in the knee."

He looks at the man, a drug dealer who sells poison to kids. He pulls out his throwaway, points it at the man's knee, and fires. The man drops to his side, screaming.

"Good work," Donny says. Then he pulls out his own pistol from his jacket pocket and shoots the man in the head. He puts the gun back in his pocket, turns to him. "Now you're all in. And once you're in, there's no getting out. Understand?"

He nods. "No problem." That night, he goes home and throws up. He's crossed a line. He's a different person.

Now he remembers that was the first time he shot a man for Donny Franco. At least now he recalls that he didn't finish the poor guy off on the ground. That was Donny. Still, he recalls his mother's remarks about how terrible he became. The railroad shooting was clearly only the beginning; he went on to do even worse.

He looks out the car window to the stone wall. *JRgonegetU!* JR—Jackson Robert. A memory pops into his head of the first time he met Donny. His future boss comes up to him while he's still in uniform, on patrol. It's about six months after he and Richie got into their shootout with the guys robbing the electronics store.

"So, you're the hero who got shot saving your partner," Donny says. "Then ran after the perp with a slug in your gut and put him down."

"It was a through-and-through," he corrects Donny. "The slug was long gone by the time I started chasing the guy."

"Still, it must have hurt like hell." Donny steps back, studies him. "Do you plan on staying on patrol all your life? Or do you have some ambition? Because if you do, I'm looking for a good man to join my squad. All you'd have to do is pass the detective exam and I'd be happy to take you."

Donny Franco's *not* a cop you want to piss off. He's reputed to have friends on both sides of the law, including two uncles watching his back in Internal Affairs. Donny's the cop equivalent of a made man.

"I'm honored to be asked, sir," he tells Donny. "But right now, I'm happy where I am." The truth is, he's not ready to leave patrol. He has enough seniority that he can work mostly day shifts and he knows that detectives are often required to work late into the night, which wouldn't go over well with Pam.

Donny shrugs, shakes his hand, and tells him to call if he changes his mind.

Now, back in the car with Andy and Ted and the fat driver, he wonders what happened to make him sign on with Donny. He tries to force the memory, but it won't come.

"Stop here," Ted says, after they've gone about half a mile on the service road, then orders everyone out of the car and they start walking.

A light rain begins to fall, more mist than drops, putting a sheen on everyone's faces.

A quarter mile ahead, another car pulls onto the service road and proceeds toward them for a short distance before stopping. The car's headlights darken and the driver's door opens.

He doesn't have to see Donny Franco to know it's him. This must be the way Donny always plays it—have his thugs drive the stooge to some remote location while Donny drives there alone so there's no chance anyone will see him with the victim.

Donny stops three feet in front of him. They face off for a long moment, then Donny breaks the silence. "The prodigal son . . ."

The word *son* triggers a memory that answers his question about why he joined up with Donny.

"I don't like living with my parents," Vanessa tells him one night about a month after he's started seeing her. "I want my own place."

And that's all it takes. The next day he meets Donny at a famous Italian place in South Philadelphia. When he arrives, Donny is sitting in front of the restaurant in an unmarked police car. Donny and the driver get out and Donny tells the driver: "Search him."

"No wire," the driver says when he's done.

Donny says, "Let's go inside, have some dinner."

After their drinks arrive, Donny asks him what made him change his mind.

Jackson doesn't mince words. "Money," he says, looking Donny in the eye. "You know what a patrolman makes. It's not enough."

Donny stares at him for a long time. "So, it's the good life you want?"

"You could say that."

"Are you thinking you'll be on Easy Street if you join up with me? Because I'm telling you up front, there'll be nothing easy about it."

"Easy's never been my thing," he answers.

"You know why I want you on board?"

"Because I'm a hero cop. Give you some cover."

Donny smiles broadly. "I like it. You're not just muscle. You have brains, too." He shovels a forkful of lasagna into his mouth, takes his time chewing and swallowing.

When the meal's over, they walk outside. "I'll make arrangements for you to take the detective exam," Donny says.

And just like that, he's in the life.

Three years later, he betrayed Donny and disappeared.

Donny pulls out a pack of smokes, lights one up, takes a long drag. Blows the smoke in his face.

"Finally," he says, "a breath of fresh air."

"You're a funny guy, Jackson. But you won't be laughing for long." Donny takes another drag. "What I want to know is why? You were sitting pretty with me. Socking enough money away you'd be set in a few more years. So why did you blow it? Why steal from me?"

Socking money away jars loose a memory . . . more than a memory, an understanding. What Donny was doing was selling protection to the local drug lords. For a taste, a percentage, Donny would make sure their warehouses weren't raided, their hustlers and mules not rounded up. It was a good deal for everyone. Everyone knew the rules, and everyone abided by them. Well, almost everyone; the guys they took to the railroad tracks didn't, and they paid the price.

"Why?" Donny repeats.

Good question. His life was in a downhill spiral of drugs, sex, and violence, and he was addicted to all three. His health was failing, his marriage had been dashed on the rocks. Still, he would have kept on racing down the proverbial highway. Except for . . . what?

The question opens something in him, triggers a memory. He's standing on the pavement in front of the Broad Street

Diner. It's close to midnight on a muggy August night. Thick clouds overhead signal an approaching thunderstorm and blot out any light from the moon or stars. After a short while, an unmarked police car pulls up in front of him; he climbs inside, takes shotgun. The driver is a stocky guy with a scar that runs along his jawline from his right ear to the right corner of his mouth.

He turns to the driver. "Who we got in the trunk?"

"That shithead gangbanger in Kensington Donny's been after? The one who's been stiffing us, told Donny to fuck himself—"

"Saulo?"

"No, his brother. Goes by *Lemon*."

"Fuck kind of name is that?"

The driver shrugs.

He turns to the driver. "Why Saulo's brother?"

"Why do you think?" the driver says. "Saulo's gone into hiding. But Donny still wants to send him a message."

He turns to face the windshield, and it doesn't take long to realize the driver isn't heading out of the city. This seems odd. He's about to ask the driver where they're headed when the answer comes to him. They're taking Lemon to his own backyard. The Kensington section of Philadelphia, the most drug-ridden area of the city. A pair of Conrail tracks run parallel to East Tusculum and East Gurney Streets, below steep embankments.

The driver parks the car along Tusculum near the B Street Bridge, then turns to him. "I can get this one down to the tracks myself," the driver says. "I'll see you down there."

Jackson leaves the car, negotiates his way down the embankment to the tracks. The underside of the B Street Bridge is pitch black, except for the small red glow of a cigarette. He approaches cautiously and is surprised to find Donny already there, waiting.

"Even without light, I can see you look like shit," Donny says.

"I went on a diet. I guess I overdid it."

Donny stares at him, says nothing.

He hears crunching on the gravel behind him and sees the stout guy with the scar dragging Lemon alongside him. When they get close, he's stunned by how young the boy is.

"How old is he?"

"Old enough to run drugs for his shit-for-brains brother," Donny answers.

"I'm fourteen," Lemon says without looking up from the ground.

He turns to Donny. "Let's talk."

Donny shrugs and they walk a few paces away.

"He's a kid," he says.

"We need to send a message," Donny answers.

"I don't feel like kneecapping a kid."

"Kneecap? We have to send a message. Not a messenger."

He stares at Donny. So far, they've taken ten guys to the railroad tracks. On Donny's direction, he shot them all in the knee. The point of it has been to send wounded messengers back to their tribes, spread the word that JR is out there, waiting to put a bad hurt on anyone who double-crosses Donny Franco. When they finish, Donny typically makes a smart-ass remark, telling the wounded stooge to "live long and prosper," or, sacrilegiously, to "spread the Good News." On two occasions, though, after he shot the stooges in the knee, Donny finished them off. Apparently, that's what Donny has planned for Lemon.

"The kid's not the problem," he tells Donny. "Saulo is."

So far, he's been able to justify what he's been doing for Donny on the grounds that the guys he's hurting are gangbanger drug dealers peddling the *slow death* to anyone stupid enough to pay for it, including children. But Lemon is a kid himself. "I'll find Saulo and we can deal with him."

Donny stares hard into his face. Then he steps into him, pokes his finger into his chest. "That's the way you want to play it, Jackson, all right, but you make sure you find Saulo, and *soon*."

He says he will, then turns and walks away. As he passes the driver and Lemon, he hears Donny shouting after him.

"Aren't you forgetting something?"

He takes a deep breath, turns around, pulls his 9mm from his shoulder holster and fires. Lemon howls in pain and crumples. They leave the kid on the ground and climb the embankment to their cars. He stands by the passenger door and watches Donny open the driver's door of his sedan, parked just ahead of their own unmarked car. Donny pauses, then signals for him to approach. He walks up to Donny and waits as Donny stares at him.

"You're not getting soft on me, are you?"

"No way."

"Because if you were, that would be bad."

He nods and turns away, and Donny calls after him "*Real* bad."

The recollection ends abruptly and his mind jets him to the early morning hours of that same night. In bed with Vanessa, he wakes up in a cold sweat and makes his way to the bathroom. His heart is pounding and he's breathing so hard he's starting to get dizzy. He splashes cold water on his face and closes his eyes. When he opens them, he stares into the mirror.

"What's the matter?"

He sees Vanessa in the mirror, walking up behind him. He shakes his head. "It's . . . what I'm doing."

"What you're doing is making money, for us." Vanessa wraps her arms around him, and he melts into her.

"Did you hear me?" Donny says. "Why'd you steal from me?"

Ignoring Donny, he thinks out loud. "The cook, in the diner, with the limp—that was Lemon."

"What the hell are you talking about?" Donny says. Then, "Look, I'm not asking you again. Why did you fuck things up with me?"

The answer is that he has no idea. He smiles and opens his arms. "One of the great mysteries."

"That's the way you want to play it? Even now, with nothing to gain, or lose, other than what you're going to lose anyway, you won't be square with me?"

He shrugs.

"What about Miami? I saw a video of you getting shot and kicked into a swamp. Yet here you are. You want to tell me how? You want to at least tell me who those Miami guys even *were*, because I never heard of them before."

"I need to know something first, and let's see how honest you can be with me," he says. "Are you the one that had my wife killed?"

Donny blinks, tilts his head. Then he smiles. "No, but if you dig her up, I'll be happy to put a couple slugs through her face."

It wasn't him.

So, who the hell *was* it?

Far down the track, a light appears rounding a corner. The train is coming.

"So, you went to see Vanessa," Donny says, and something about the way he says it takes Jackson back to a time he and Donny and the rest of the crew are all having dinner at Ralph's in South Philadelphia with their girls—not their wives. He looks around the table thinking it's like a scene out of *Goodfellas* except they are all cops, not wise guys. His eyes land on Donny and he sees that Donny's eyes are parked on Vanessa. The memory triggers another—Donny saying, "I can tell she's a wild one," hoping he'll take the bait, talk about Vanessa's tricks in bed.

And it hits him: "You're the one paying for Vanessa to live at Symphony House."

"Would it make you feel better to know that I was screwing her even before you left?"

"It makes me feel better to know that you feel you have to lie to me. You made your play, more than once, but she rejected you flat-out. We used to laugh about it."

Donny's face turns sour. "Well, I'm the one laughing now. And it's me fucking the hell out of her."

Jackson smiles. "Yeah and she's seeing my face every time she's with you. Every time your dick is inside her, she's thinking how much better mine felt."

Donny punches him in the gut, and he doubles over, and it's only now that Donny seems to notice his hands.

"He's not cuffed?" Donny shouts at Ted. "Goddamnit! I told you to make sure he was cuffed."

Ted and Andy both walk up to him, Ted holding out a set of plasticuffs, Andy with a pistol. A split second later, Jackson has Andy's right arm in his grip, the elbow bent ninety degrees in the wrong direction; his gun discharges and Ted's moaning on the ground, gut-shot. He shoves Andy onto the track, taking his pistol as he falls, and puts Donny down with a slug to the knee before he has time to reach for his weapon.

A huge blast of air smacks him in the face as the train races past, turning Andy into chopped tomato. Meanwhile, the fat driver is slowly backing away, hands in the air.

"Keep on moving," he tells the driver. "Get to the car and drive away."

The man nods, turns, and runs for the car.

He walks calmly to Donny, removes Donny's gun from his jacket.

"I'll fucking kill you for this, Jackson."

"You know what's funny," he says. "Even now, if I asked Vanessa to run away with me, I know she would. Hell, she'd drive the car and run you over along the way." He walks up to Donny and presses the barrel of Donny's pistol into the side of Donny's head.

"Go ahead. Pull the trigger," Donny growls. "Just remember, I'm the man who made you into a killer. Into JR."

He removes the clip from Donny's gun, empties it, and the chamber, too. He tosses the pistol into the weeds.

"Haven't you heard," he tells Donny. "JR's dead. Which means that tonight, you're not."

He reaches into Donny's jacket pocket, takes his keys, and walks to Donny's car. From behind him, he hears Donny shouting in the dark.

"I'm gonna come for you, Jackson. I'm gonna fucking kill you."

He opens the door and shouts back. "Live long and prosper, Donny."

CHAPTER EIGHTEEN

HE TAKES DONNY'S car to the garage of the DoubleTree on Broad Street, parks it, and picks up his F-150. Two hours after leaving Donny, he's back at the diner where he had lunch after he met with Richie. He's taking stock of where things stand. He came back east looking for Helen's killer, and Donny seemed the perfect suspect. But it wasn't Donny and all he's succeeded in doing is to alert his old boss that he's still alive and create a cluster-fuck along the tracks that left one cop dead and two shot, including Donny himself.

And what has he achieved with Vanessa? "You left me," she said when Donny's boys came to take him. All the excuse she needed to feed him to the wolves.

Meanwhile, Helen's still dead and gone and he feels no closer to finding her killer than before. He glances at his hands, now empty, no cards left to play, and he worries he's reached a dead end.

The waitress approaches and asks if he's ready to order.

He's hungry but too worked up to eat. "Just coffee."

When the waitress walks away, he spots a man standing in the doorway, staring at him. The man is wearing a gray business suit that hangs on his thin frame. His top button is open and his tie is loose around his neck. He looks tired. Worn.

The man approaches and slides into the booth. "The last time you caught me looking at you," the man says, "you beat me up, put a gun in my face."

Jackson says nothing. He has no idea what the man is talking about, who the man is.

"I was angry at you for a long time," the man says. "I'd thought you kept the money. Then Jackie disappeared and called me a week later from wherever she was and told me *he* had the money, that he had her and Penny, too. I knew then you'd told us the truth, but you were long gone yourself. Gone, and then dead. Or so everyone thought."

He repeats the names. "Jackie. Penny."

The man's eyes tear up. "It's killing me—not knowing where they are. What he's done with them." He leans forward, his arms open on the table. "Please. Please help me find them."

He stares at the man.

"I didn't even know you were back in town until the guy came asking questions about you."

"The guy?"

"He asked if I'd heard from you. If you'd told me why you'd come back."

"How long ago was this?"

"Yesterday."

"Did you see what he was driving?"

"Through this window," the man says, pointing to the window next to their booth. "I was grabbing a quick bite after work and he asked if he could talk to me. I said sure and he sat down. He asked me about you, and after he left, I saw him get into his car and drive away. It was one of those cars that always reminded me of an old-fashioned gangster car."

"A Chrysler 300."

"That's right. Do you know who he is?"

I don't even know you. How can he explain to this stranger that he can't remember whole blocks of his life? "I suffered a head injury. I have some memory loss."

"Oh. Damn."

"Let's start with some basics. How do I know you?"

"I'm married to Jackie. Your sister."

Sister? The word triggers a memory of this same guy following him years ago. He sees the guy watching him at a club on Delaware Avenue. When he leaves the club, he lets the guy tail him into the parking lot. Then he doubles back and clocks the guy, he kneels over him, and puts his pistol in his face.

"You have two seconds to tell me why you're following me."

The guy is terrified, his eyes are bulging. "I'm married to your sister. We need your help, for our daughter."

"I don't have a sister."

"Yes, you do. A half-sister."

He stands and lets the guy get up too. "Why did you follow me? Why not just come up to me and talk?"

"Because of who you are. I was working up the nerve."

Across the table now, the man watches him. "You're remembering. I can tell."

"You're Owen," he says, as the name flashes into his mind. "Owen Brenner. You're an accountant. Jackie is my half-sister, and you have a ten-year-old daughter. Penelope."

"Penny would be twenty now. Assuming she's still alive." Owen starts to tear up again. "She was so sickly when Jackie took her to him."

"Him?"

"Jackie's father. *Your* father."

"My father." The words take him to the back seat of a Cadillac. He and Jimmy are six or seven years old and their father drives them to a park. He and Jimmy jump out of the car and run to the sandbox. They play in the sand and, after a while, he looks up and spots his father talking with a woman near a bench. A girl about his age is with the woman, who motions toward the sandbox. The girl approaches and joins them in their play. She's pretty, long dark hair, dark eyes and olive skin, and he catches himself stealing glances at her. She catches him, too, and smiles shyly. Playing beside him, Jimmy seems oblivious.

The memory is followed by two or three other instances of his father driving Jimmy and him to the park, meeting up with the girl. In one memory, Jimmy walks away from the sandbox, leaving him and the girl alone.

"My mom says he likes you better," the girl says.

"What?"

"He told her you and Jimmy look alike, but you're different as night and day."

"He who?"

The girl looks up from the sand and nods at his father, who is now standing in the center of a group of adults, his back to him. His father seems to be making the other adults laugh.

He glances from the adults to Jimmy, now by the jungle gym, waiting to be noticed by the other kids, waiting to be invited to play. Waiting is something Jackson would never do. If he sees a bunch of kids playing, he just jumps in.

On the drive home that day, he stares at the back of his father's head, Jimmy sitting next to him in the rear seat of the Caddy.

"Did you boys have fun?" his father asks over his shoulder. "It sure looked like you did."

He hears his father's words, but he's thinking about the girl, wondering how she knew what his father thinks about him and Jimmy. Wondering if what she said was true.

"Who is that girl?" he asks his dad.

"What girl?"

"The girl who's always in the park."

His father says he doesn't know. "Just some girl who plays in the park, it seems."

They drive on for a while, and his father says, "Don't tell your mother about that girl. You, too, Jimmy. I mean it."

Looking across the table at Owen, he realizes that the girl was his sister, Jackie. "I want you to start at the beginning. Tell me what you know about my sister, the money, my father. Pretend like this is the first time we ever talked about it."

Owen takes a deep breath. "It all started when Penny got sick. She was eight years old and she was getting debilitating headaches, stomach pain so bad it doubled her over. Vision problems, dizziness, nausea. We took her to one doctor after another, in Philadelphia, New York. But the doctors couldn't figure out what was wrong. Finally, a doctor in Chicago told us it was an autoimmune disorder, but he wasn't sure how to treat it. For two years, we tried everything—medicines, antibiotics, even having her blood drained, replaced by the blood of people with normal immune systems.

"Most of it wasn't covered by insurance, and before we knew it, we'd drained our 401(k) and borrowed everything we could against the house. We were flat broke, and Penny still needed medical care. Jackie went to her mother, Amanda, who didn't have much money but gave what she could. One night, the three of us—Jackie, her mother, and I—were sitting around crying and Jackie said she was going to get ahold of your father."

"He had money?"

"Jackie's mother said he did. Tons."

"Tell me about him."

"I don't know much. Only that he was screwing around with Jackie's mother at the same time he was married to your mother. Jackie's your age, born the same day, in fact."

"Jackson and Jackie?"

"Jackie's mother was against you and her having pretty much the same name, but your dad was insistent."

"My father told Jackie's mother about me? My family?"

"Yes, and Amanda told Jackie."

The talk about Jackie's mother triggers a memory of him in the living room of Owen and Jackie's house. Jackie's mother, Amanda, is with him. She has a cigarette in one hand and a tumbler with some kind of liquor in the other. Amanda paces the room, her eyes flicking from one thing to the other. She forces herself to stand still for a minute, looks him over.

"I'm the one he loved, you know," Amanda says.

"What?"

"He met and married your mother first. Then he met me and lost himself."

Jackson feels angry inside, wants to say something cruel, like his father's left Amanda behind just like everyone else, so how special could she have been to him? But like Jackie and Owen, Amanda is in pain over what's happening to Penny, who is suffering upstairs in bed.

Back in the diner, Owen pauses, calls the waitress over, asks for some coffee. Then, to him, "I'm not used to being up so late. I wouldn't be here right now except the guy who was asking me about you told me you were still alive and back in Philly. He said you liked to come to this diner, late at night. So I took a chance and came here myself."

"Getting back to my father . . ."

"Jackie's mother hadn't heard from him in years, but she had a phone number she said he could be reached at in an emergency. She gave it to Jackie and Jackie called him."

"And he offered to help pay for the medical expenses, but only if Jackie and Penny came to live with him." It's a hunch, but it turns out to be a bad one.

"No. He turned Jackie down. But he did tell her to call you. He said you had access to lots of money. He said you were . . ."

"A crooked cop," he finishes the sentence.

"Worse. He said you were the boogeyman all the drug dealers were afraid of, tagged in graffiti all around the city. You told me later that Donny Franco paid graffiti artists to do it. Did you know some Philly rapper wrote a song about you?" Owen's coffee arrives and he stirs in cream and sugar.

"So, I came to you. I told you about Jackie and Penny and the bind we were all in. You told me to get lost, said you didn't believe me. Then, a week later, Jackie saw you watching her and Penny in the park by our house, and—"

Penny. The image of a young girl with freckles and a blond ponytail blasts its way into his mind, trailing a dozen other memories and images behind it. He winces and clamps his head with both hands.

"Are you okay?" Owen asks.

"My head hurts." After a few minutes, the pain passes and he sees himself sitting on a park bench with little Penny next to him, explaining to her that he's her Uncle Jackson. He sees her in the passenger seat of the Jag, laughing wildly as he speeds down I-95. Sees her waiting in line with him at Dairy Queen. Those were good days for Penny.

More often, her days were rough. He remembers her lying motionless on her bed, face contorted in pain. Jackie walks in, lowers herself onto the bed next to him.

"I'm so worried for her. What if she never gets past this? What if this is what her life is going to be? These terrible episodes where she's so sick she can't even stand without getting dizzy. Throwing up all the time. Unable to eat normal food."

Jackie starts to cry and he wraps an arm around her. He looks at his niece, thinks that he'll never be able to make up for all the terrible things he's done, still does, but maybe he can save this one little girl.

Back in the diner, Owen says, "I had my doubts about you, at first. You were like a charged wire. Nervous and jittery, on edge all the time, the anger always just below the surface. Jackie told me she thought you were on drugs, and we both knew you were mixed up with some crazy woman. I told you that if you couldn't help with the medical bills, you shouldn't spend time with Penny because of who you were. She needed good role models, not bad ones. It scared the hell out of me to say that to you, but I had to look out for my daughter."

"I know you did," he says, remembering it now.

"So, you remember that conversation?" Owen asks. "How about the rest, what went down with the money?"

"There are still holes," he tells Owen. "Fill me in."

"You started giving us money—a thousand here, five thousand there. Ten thousand one time. But it wasn't enough. Some of the alternative medicine clinics we wanted to take Penny to were crazy expensive. Their treatments weren't covered by insurance, so we had to come up with cash. Up front. And Penny was getting worse."

He sits up, suddenly remembering Donny's $1.2 million. "I told you I was about to make a big score. One of the bigger gang-bangers had screwed Donny, and he was going to set an example. A fat shipment of cocaine was coming in and Donny found out when and where. He brought me and his other top guys together and told us this time there wasn't going to be any percentage, that we were taking it all. When the shipment came in, we'd be there to meet it. Donny had a buyer lined up and me and the other guys would make the sale, then I was to take the money to Donny. That was the plan."

"Donny's plan," Owen says. "Our plan—yours and mine—was that you were going to bring the money to Jackie and me. But when you showed up—"

"I told you I'd been rolled, the money stolen." He remembers walking from his car with the bags in his hands. Then . . . stars, blackness. Waking up on the ground with a pounding headache and a lump the size of a cantaloupe on the back of his head.

"Jackie believed you," Owen says. "But I didn't. I stewed for days and I was ready to confront you. But, of course, you'd left by then for Miami. You still had to go through with that part of our plan, even though you didn't have the money, so that Donny wouldn't come looking for you."

"The Miami thing is still hazy to me."

Owen smiles. "That was my favorite part of the plan. A complete charade. There were no Miami guys. I mean, there were guys, but they weren't after you. My company does accounting work for some shady characters and one of them owed me big for a tax-fraud case I helped him with. I called in the favor and we set up a scene that looked like you tried to buy your way out of trouble with some bad guys but they double-crossed you, took the money, and killed you. They sent a video to Donny to make him think you were dead and the money was gone."

His mind carries him back to the hot night in Florida. He's in the back seat of the car next to a big guy as it pulls into the swamp, bounces its way down an access road and stops. It's all worked out, what is going to happen. The guy in the car is going to pull him out roughly, stand him up before two other guys. They'll pretend he brought them money to buy his way out of a jam. But the other guys will double-cross him, shoot him. One of the guys will film the scene. It plays out as he expects. He does his part, tells the other guys he's brought the money, gets panicked when it looks like they're going to kill him anyway, drops to the ground when one of the guys fires on him with blanks. They kick him into the swamp. He stays underwater for half a minute, then surfaces and they help him out, give him some dry clothes from the trunk of the car. They let him view the video on the camera, make sure it's good, then drive him back to Miami, where he picks up his car and makes tracks.

"So, I was going to disappear all along." He gets it now. Saving his niece was the thing that finally motivated him to turn his back on the life, to double-cross Donny Franco, and leave Vanessa before he was totally consumed by the drugs, the sex, the guilt.

"You said you don't know where Jackie is, or Penny."

Owen shakes his head. "After you came to us and said you'd been waylaid and the money taken, Jackie said she was going to call your father again, and we got into a big fight. No disrespect to you, but your old man is a prick. I mean, I never met him, but he was married to one woman, screwing around with another, and ended up leaving them both."

The words sting. He did the same thing to Pam and Vanessa.

"He left them and their children—you and your brother and Jackie." Owen nods. "Two days after my fight with Jackie, I came home from the office and Jackie and Penny were gone. A week later, Jackie called me, said she and our daughter were with *him*, and Penny was getting all the medical help she needed."

Owen pauses, looks out the window, then back at him. "That was ten years ago. I haven't heard a word from them since."

They sit quietly for a while.

"Tell me about my father. What do you know?"

"Almost nothing," Owen says. "Only that Jackie's mother was enthralled with him, and that his leaving broke something inside her."

"When did he leave?"

"Jackie was ten. She came home from school and her mother sat her down and said that her father had moved away. Jackie told me she was upset by it, confused. She wondered if she'd done something wrong. It messed her up."

Jackson senses motion on the other side of the window next to their table. Outside the diner, two patrol cars pull up, and his pulse accelerates. Has Donny already called the dogs on him? He doesn't think so; it's too soon. Best case scenario for Donny is that he's at the hospital, getting his knee repaired. Even once he was released, Donny would need time to plan. And he wouldn't bring the uniforms into it. He'd rely on his crew, his detectives, the bad apples he'd personally recruited. He watches the squad cars park next to an SUV, sees the driver slumped over, eyes open. Just another C&C.

Still, he no longer feels safe hanging around the city.

"Come on." He stands, tosses a twenty onto the table. "We need to go."

"Where?"

He gives Owen the address of Richie's garage. "Meet me there in ten minutes."

In his truck, he calls Richie, tells him what he's going to do. When he gets to Richie's garage, he parks his truck near the building that houses the Jag. He glances up at the train trestle—*JRgonegetU!* His thoughts jump to the skull and crossbones on his arm and he remembers now that the tattoo wasn't something he and Vanessa did together. It was Donny's idea, something to go with the *JR* messaging. JR originally stood for Jackson Robert, but now it took on the added meaning of "Jolly Roger." A pirate murdering other pirates. He never asked Vanessa to get a matching tattoo; she did that on her own, a gesture of her love for him, more proof that their relationship went both ways: Vanessa had been as much his puppet as he'd been hers.

"Waxing nostalgic?" Richie asks, moving up to him as he looks at the graffiti.

"Something like that."

"Come on," Richie says, then leads him into the garage where the Jaguar is stored. As soon as they're inside, Richie whips off the tarp, and his mind carries him back to the first time he saw the car finished. Eighteen months after he first saw it all junked up in Richie's garage and the morning after his first night out with Vanessa. He brings Vanessa with him to pick up the car. When they arrive, it's plain that Richie doesn't like what he's seeing. He shakes Vanessa's hand, but he does so with a tight face. He asks Vanessa to wait with the car while he takes Jackson to his office in the back of the garage.

"I've known your wife for a long time," Richie says. "Pam's a good woman, and I don't mind telling you that I don't like this one bit. Something tells me I should take a sledgehammer to that car right now. Then turn it on you and beat some sense into your head."

His blood starts to warm, but he holds his tongue.

"I don't like what I'm seeing in your eyes, Jackson. You want to tell me what it is?"

Again, Jackson remains silent, and Richie shrugs and leads him back to the car. Richie whisks away the tarp and Jackson and Vanessa both gasp, that's how beautiful the car is, even unpainted and sanded down to the bare metal.

"What color do you want it?" Richie asks.

He doesn't hesitate. "Black."

"And the finish? Matte, glossy, lustrous—"

"Make it shine, like polished coal." He feels Vanessa's grip on his bicep tighten.

Looking back at it now, he remembers that Vanessa drove a wedge between him and Richie. It didn't ruin their friendship, but it strained it, paving the way for Richie's increasing ire at Jackson's decision to work for Donny Franco. Still, in the end, after he'd stolen Donny's money and was about to go on the lam, it was Richie he turned to. To hold onto the Jaguar and, later, to keep his ear to the ground, listen for signs that Donny had found out he was still alive.

Richie turns to him now. "The car's all yours again. I'd tell you to be gentle with her, but . . ."

Owen pulls into the lot and parks next to Jackson's truck.

Richie stiffens. "Who's this?"

"My brother-in-law, it turns out."

After Richie and Owen shake hands, Richie says he'll hide the pickup under the tarp in the outbuilding and put Owen's car on one of the lifts in the main garage. "You'll get it back in tip-top shape, with a new inspection sticker on it," Richie tells Owen. Then, to Jackson, "As for your truck . . ."

"It's yours."

Richie's face darkens. "I get the feeling this is it. I won't be seeing you again."

"Donny's gonna make things hot for me here," he says.

"It's more than that," Richie says. "I know there's somewhere you think you have to be, but I'm worried when it gets its hands on you, it's not gonna let go."

He looks away, doesn't answer.

"You know, Jackson, if it's just about revenge, it's not worth it. Never is."

He shakes his head. He no longer knows *what* this is about. He shakes hands with Richie, climbs into the Jag, tells Owen to do the same. He starts the engine and pulls away.

"You want to give me a clue where we're going?" Owen asks as they head for the interstate.

"To see the one person who might know where my father is. And we're not going alone." He picks up the cellphone, punches the number.

"It's me. Jackson."

"Do you know what time it is?" Jimmy's sleepy voice on the other end. "Why are you calling me?"

"I'm calling to let you know I'm going to find our father." He glances at Owen. "Our father, our sister, and our niece."

Silence on the other end. "The hell are you talking about?"

"Meet me at Mom's house. I'll explain everything."

"Meet . . . you mean at the Governor's Mansion?"

"Yes, and hurry. I'm on my way there now. And bring Pam."

He's remembered something that he needs to tell both of them.

CHAPTER NINETEEN

IT'S AFTER MIDNIGHT when they get to the Governor's Residence. A security guard escorts Owen and him to the same sitting room in which he met his mother. Jimmy and Pam are already there, which means that his mother did as he requested and urged them to come. He called Evelyn as soon as he hung up with Jimmy, asked her to persuade his brother and ex-wife to come to the Governor's Residence. He knew that otherwise there was no way Jimmy and Pam would make the trip to Harrisburg to meet him.

"What's going on, Jackson?" Jimmy stands as soon as he enters the room. "Why was it so important we come here tonight?"

"Good to see you again, too, brother." He turns to Pam. "Sorry we missed each other when I was at your house."

Pam glares at him, and he can tell she's working out what to say when Evelyn swishes into the room.

"Where's Randy?" Evelyn asks Jimmy and Pam of their son.

"We left him with our next-door neighbor," Jimmy answers. "She wasn't any happier to be woken up in the middle of the night than we were."

"I wasn't going to let my son anywhere near you," Pam tells Jackson.

"Enough." It's Evelyn. "There are a lot of hard feelings in this room, but we're all going to be civil about this." She walks to Owen and extends her hand. They shake and Evelyn tells everyone to sit. "I've ordered coffee," she says. "I expect this will be a long night for all of us."

They take their seats and Evelyn turns to Jackson. "The stage is yours."

He nods to his mother, then tells the tale—the murder of his wife, his decision to come back east to find and confront her killer. His initial belief that Donny Franco was behind it. He describes his meeting with Vanessa, which causes Pam and Jimmy to stiffen. He tells them everything about his rail-side confrontation with Donny. Finally, he mentions Jackie and Penny.

"That's where I come in," Owen pipes up. "My wife, Jackie, is your half-sister," he tells Jimmy. "Your father was seeing Jackie's mother while she was married to . . ." Owen glances at Evelyn and his words trail off.

The news seems to knock Evelyn back. "My husband had a second family?" She takes a deep breath. "I suppose I shouldn't be surprised. I figured he stepped out on me."

"Like father like son," Pam interjects, throwing Jackson a nasty look.

"*Sons*," he answers, looking at his brother.

Pam takes Jimmy's hands in her own. "Jimmy and I weren't just screwing around. We fell in love."

Jackson looks at his brother, knowing that Jimmy didn't "fall" in love with Pam; he'd always been in love with her.

"I know," he says. "And I knew back then. And to be honest"— he looks from Pam to Jimmy—"I was glad about it. One of the things I counted on when I was about to make my big exit ten years ago, Pam, was that I wasn't going to leave you alone, but with Jimmy. I knew he'd be good to you, and I knew you'd be good to him. I'm happy you ended up together and that you have a son." He exhales. "There, I've gotten that out."

The room goes quiet. He sees Pam's face soften, and it triggers a flood of memories of their early marriage, before the madness with Vanessa. He and Pam would take weekend trips to Cape May, stay at the bed-and-breakfasts. They'd ride the haunted tour bus, do the dinner theater. When they stayed for a whole week, they'd take a room at Congress Hall, enjoy breakfasts at the Blue Pig, dance into the wee hours in the hotel's basement bar, the Boiler Room. Wherever they stayed, they'd begin their day by grabbing coffee and sitting on the lifeguard chair, watching the dolphins. After that, they'd rent kayaks or go for long bike rides or simply waste the whole day on the beach. He wonders if Pam's remembering the same things.

Evelyn turns to Owen. "How old is she? Jackie? And your daughter?"

"Jackie is forty-one, Penny is twenty, assuming she's still alive," Owen answers.

"You don't know?"

"Let me jump in again," Jackson says and tells the story of Penny's illness, the need for money for her medical care, his scheme to steal the million from Donny Franco, the Miami scam, and, finally, how he was attacked and the money stolen from him.

Owen completes the tale: After Jackson was waylaid, Jackie called their father, who said he'd provide the money for Penny's care on the condition that Jackie and Penny both come to live with him. "A week after Jackie and Penny disappeared, Jackie called and said they were with her father. But she wouldn't tell me where."

"Which is why I'm here now," Jackson tells his mother. "I'm thinking you know where he is."

The door to the sitting room opens and the governor walks in. "I just returned from the conference," he says to Evelyn. "Hello, Jimmy. Pam. *Jackson?* Is that really you? Does someone want to tell me what's going on here?"

"Put a lid on it, Howard," Evelyn says. "This is a family meeting, and we need some privacy."

"Well, I'm family."

Evelyn rolls her eyes. "Go to bed. You have an early breakfast meeting and you know how your eyes sag when you don't get enough sleep."

The governor's face falls, but he leaves, muttering as he closes the door a little too hard on the way out.

"I'm impressed," Jackson says to his mother.

"I learned from the best," she replies. "I'll grant your father that. Enough to turn a socially inept prosecutor into the district attorney, then the mayor, attorney general, and governor."

*   *   *

He remembers now that, after his father left, his mother was forced to sell their home, move them into an apartment. A vision appears of him and Jimmy late at night, lying in their creaky double beds in their shared bedroom, the ancient window air-conditioner struggling against the sweltering August air. The next morning, they would start sixth grade in a new school.

He hears Jimmy stirring and whispers to him. "What's wrong?"

"Nothing."

"Don't be scared about tomorrow. It'll be all right."

The room is quiet for a long while. "Are you scared?" Jimmy asks.

The truth is he isn't afraid. Not at all. "A little," he tells Jimmy, hoping to make his brother feel better.

"I don't like going to a new school, where I don't know anyone," Jimmy says.

"You know me. All we have to do is stick together and we'll be okay."

"That's what Mom always says."

"Well, she's right sometimes. And she's right about that."

Another long silence. Then he hears Jimmy's bed creak and he knows Jimmy has turned on his side to face him. "Why did Dad leave?"

Jimmy has asked him that a hundred times. Asked their mother a hundred more. The answer is always the same. "Not because of us," he tells his brother.

Money was tight for a long time after his father left, but things eventually got better when his mother landed a job as a secretary at the district attorney's office. A few years later, things got better still once his mother had her hooks in Howard. Then they had to move to Kournfield for a couple years.

*　*　*

He glances at Jimmy and Pam, then turns to his mother. "What was he like? My father?"

"He was a piece of shit," Jimmy interjects. "He left you and me and Mom. And a whole other family, it seems."

He watches his mother weigh how to answer him. "I first met your father at the Union League. I was there with one of my girlfriends, whose own father was a member, and she was giving me a tour. She opened the door to one of the small conference rooms and there he was, addressing a group of people. I watched for a while and it was something to see. He had them laughing, then crying, then laughing again."

"What exactly was he doing?" he asks. "I mean, what did he do for a living?"

"He was a con artist, wasn't he," Jimmy says—an accusation rather than a question.

Evelyn nods. "Your father was in commercial real estate. He started out as a broker, then brought together some investors and started a company that managed office buildings for institutional owners. He made a lot of money but wanted to make more, so he gathered another group of investors and started a second company that bought broken-down office buildings and industrial properties, rehabilitated them, and then sold them. Everything was going well, until he bought a huge property that turned into a money pit. He hit up his investors for more capital and borrowed as much as the banks would lend him. Then, when that wasn't enough, he turned to another group of lenders for 'off-the-book' loans."

"He went to the mob," Jackson says.

Evelyn nods. "And that's when things went really bad. The property he'd bought turned out to have major environmental issues, chemicals in the ground. That meant he'd have to pour millions into it to remediate the hazmat issues before ever getting a penny back on it."

"So he skipped and left all of us behind." Jimmy's face is tight with anger.

"Why didn't you tell us this before?" he asks, thinking maybe she had. How would he know? He remembers almost nothing.

Evelyn sighs. "I didn't know myself, at the time." She looks from Jimmy to him. "I only found out a couple months later, when your father wrote me. He said he'd turned over a new leaf and laid out what happened in the letter."

"If he wrote you, why didn't you take us to him?" Jimmy asks.

Evelyn's eyes harden. "Because he didn't ask."

"Is he dangerous?" Jackson changes the topic. "Would he have someone killed?"

Evelyn blows out air. "Your father had a partner. They were thick as thieves. Like Scrooge and Marley, those two." She pauses. "Just before your father left town, the partner was found dead. His throat had been slit."

"It could have been the wise guys they borrowed from," Jackson says.

Evelyn stares at him.

"But you don't think so."

Evelyn looks away, then, after a minute, looks back at him. "I think your father's partner knew too much about him, about how they ran their business. He was a threat. And if there's one thing your father couldn't take, it was being threatened. It brought out a side of him that was . . . hideous."

The room falls quiet as everyone takes in Evelyn's words.

"The worst thing about your father, though, was how he could change people. He changed me, and not for the better. I hate to say this, Owen, but if your wife and daughter have been with him for ten years, you might not recognize them."

A vision of a giggling, ten-year-old Penny pops into his head. It makes him sick to think his father—Penny's grandfather—is grooming her to become like him. And God knows what his father has manipulated Jackie into doing all this time. "I have to find my niece and my sister," he tells Evelyn. "Which means you have to tell me where they are." He stands and faces his mother. "Where is he?"

Evelyn lowers her head, closes her eyes for a long moment. "Your father lives in the city where sin never sleeps."

He and Jimmy exchange glances. "He's in—"

"Las Vegas." Evelyn completes the sentence just as the coffee service arrives. Everyone serves themselves, then settles back in. Seated in a wing chair now, Evelyn resumes. "My position in politics gives me access to information not available to most people. Your father told me in his letter that he'd moved to Las Vegas, and I know that he's been there since. Beyond that, I can't tell you much about him other than that he's thriving."

"That's not much help," he says. "Can you be a little more specific?"

Evelyn sips her coffee. "Vegas is controlled from the shadows by a handful of men. Your father is one of them. What exactly his role is, I can't tell you. I don't even know what name he's going by now."

"How will I find him?" he asks.

"You told me you were sitting in a diner with no idea where to turn when you realized Donny Franco wasn't behind your wife's death. Then, all of a sudden, Owen shows up and tells you Jackie and Penny have been gone for ten years, lured by your father, whom you hadn't even thought of until then. Am I right so far?"

"And I only knew about the diner," Owen adds, "because I was told Jackson might be there by a man who approached me asking questions about him."

"Are you saying my father set it up so Owen would meet me?"

Evelyn nods. "You won't have to find your father. He knows you're coming for him, and he'll find you."

He leans over, puts his head in his hands, and mulls what his mother has told him. After a while, he looks up at her. "The only reason Owen was able to come to me was because I was back in Philadelphia. And the reason I did that was because I was looking for my wife's killer." He lets the words hang in the air.

Evelyn takes a deep breath, turns to Owen. "Whose idea, again, was it that your wife reach out to Jackson ten years ago for the money to help your daughter?"

Owen's face drains of color. "It was *his* idea. Jackie's father. Jackson's."

Jackson shoots to his feet. "So, he knew I'd go after the money. Then when I got it, I'm attacked from behind and the money's stolen. It was *him*, wasn't it? He forced Jackie to go back to him again for money for Penny's treatment."

On the sofa, Owen stares into space. "So, the thing ten years ago was a scheme to get control over his daughter and granddaughter."

"And maybe you, too, Jackson." It's Evelyn. "Think about it. Your father would have known that once you stole a million bucks from Donny Franco, you'd have to flee. He might've expected that you'd try to follow Jackie and Penny. That you'd ask Jackie's mother or me how to find him. Instead, you struck out for the Midwest."

The implication of what Evelyn and Owen are saying is clear: what has happened in the past few weeks is only the latest stage in a plot that goes far back in time, a plan to bring him to his father, just like his father snared Jackie and Penny. But that notion raises a question.

"Why now, after all these years? I've been living in Kournfield for a decade, and until my wife's death, no one ever came around asking about me. Until these past few days, my father never tried to get me to connect with Owen. So why is he trying to reel me in now? And why is he doing it in such a roundabout way? Why not just call me?"

"The answer to the first question isn't hard to figure out," Evelyn says. "He wants something from you. As for his methods? I don't know. Maybe he feels he needs more information before reaching out to you."

He feels on the verge of swooning and braces himself on the back of the sofa for support. He straightens up, paces the room, then turns to face the others. "That does it. I'm going to find him, and he's going to answer my questions. And if I don't like what I hear . . ."

Jimmy and Owen excuse themselves to use the restroom. His mother follows moments later, leaving Jackson alone with Pam. They sit in uncomfortable silence until Pam speaks.

"I just don't understand," she says.

She doesn't need to expound; he knows what she's talking about. He looks at her, takes a deep breath. "You were a good wife to me. A great wife."

"Then why?"

He shakes his head. What can he say that could possibly justify how he treated her? That he'd thought he was happy with Pam until he met his soulmate, Vanessa, who showed him what real happiness was? The soul mate part was true, partly true, anyway—Vanessa was the other half of the darkest part of his soul. But the happiness part? Was he ever truly happy with Vanessa? That's like asking if an addict is happy with his addiction. But an addict's craving has nothing to do with happiness. For some, it's the temptation of excitement. For others, it's a desire to cover despair that's so deep it has no bottom. For others still, it's an escape from loneliness. What was his need that only Vanessa could sate?

Pam pulls him from his thoughts. "I'd have given anything—"

"You gave me *everything*—"

"Everything but what you really needed." She locks eyes with him, and he finds pain in her stare, confusion.

He wants to tell her he doesn't understand it himself, tell her how truly sorry he is. He opens his mouth, hoping the words will come, but Owen returns first. Jackson and Pam hold each other's gaze, but both know the conversation is over. What happened between them will never be resolved.

He stands and leaves the room, walks into the hall, where he finds Jimmy and his mother in quiet conversation. He tells his mother that he'd like a moment with his brother, and Evelyn leaves them. When he and Jimmy are alone, he says, "One thing I never understood is why you let me have Pam. I came to love her after we were married, but you'd loved her since we were kids."

Jimmy looks away from him, taking time to gather his thoughts. "When we were young, before you became a total asshole, you were a good brother. You remember the Klein brothers? The bullies who always came looking for me? They had it in for me, I never knew why. But you stuck with me—even though they beat both of us up."

He doesn't remember but nods as though he does.

"And when Mom brought us back from Kansas and we played football together? We were both running backs and you were faster than me, better at finding holes. But you held back in practice and convinced Coach that I was better, so you ended up blocking for me. How many times did I break for a long run because of your blocking? How many touchdowns did I score thanks to you? I got a scholarship to college because of you."

Jackson recalls playing high-school football generally, but none of the details. "You were better than me—"

"Bullshit. And we both know it." They stare at each other until Jimmy continues. "And when Dad left, I was devastated. I would have fallen apart completely if it wasn't for you. All that stuff you said about you and me being a team, that nothing was going to break us apart, not even what Dad had done."

"But you loved her . . ."

"I loved you, too, Jackson."

He sees Jimmy tear up and can tell his brother's fighting himself. He needs to stay angry to keep going.

"And when you came home from college, you were falling down the rabbit hole so fast if something wasn't done, you'd end up dead."

"I almost did end up dead. The overdose . . ."

The overdose.

⁜   ⁜   ⁜

It comes back to him in a rush, starting when he hears a loud knock at the door to his bedroom but can't move to answer it. A series of loud knocks follows and someone shouts but he still can't move. Finally, the door is kicked open and Jimmy rushes in.

"*Jackson?* Jesus!"

He's on the floor by the sofa and his brother kneels over him, slaps his face, yells for him to wake up. He sees Jimmy for a second before his eyes roll back in his head. From a thousand miles away, he hears Jimmy on the phone to 911, telling them that someone has overdosed. Jimmy asks them what to do, then roughly lifts him off the floor, huffing and puffing as he drags him around the room.

"Try to walk!" Jimmy yells. "Stay awake!"

But he falls unconscious and the next thing he knows he's on his back in an enclosed space with two people hovering over him. He realizes he's in an ambulance and wonders how he got there.

"What did you take?" One of the EMTs is leaning into him.

He tries to answer, but the world goes black.

He wakes up in bed in a bright room with sunlight washing through the windows. He looks around and sees Jimmy and Pam and his mother. Pam reaches for his hand while Jimmy and Evelyn stand back.

"How are you feeling?" Pam asks.

He closes his eyes, shakes his head. *Like shit.*

A voice on the other side of the bed says, "He's out of danger now." He turns and sees a doctor in a white coat.

"Like hell he is," Jimmy says.

The doctor talks with his mother and brother then leaves the room. When he's gone, his mother moves up to the bed.

"This has to stop, Jackson. You've been going downhill since you returned from college and no one knows why."

"You're *killing* yourself." Jimmy's furious.

"You got yourself fired yesterday," his mother adds and he remembers a nasty scene at work with his boss. "What's behind all this?"

Now in the hallway at the Governor's Residence, he remembers his overdose like it was yesterday. Taking the pills, the hospital stay, being questioned by his mother. He recalls everything but *why* he poisoned himself. What caused him to race down the path to self-destruction.

"No wonder Pam hates me."

"No. She's better than that. She doesn't hate. She's angry, but how could she *not* be? She's confused, too. She doesn't understand. Hell, I don't understand." Jimmy pauses. "You asked me why I let you have Pam. But the real question is why you accepted her. Knowing I loved her. And knowing whatever the fuck you really are inside, how much it was going to cost her. Why didn't you turn her away when she was still whole? *Damn it.*"

He sees the fury rising inside Jimmy's eyes before Jimmy turns and leaves him alone in the hall. Watching his brother walk away, he realizes he's not the type of man other people will look back on fondly. They'll recall him as someone they survived. Endured. Lived through. Unless they didn't.

Helen didn't.

*   *   *

His mother sees him to the front door of the mansion.

"It's dangerous for you to look for your father," Evelyn says. "But I won't try to talk you out of it. Not just because I know you won't listen, but because you should try to save your half-sister and niece if you can, at least save what's left of them. At some point, your father has to be held accountable for what he does—using people as his personal pawns. Maybe you're the man to do it, maybe not. Maybe no one can stop him."

Evelyn looks up and he follows her gaze to the moon—a blood moon, a talisman, he knows, but of what, he cannot remember.

"I just want you to be prepared," she tells him. "I've done my best to forget about your father, put him behind me. I had to, as a matter of survival. The memories of what we shared were too painful. And that's what I'm getting at. Your father has a way of winning people over. Sucking them in. It's how he makes his money. What's even worse, though, is that he's able to remake people in his image. I saw him do it to men and women he brought into his business. Toward the end of our marriage, I was letting him do it to me. When you do finally cross paths with him, be careful. Don't let him turn you."

His mother locks eyes with him, then leans into him, kisses him on the cheek, hugs him.

Taking a step back, she smiles sadly. "Goodbye."

The door closes behind her, and he knows in his bones that he will never see her again.

BOOK III

BREAK FREE

CHAPTER TWENTY

IN THE COURSE of the past twenty hours, he has met with the mother, brother, and "widow" he hadn't seen in ten years. He has confronted his personal *femme fatale*, gotten into a shootout with his ex-boss, leaving the ex-boss and another cop shot and a third cop turned to jelly on the tracks. He's learned about a whole other side of his family, including a father who seems to have been pulling the strings of his life from hiding for much of his life.

The stress of it all, the confusion, the exhaustion from lack of sleep, are all taking their toll and he's finding it hard to keep his eyes open.

He spots a sign announcing an exit, and when he reaches it, he takes it and turns into the first motel he gets to. It's a one-story structure with a dozen or so rooms. The kind of place patronized by truckers and men sneaking off for nooners with their secretaries. The rooms sit across a cracked parking lot from a separate pill-box building hosting the front desk.

The lobby is a shabby space with a couch and a vending machine. Behind the front desk, a twenty-something is asleep in the chair, mouth open, drool down one side of his chin. The kid is rail-thin with arms covered in artless monochromatic tattoos. His long hair is two-toned—blond and brown.

An old-fashioned bell sits on the counter. He rings it. The desk clerk doesn't stir so he rings it again, three times in quick succession. The kid startles awake, almost falling off the chair.

"I'd like a room."

The kid pulls out a slip of paper, writes something on it, hands it to him. "Just sign your name."

He signs, slides the paper back to the kid, who tells him the room will be $54, including tax. Without thinking, he reaches into his overnight bag and pulls out a brick of hundreds, peels one off, and hands it to the kid, who is suddenly wide awake.

"Do you have change?"

"Wow. That's a hundred-dollar bill."

"I don't carry credit cards."

The kid stares at the Franklin. "Can I give you the change in the morning?"

He says sure, takes the key, and walks across the lot to his room. It's everything he expected. Worn carpet, cheap laminated furniture. A faded duvet over sheets he'll probably stick to. The air is thick with must. But he's so tired he doesn't care. After using the bathroom, he peels off his shirt and jeans and climbs into bed.

He closes his eyes and sinks into luxurious blackness. His senses shut down and he loses awareness of everything but the darkness surrounding him.

With a start, he awakens. He springs up in bed, looks around the dingy motel room, and sighs.

He forces himself to put his feet on the floor. He'd forgotten to close the curtains last night and he has a clear view of the parking lot and the office across the way. Standing behind the counter, the kid glances in his direction but quickly looks away when he sees him looking back.

He scratches his balls and stands. At the counter the night before, he'd stuffed the brick of hundreds into one of his front pockets, but the money isn't there when he pulls on the jeans. It's not on the floor, either, or on the chair he'd thrown the jeans over.

"Unbelievable." He throws his shirt over his head, puts on his boots, and walks across the parking lot.

"Can I help you?" the kid asks.

He doesn't answer, just stands there, his eyes boring into the kid.

"Um . . ." the kids says.

He sighs. "I'm going to give you three seconds to hand over the money you took last night when you used your master key to come into my room while I slept." He doesn't know for a fact that that's what happened, but he's pretty sure. "If you don't give me the dough before I'm done counting, I'm going to break your neck. Kill you, literally. Then I'm going to find out where you live and do the same thing to everyone I find there."

He never would've made a threat like that when he was Middle America Bob. But he has no doubt that he made them all the time as Jackson, the crooked cop. And followed through on them.

The kid stares at him.

"One," he begins. "Two . . ."

"Oh, man." The kid turns, reaches into a rain slicker hanging off the back of his chair, pulls out the money, and lays it on the counter.

He picks up the bills. "Taking that money was a dumb move on your part," he tells the kid. "But it was stupid of me, too, to pull it out where you could see it. So, you taught me a lesson." He peels off a couple of bills, slides them across the counter to the kid. "Consider this a finder's fee."

"Oh, wow! Thank you!"

"Where can I get something to eat around here?"

"There's a diner down the road, about two miles."

"Is it as nice as this place?"

The kid looks around. "Uh . . ."

"Never mind."

He returns to his room, takes a quick shower, puts on fresh clothes. At the diner, he slides into a booth, asks the waitress to bring him some coffee. When she returns, he orders the country breakfast—three eggs, sausage, hash browns, a short stack of pancakes, toast. While he waits for his food, he closes his eyes and nods off.

"Bad night? Or maybe a *good* night?"

He opens his eyes, sees the waitress standing next to him, holding his plate, a wry smile on her face. He knows what she's insinuating, but he's not in the mood for it.

"How about you just hand me my food."

While eating his breakfast, he chews on some of the things he still doesn't know. Apart from standing next to Jimmy at the zoo and playing with him in the sandbox at the park where he met the girl who turned out to be his half-sister, Jackie, he still has precious few memories of growing up with Jimmy before their mother relocated them to Kournfield. He doesn't recall any of their football games or being beaten up by the Klein brothers. Still, it seems he was a good brother to Jimmy when they were younger. So why did he become so selfish toward Jimmy when they were older? And why on earth did he drag Pam into his life?

He also knows he fell apart after college—overdosed and almost died—but he doesn't know why.

He hated his desk job in corporate world. Spending ten hours a day behind a computer screen was suffocating. But there was more to his decision to burn the suit and tie than his need to be out in the fresh air, on his feet. He just doesn't know what.

The biggest questions he has, though, are about his father. The man walked away from him thirty years ago. Then, ten years ago, when he was a crooked cop working for Donny Franco, his father helped drive a wedge between them by telling Owen and Jackie to look to him for the money they needed for Penny's treatment. And once he'd double-crossed Donny, his father stole the money he'd stolen from Donny. Then . . . nothing. He fled from Philadelphia, planted himself in Kournfield, Kansas, and lived there for a decade. Then some guy in a Chrysler 300 shows up asking questions about him, his wife is murdered, and when he returns to Philly thinking Donny was behind it all, his father hooks him up with Owen, putting him on notice that his old man is the one he should be looking for.

It all brings him back to the question he posed at the Governor's Mansion: *Why now?*

He finishes eating, pays the bill, and walks outside to the car. He takes a deep breath, opens the door, and climbs in, sinking back into the leather seat, lets it wrap itself around him. He's well rested, well fed, but he feels like an electric wire humming with ten thousand volts. He is angry and confused. And worried.

What other surprises are waiting for me?

CHAPTER TWENTY-ONE

TWELVE HOURS LATER, just before 9:00 p.m., he pulls up to the Holiday Inn Express seven miles south of I-70 near O'Fallon, Missouri. He checks in at the front desk and turns to cross the lobby when he hears a voice ring out to his right.

"Jackson? Hunter?"

He turns to see a big blond guy walking toward him, a smile plastered on his face. "It's me, Jonah!"

The guy grabs him in a bear hug, then releases him and steps back. "How have you been, man?"

He studies Jonah's face, trying to place him.

"I heard you hired on with a big tech company, in sales or something. Then someone told me you became a cop."

What does he say to this guy? He has decided to work the brain-injury angle when his head is suddenly flooded with scenes of him and Jonah—Jonah Zahn!—at parties, ball games, in clubs, and in class. He went to college at Temple University, in Philly. Jonah was one of his housemates. The two of them and two other guys rented a four-bedroom house on North 17th Street.

"Hey, I'm starving," Jonah says. "There's a Mexican place nearby. Let's grab a bite and catch up."

He agrees and they meet again in the lobby after he deposits his bags in his room.

"Come on," he tells Jonah. "We'll take my car."

Jonah's eyes bulge when he sees the Jag. "Damn, dude! Hey, can I drive?"

"Not a chance."

Jonah shrugs. "Had to ask."

The restaurant is two minutes away and before he knows it, he and Jonah are wolfing down nachos, tacos, and refried beans. His reunion with his old friend is different from all that has gone before because he can remember everything about college—where they lived, who he hung out with, his courses—at least the ones he showed up for. He even remembers the first frat party he went to, puking his guts out afterward. It's as though someone installed a hundred gigs of new memory into his brain.

He and Jonah go back and forth and what strikes him is that his memories are so vivid, he actually *feels* like he's back at school, a twenty-year-old happy idiot again. He and Jonah are certainly behaving like idiots—the looks they're getting from some of the other diners make that clear.

Jonah leans back in his chair, shakes his head. "You know, I'm not surprised one bit that the suit and tie thing didn't work for you."

"No?"

"You were a caged animal, dude. You could never sit still. I think you skipped half your classes. And you were always up half the night, except of course when you were up *all night*. Man, I'd get so jealous of all that tail you'd bring home."

"Good times," he says. "So, what are you doing now?"

"Manufacturer's rep. Farming equipment. Exciting, right? But I can't complain. I have three great kids, a fourth on the way. A wife who puts up with my bullshit. How about you? Married? Kids?"

"Divorced from wife number one. Second time around, a widower. No kids." *Just a niece I found out about yesterday.*

"Oh, well . . ." Jonah looks away.

"I'm good with it. I like my freedom."

"How's that hot mom of yours? I remember her coming around and all the guys would be drooling."

"She's married to the Governor of Pennsylvania."

"Doesn't surprise me. She was tough."

"She had to be. Our father left us, you know. Did I ever tell you that?"

"Maybe." Jonah scratches his chin. "I think I remember you saying something about it, once. Other than that, you never talked about your old man. Do you know what happened to him? Where he is?"

He nods. "As a matter of fact, I'm on my way west to see him. He lives in Vegas."

"Gambling?"

He's a player, that's for sure. "I'll soon find out. I don't know much about him."

Jonah tips his margarita glass. "So, what are you hoping to find?" he asks. "With your father, I mean."

"What am I hoping to find?" The question doesn't feel right; it's like one minute he and his old roommate are yukking it up and the next minute Jonah is trying to get inside his head. He gives Jonah a look, but at the same time, he questions himself, wondering whether he's being paranoid, reading into things.

"No problem," Jonah says. "You don't want to talk about it. I get it."

They finish, split the bill, and he drives Jonah back to the hotel. They exchange numbers in the lobby, take the elevator—Jonah to the second floor, him to three.

In his room, he mulls Jonah's question about what he's hoping to find with his father and decides he was being paranoid. He lifts the room phone and asks to be connected to Jonah Zahn.

"I'm sorry," the hotel operator says. "But Mr. Zahn is in the lobby, checking out."

At midnight?

He leaves his room and makes his way to the first floor. Through the lobby windows, he sees Jonah loading his belongings into the trunk of a Chrysler 300.

Son-of-a-bitch. Is Jonah the mystery guy who's been asking around about him? The guy he thought was working for Donny Franco but is probably working for his father? Was his "chance meeting" with his old college friend something other than a coincidence? Was it, in fact, a setup? He strides through the front doors.

"What the hell, Jonah?"

"Jackson . . . what's the matter?"

"That's what you're driving?"

"Yeah. So what?"

"So, it's true—you're the one who's been asking around about me."

"You better step back, Jackson."

Jonah is a big boy. Jackson has seen Jonah fight and knows the man can handle himself.

"What are you up to?"

"I don't know what the hell you're talking about, but I'm not going to warn you again." Jonah's tone is sharp now; his hackles are up.

He steps up to Jonah, gets right in his face. "If you had anything to do with her death, I swear—"

Jonah's had enough and he shoves him, a bad move for Jonah, who ends up on the ground.

"Get off me!"

"Not until you tell me what's going on. Why are you asking around about me? I know it's you because the guy who's been doing it has been driving *that* car."

"Damn, man! I'm just renting that car. I picked it up this afternoon, at the airport. Look at the rental contract in the glove compartment if you don't believe me."

He climbs off Jonah, strides to the car, and finds the contract. Jonah was telling the truth about picking it up earlier today. He also notices the car is a slightly different shade of gray than the one that's been following him around, and it doesn't have tinted windows.

"Why are you leaving at midnight?" he asks Jonah.

"I got a call from my wife. Her water broke and she's on the way to the hospital to deliver a baby. I have to catch a flight ASAP."

He looks down, shakes his head. "Fuck. Jonah, I'm sorry. I'm . . ."

"You're fucked up is what you are. I know you lost it at the end, because of Kimmie. We were all upset. But I figured you'd gotten your shit together by now. Looks like I was wrong."

He offers to help Jonah load the car, but Jonah tells him to forget it.

"The reunion's over, Jackson. Nice seeing you."

He's back in his room, getting ready for bed, when an image of a young woman pops into his mind. She's thin, almost lanky, with long brown hair, a heart-shaped face, and deep-brown doe eyes.

"Kimmie," he says. He climbs into bed and turns out the light. It doesn't take him long to fall asleep, and when he does, he meets her.

It's a Saturday night and the house is hopping. He, Jonah, and their roommates are throwing a party during the first semester of their senior year. They've rented the house for three years and it's become famous as a place to party. Tonight, the house is packed, the music blaring. He's serving drinks from a makeshift bar in the basement. In the kitchen, there's a punchbowl filled with fruit and grain alcohol. The air is thick with the smell of weed.

The party runs late, as always, and the last stragglers leave around two. He and his roommate Tony make a half-hearted effort to clean up, then decide to call it quits. He asks Tony where Jonah and their other roommate, Mike, are.

"Jonah left a while ago. I think he walked some girl home. Mike has a girl in his room."

He leaves Tony on the second floor and climbs the stairs to the third floor, where his bedroom is. He has his own bathroom and when he walks in, he finds a girl from the party curled up next to the toilet. She's conscious, barely, and covered in puke.

The girl's eyes are unfocused, but she must see him, because she says, "I don't feel well."

"I guess not," he says. He reaches down and lifts her into the tub. "You need to get clean. Can you get your clothes off, take a shower?"

With great effort, she lifts her head. "Sure." Then her head flops back down.

"Shit." He can't leave her in the bathtub covered in vomit, but he doesn't want to undress her and bathe her himself. He tries to figure out what to do and remembers there's a girl in Mike's room.

"I'll get someone to help," he tells her. "Wait here." His words make him laugh: of course she's going to wait—she can't stand up.

He knocks on Mike's door and when his roommate opens it, he's not happy.

"I have someone in here," Mike says.

"I know. I need her."

"Huh?"

"There's a chick upstairs in my room—"

"Wait, so what do you need my girl for?"

"She's covered in hurl. Needs a shower."

"So, give her a shower."

"Come on, man. She's drunk as a skunk. I can't do that kind of shit."

Mike closes the door and a few minutes later, a girl opens it and follows him upstairs. Mike's friend undresses the drunk girl, uses the shower hose to spray water on her, while he waits outside the bathroom.

"You'll have to help me lift her," Mike's girl says. "Carry her to the bed."

The drunk girl is covered with a towel, which slips off as he hoists her from the tub. Once she's on the bed, he pulls one of his t-shirts from a drawer and puts it on her, then covers her with a blanket.

"You need to turn her on her side," Mike's girl says. "In case she throws up again. And you have to stay and watch her sleep to make sure she doesn't roll onto her back. She could choke to death."

Mike's girl disappears downstairs, and he hears Mike trying to talk her into staying. She says she doesn't want to and calls a taxi to pick her up.

"You owe me!" Mike shouts up the stairs, before slamming his door.

He spends the night in a chair, watching the girl breathe. She first stirs when the sun rises but another hour passes before she opens her eyes. Then she bolts upright in the bed.

"Oh, no!"

"Morning, sunshine."

"Oh, no," she repeats. Then she looks down, sees she's wearing his shirt. "Who put me in this?"

"Mike's girlfriend dressed you. She showered you, too."

"I have to go," she says. "Where are my clothes?"

"Hanging in the bathroom. I washed the puke off. I don't know if the clothes are dry yet."

"I threw up?"

"Not a pretty sight."

"Oh, no."

He stands. "Come on, we can put your clothes in the dryer. I'll make you some breakfast while they dry."

Her face sours.

"You have to eat. There's nothing in your stomach. Believe me."

She takes the clothes to the basement while he starts breakfast. She joins him in the kitchen and he scrambles some eggs, brews coffee, pours them both some orange juice.

"I'm Jackson," he says, sitting across the table from her. "I live here."

"Kim," she says. "Kim Cacciacarro. But everyone calls me Kimmie Cappuccino, because they can't pronounce my last name."

They talk and he tells her he was born in Philadelphia, that his parents are divorced, and his mother now lives with her new husband in Chestnut Hill.

Kimmie Cappuccino says she's from a small town in the western part of the state. "Latrobe. You ever drink Rolling Rock? That's our claim to fame. Plus, Arnold Palmer grew up there."

It turns out Kimmie is a sophomore who shares an apartment with another girl a few blocks away. "I didn't party much when I was a freshman," she tells him. "I was afraid it would affect my grades. But it made me feel left out so over the summer I figured I'd have more fun this year. My roommate told me your house is a big party place, so we came last night." She pauses. "What was in that punch?"

He shakes his head. "Poor judgment."

They talk some more, then fall quiet. He decides of this doe-eyed innocent that he's going to be her big brother. He'll watch over her, protect her from the predators.

"I think next weekend you should take it easy," he says. "Maybe go to a movie instead of a place like this."

The dream ends there, and he realizes that it wasn't a dream at all, but a memory, and he's been awake all along. He sits up in bed. *So, what happened to you, Kimmie? What happened that made me lose it?*

CHAPTER TWENTY-TWO

HE'S HEADING WEST on I-70 now, and the exit for Kournfield is two miles ahead. He's been going back and forth with himself about whether to stop at the cabin to see if any new memories reveal themselves. He's also gone back and forth about whether he should meet up with Juke and tell him that his little sister was murdered. That the real reason he left town was to find Helen's killer, who he'd thought was his old boss, but who actually might turn out to be his father, or someone his father put up to it.

He takes the exit and travels south on 99. He decides that he made the right call with Juke when he left town. Juke is in enough pain already and doesn't need to hear that his sister was murdered. So he passes through town without stopping and continues toward the cabin. A "For Sale" sign stands at the entrance to the driveway. Quite a few potential buyers have come through the house and his real-estate agent has texted every time. So far, no one's made an offer, and he expects it's because the house is known as a place where the previous owner committed suicide. He's lowered the price twice and will keep on lowering it until someone bites.

He enters the front door and finds the house staged exactly as he left it. Because it's been shuttered, the air is damp, musty; he opens a couple windows. He takes his time walking through the rooms upstairs, lingering in the bedroom, staring at Helen's deathbed, the place her killer chose to steal her from this world. His mind brings up the torn-in-half picture of Helen and him that her killer had left to highlight that he was tearing their marriage asunder. Fighting back tears, he leaves the room and walks onto the upper deck, stares out at the lake for a long time. His mind brings up the two memories of him and Helen out on the boat—the one where she's happy and laughing, the one where her mood is black and she asks him to take her back.

From the upper deck, he stares down at the boathouse. The rowboat, he knows, is back in the boathouse, hanging from its chains. For a brief moment, he considers lowering it into the water, rowing out onto the lake. He sighs and the moment passes.

On impulse, he pulls out his cellphone and dials his home number. The phone rings twice, then Helen's voice comes on: *Helen and Bob aren't here right now, but please leave a message and we'll get back to you as soon as we can. Have a nice day.* In the early weeks following Helen's death, he now remembers, he called to hear that announcement many times.

The sound of her voice makes his heart smile, but when the message ends, he's left feeling hollow again. He stands at the front door, takes one more look around. He turns to leave when he feels something pulling him toward the hallway, and the bedrooms beyond. Feeling uneasy, he crosses the living room, walks down the hall. He turns into the master bedroom, and there they are—Helen and him, her sitting in her chair, staring blankly into the corner, him behind her. His right hand is on Helen's shoulder and he's leaning into her, slightly, talking into her ear. He's telling her about something funny that happened at work, in the cafeteria. Someone they both know accidentally spilled something on someone else they know. The tone of his voice is light, happy. But tears are rolling down his eyes and his face is tight with pain. He's hurting but he doesn't want Helen to know it, doesn't want her to feel his pain. His heart is breaking inside.

Don't do it, baby. Don't leave. Please don't leave.

The memory ends and he's back on the bed, shaken up now. So, Helen was going to leave him? Why? What was going on between them? His pace quickens and he has a hard time catching his breath. With great effort, he forces himself off the bed, down the hall, out of the house. His breathing is labored, and he tries to still himself.

Inhale. Hold for ten. Exhale.

Back on the road, he approaches the Welcome to Kournfield sign and pulls over. He sits in the Jag for a few minutes, then gets out, takes a few steps toward the sign. In the distance, he sees a white pickup heading toward him, going fast. It speeds by and when it does, he sees his own worried face on the driver. An instant later, he's behind that face, inside his pickup. Heat pours through the vents because it's bitter cold outside. There's a coating of snow on the fields along the road, and the sky is filled with a cover of gray clouds.

He's just come from town, from Juke's Place, where he met up with Juke and some others who'd been out looking for Helen. Over the course of the previous week, Helen had grown quiet, listless, called in sick from work. He knew one of her episodes was coming on and made a point of coming directly home from work. He expected he'd find Helen sitting in her chair in their bedroom, staring at the wall. But when he arrived home, her car wasn't in the garage and she wasn't inside the house. He called her cellphone, and when she didn't answer, he told himself that her spell had broken and she was at the grocery store, or out with friends. When she didn't return his message or return home after an hour, he grew concerned and started making calls, to Juke, to friends, to some of the neighbors. They all said they hadn't seen Helen. He started pacing the house and, after another hour, placed calls to the local hospitals. He learned that Helen hadn't been brought in, and he called Juke again. Then he called the sheriff's office and was told they couldn't do anything officially until Helen was missing for twenty-four hours, but that they'd keep an eye out for her.

He started driving around, looking for Helen's car, and Juke did the same thing. They searched for hours, until the sun came up, but didn't find her. Finally, his eyes bleary from lack of sleep, he decided to return home.

He pulls the truck down the dirt and gravel driveway, past the house to the detached garage. The garage door is open, and Helen's car is sitting inside. He races to the driver's-side door and sees Helen, staring straight ahead, through the windshield. She sits perfectly motionless, as though she has no idea he's standing right next to her.

He raps on the window. After a moment, Helen slowly turns her head, looks up at him. Her eyes are flat and far away. He stares at her, then moves around the back of the car to the passenger's side, opens the door, and climbs in. He shuts the door and they sit in silence.

"I looked everywhere for you," he says. "Called everyone we know."

She doesn't answer.

"Where were you?"

She sighs. "I went to a hotel."

He holds his breath. "Were you . . . alone?"

No answer.

"Helen?"

Another sigh. "No."

"Who?" The only word he can force out.

She turns to him. "My seducer."

"Bob?"

A man's voice, coming from far away.

"Bob? Are you all right?"

He finds himself sitting on the ground, between his truck and the Welcome to Kournfield sign. He looks up, sees a man in a tan uniform. It's Jerry Trimble, a sheriff's deputy, the one he spoke to when he first woke up in Juke's Place after the assault.

"What happened? Can you stand up?" Deputy Trimble extends a hand.

He accepts and lets the deputy help him get to his feet.

"You want me to take you to Juke's? Or a hospital?"

He hears the words but doesn't know how to respond to him. He's just learned that his wife had been having an affair. How long had it been going on? What had made Helen do it? Did he drive her into the arms of another man? Had he been that neglectful?

"Jesus, Bob. You look like shit."

He takes a couple deep breaths, thanks Trimble, pats him on the shoulder, and walks back to his truck. He climbs inside, starts up, and pulls onto the road, noting that the deputy's eyes are following him the whole way.

A few minutes later, he spots his own truck racing toward him in the southbound lane. When it passes, he sees himself, as "Bob," wearing a t-shirt and looking terrified. That's when he realizes that he's seeing himself speeding toward his house on the day Helen took her life. But why the fear? He's returning home from work, expecting to find Helen in a joyous mood over the "surprise" she promised him. He should be in a good mood. But he's clearly weathering a storm inside.

"What the fuck . . ."

He tries to force his mind to bring up the *whole* memory, including what he's thinking, but he's locked out. He curses again, smashes the palms of his hands against his steering wheel.

He reaches the entrance to I-70 west and takes it. Once he's on the interstate, he presses hard on the accelerator, until the speedometer is well over a hundred and the engine is roaring, his body vibrating with the car, his heart thumping like he's had ten cups of coffee.

After a while, he doesn't know how long, he hears a siren and glances in his rearview mirror to see a police cruiser coming up behind him.

"Shit." He slows to pull over and at the same time takes out his Philly cop badge and places it where the trooper will see it, maybe cut him a break.

"License and registration," the trooper says when he gets to the car.

He hands both over and waits.

"Kansas driver's license but you're driving a car registered in Pennsylvania, to somebody else. Richard Francis. How does that happen?"

"Richie was my partner with the Philly PD, back in the day. Before I moved out here ten years ago. He's been holding the car for me since then. I went back and picked it up, to bring it home."

"Home . . . to Kournfield?"

"Exactly," he says.

"Kournfield being twenty miles behind you." The trooper's eyes bore into him.

"I'm on my way to Vegas, to see my father. He couldn't get in for my wife's funeral, so I'm going to him." He plays the sympathy card, given that the cop angle doesn't appear to have worked.

"Do you know how fast you were going?" the cop asks him.

He shakes his head. "Too fast, I know." Contrition. Cops love contrition, especially the staties.

The trooper stares at him, then glances down at his license and back at him again. "I know you. You work at Goodyear, with my brother. He's on your company baseball team." The officer says the brother's name, and his memory offers up a face.

"Your brother's a hell of a second baseman," he says.

The trooper nods his head. Smiles. Hands back the license and registration. "Just a warning this time."

He thanks the trooper, who looks over the Jag.

"Nice car. V-8?"

"V-12," he answers. "Gets terrible mileage."

"But goes like hell," the cop says, adding a wry, "from what I saw."

He shakes his head again. "Sorry about that. I got distracted. Too much stress. No excuse, I know."

"Highway's not the place to work off stress," the cop says. "Get yourself to a gym. And sorry about your wife."

He exhales as the trooper returns to his car, then wonders why he was nervous in the first place. What does he care whether he gets a fucking ticket? What are a few points and a fine compared to what he's gone through in the past few weeks? Compared to what he's facing?

"Man, I really do need to get to a gym." As soon as he says the words, he knows what he's going to do.

*   *   *

"Three weeks." The first words out of Walt's mouth when he walks in. Walt's Boxing Gym is only twenty minutes west of where the state trooper pulled him over on I-70.

The three-weeks thing tells him he doesn't usually go that long between sessions. "Had some things to take care of," he says.

From behind the counter, Walt stares at him. The gym owner is a big man, a former fighter who won a belt or two before hanging up his gloves twenty years ago. He has the saggy look that musclebound guys get once they stop working out.

"Anyone here you think might want to mix it up?" he asks.

Walt tilts his head, looks toward the ceiling. "Got a mean buck in the ring upstairs. Says he boxes for the Navy. He's home on leave a couple weeks, visiting his sister. He cleaned up the ring with a guy two days back; now no one wants to spar with him."

He smiles. "Made to order."

"Here we go." Walt hands him the key to a locker. "Number 111, in case you forgot." Walt is joking, but Bob appreciates the memory prompt.

He changes, then takes the steps upstairs. The guy in the ring looks to be fifteen years younger than him and outweighs him by an easy twenty pounds. His footwork is good. He seems fast.

Walking up to the ring, he calls out to the guy. "You want to dance a little?"

The fighter says sure, so he gloves up, puts on his headgear. They bounce around a while, jab at each other. He holds back and he can tell the kid is holding back, too.

"You want to go a few rounds?" the kid asks. "Say three? Unless you put me down before that." The kid smiles, feigning humility.

"Sure," he answers. "Go easy on me."

Walt's assistant is watching and he agrees to time the rounds, do the bell. "I'm not going to referee, though," he says. "I expect you guys to fight clean."

He and the kid are standing close to each other. "Rules?" Jackson asks, his voice low.

The kid smiles. "Sheeyit."

He nods and knows they have an understanding.

The kid advances on him as soon as the bell rings, and lands a couple solid blows to his torso, one of them just below the belt. He returns the favor and they go at it. By the time the bell rings, they're both huffing and puffing, sweat pouring off of them. In his corner, he glances toward the kid, finds him staring at him, maybe wondering what he's gotten himself into. This time, when Walt's assistant rings the bell, it's his turn to rush the kid.

Round two costs him a cut under his left eye. The price the younger fighter pays, though, will be higher. Both of the kid's eyes are swelling shut and the muscles around his rib cage must be tender as veal. When Walt's assistant rings the bell, the kid turns away in anger.

The third round starts with him and the kid both rushing to meet in the center. It ends after a minute and a half with the kid on the mat, struggling to get up. He does make it to his feet, but by then Walt himself has entered the ring and tells them the fight's over.

"Another round," the kid insists, trying to push past Walt.

"Back off before I put you down myself," Walt tells him. "I don't got insurance for this." He turns to Jackson. "Get yourself to the locker room, Jackson," he says.

After he showers, he sits on the bench in front of the lockers, feeling spent and sore and *great* . . . for the first time in quite a while. When the Navy fighter walks in, he looks up at him. "Good fight. Thanks."

The young buck nods, mumbles something like "no problem" or "whatever," then walks out of sight to a second line of lockers.

At the front desk, he hands his key back to Walt.

"Feel better?" Walt asks.

He doesn't answer.

"You were pretty revved up when you walked in here."

"Lot on my mind."

"What's that song about drivin' down the road trying to loosen the load of all those women on your mind?"

"'Take It Easy.' The Eagles."

"Speaking of which," Walt says. "One of your fans stopped by."

"My fans?"

"Look, I'm not one to stick my nose into other people's business, but that brunette, there's something not right with her."

Walt's words bring up the image of a tall woman, a little too thin, but with large breasts. She has mousy brown hair over dull eyes and a crooked smile.

"She came in last week, asked if you'd been around. I told her I hadn't seen you and she said she put a balloon on your trailer to let you know she'd been by."

His *trailer*? *What the fuck*?

"It's still there," Walt says. "You'll see it when you walk outside."

He thanks the man and leaves the building, focusing his attention on the trailer court on the far side of the parking lot. There are three rows of single-wides, each with its own narrow driveway. The first trailer in the middle row has tan siding, a slightly peaked roof, and a small porch outside the door. Hanging limply on a string tied to the porch's railing is a deflated silver balloon. He passes the Jaguar and walks up to the trailer. As he gets there, he remembers that he keeps a key in a small metal box hidden under the bottom step leading to the porch.

He opens the front door to a small living room with worn shag carpeting and faux wood paneling. Sitting in the middle of the room is a ratty plaid couch. A ratty couch in a ratty living room. His mind pulls up the video he'd seen before—him sitting on the couch, leaning forward to inhale lines of cocaine, a woman sitting next to him, telling him to save some for her. This time, he turns to look at the woman and sees the mousy brunette.

Fuck me.

He'd thought that memory came from a time years ago, before he even met Vanessa. But it was during his marriage to Helen!

He feels sick inside. He knew he'd kept the boxing gym, his need to fight, secret from Helen. He'd tell her he was going somewhere for batting practice, a lie that meshed with his being captain of his company's baseball team. Now, it turns out, he was deceiving Helen wholesale. Had their entire marriage been a lie? Had he been Jackson the whole time he was disguised as good-guy Bob? Didn't Walt just call him *Jackson*?

Standing in the living room, he takes in the trailer, shakes his head. Then he notices for the first time an envelope on the coffee table. He walks over and opens it. Inside are photographs of a naked woman from the neck down. Sticking to the top picture is a yellow note with a smiley face drawn on it.

"Unbelievable." He tosses the envelope and pictures onto the table and turns away.

He leaves the mobile home, hides the key, and returns to the gym.

"Back so soon?" Walt looks up from his desk behind the counter.

"I have a question. How long have I had that trailer?"

"How long?"

"It's for tax purposes. My accountant needs to know exactly."

"Uh-huh," Walt mumbles. Then he leans over and pulls a file from one of his desk drawers. Walt opens the file and hands over three stapled pages.

He takes the papers and sees they constitute the lease for the trailer. According to the date at the top, he's been renting the mobile home from Walt for almost two years. He doesn't know how to feel about that. On one hand, it proves for sure he'd been living a double life for quite some time. On the other hand, it's evidence that he'd been able to live the "Bob" life with Helen for eight of their ten years together. Not conclusive evidence, because for all he knows, he had some other fuck-pad before he'd leased with Walt.

"Thanks," he says, handing the lease back to Walt.

"It expires next month. You want to re-sign for twenty-four months? Or go month to month?"

He shakes his head. "Neither. I'm headed west."

Walt leans back in his seat, looks up at him, then back down at his desk. "Good luck."

Back in the Jaguar, he sits for a long time, staring at the trailer with the empty balloon. Memories of him there with the brunette—and other women, drinking, laughing, drugging, screwing—bubble up in his brain. So, he betrayed Helen exactly as he did Pam. He feels worse about himself than ever. And he has a bad feeling that once his memory returns in full, he'll be faced with more betrayals. More violence. And God knows what else . . .

CHAPTER TWENTY-THREE

HE LEANS OVER, adjusts the radio. It's just before 2:00 p.m. His plan is to drive through to Denver, arriving around 8:30 or 9:00. He'll stay the night there and drive to Las Vegas in the morning, which should take him about eleven hours.

*   *   *

He hears a sigh, turns from the windshield, and sees a vision from his past. Kimmie Cappuccino is sitting on her front step, a cigarette in her hand, a hangdog look on her face. Kimmie and her roommate live on the top floor of a three-story walk-up about four blocks from his condo. He passes it on the way home from the gym.

"Why so glum, Kimmie?"

She shrugs.

"Didn't you have fun at the party last night?"

"Sure. Always."

He's not so certain. Kimmie has come to all the parties he and his roommates have thrown during the semester. He noted early on that Kimmie is on the shy side, so he invited her to help him run the bar in the basement. She's proven to be a great second mate and he enjoys having her by his side. Last night, though, Jonah ran the basement bar while Jackson worked the rest of the party upstairs. A couple of times during the night, he saw Kimmie wandering aimlessly, standing by herself. He smiled at her and she always smiled back, but he detected sadness in her eyes. A girl from one of his classes showed up at the party and he spent most of the night with her and then took her up to his room. He didn't see Kimmie after that.

"You got home okay last night?"

"Of course," Kimmie answers. "I left a little early. I had a headache."

He studies her. She's hiding something. "Did anyone try something inappropriate with you?"

She looks away.

"You know you can tell me about anything. I *want* you to. I'm your big brother, remember?"

She smiles, nods quickly, takes a drag of her cigarette.

"And since when do you smoke?"

"I smoke when I'm upset."

"So something is wrong?"

"Just girl stuff."

He looks her over. "You're not pregnant, are you?"

"Jeez, Jackson!"

He dishes up his million-dollar smile, sits down beside Kimmie, takes a drag from her cigarette, and gives her a friendly hug. And that's all it takes. Kimmie's mood lightens and they spend the next half hour talking and laughing.

*   *   *

The memory fades and he tries to mine it for clues as to what eventually *happened* to Kimmie, why it messed him up, as Jonah claimed. He finds nothing.

The radio is tuned to a contemporary rock station, and he turns up the volume. It's a song about a wedding, and his mind carries him to Pam's beaming face on their wedding day. With Jimmy, his best man, standing next to him at the altar, he watches Pam float down the aisle. The memory flickers and he and Jimmy are in the minister's vestry room just before the ceremony. Jimmy has been quiet the whole day, the past few weeks, actually. His brother's looking away from him, through the window, to a wooded lot behind the church.

"Thank you, Jimmy," he says. "You saved my life. You and Pam."

Still looking through the window, Jimmy says, "It will be good for you to settle down."

They sit in silence until Jimmy turns to him. "Be good to her, Jackson."

"What kind of thing is that to say? Of course, I'll be good to her."

Back in the Jag again, he shakes his head . . . He wasn't good to Pam, not in the end.

"But it wasn't the end," he says aloud. "Just the end of us. It was the beginning for you and Jimmy."

*   *   *

He drives for four hours on Kansas I-70, getting close to Colby. Then the brake lights of the tractor-trailer ahead of him light up. He downshifts until he's a few car lengths from the truck, which has come to a complete stop. He swerves a little to the left and sees that all the traffic in front of the truck is stopped as well. Something's happening on the road ahead. Construction, or an accident. After a few minutes, he hears the scream of sirens behind him, low at first but growing louder. In short order, a line of police cars race past him along the berm of the road. He turns off his engine to save gas and waits. Shortly after the cruisers pass him on the right, a helicopter whizzes by above. He leans forward to look out of the windshield. *Chopper 6* is painted on the bottom of the helicopter.

"Shit." News helicopters are like turkey vultures, appearing out of nowhere when the scent of fresh carrion reaches them downwind. Which means that traffic is stalled because of an accident. If it's bad enough, it could be hours before the road reopens. He tunes his AM radio to the news channel, but all he gets is static, so he turns off the radio to save battery. Ahead of him, he sees people getting out of their cars, and he does the same.

"Any idea what's going on?" he asks the nearby motorists.

"I can't get anything on my radio," a man in his sixties answers.

"I heard there was a two-mile backup," a younger man says. "But my radio went to static before they said what was causing it."

More police cars pass by, followed by a line of ambulances. Overhead, three more helicopters zoom by.

"Fucking newshounds," the younger man says.

"Those aren't news choppers," the older man answers. "Those are medical helicopters."

"Three of them?" a woman asks.

"Must be bad," the younger man says.

The older man turns to his wife. "Well, Mother, looks like a job for the drone." He opens his trunk, revealing a white drone with four blades. He pulls it out, along with a remote control and a separate monitor. "This baby's a Gen-7 DJI Mavic Pro," he beams. "Has a range of four miles." He turns on the power, launches the drone. A small crowd gathers by the monitor, which he has propped up on his closed trunk.

The drone flies at a good clip about fifty feet above the line of cars and trucks. When it reaches the front of the line and they can see what's happened, they stand back in shocked horror. The line of vehicles leads smack into the side of the smoldering ruins of a passenger jet. Directly to its right is a large billboard displaying the face of Cornfield Jesus.

"My God," a woman gasps.

"We should go up there and help," Jackson says.

"We'd just get in the way." It's the drone operator. "Best to stay here and watch."

"I can't just stand here," he says. He walks back to the Jag, locks it, and starts forward. When finally he reaches the crash site, he comes upon scores of people working with emergency responders to help the survivors, both the ones from the plane and those from the pileup of trucks and cars on the ground.

Helping a crash victim hobble toward the ring of ambulances, he overhears one of the pilots from the downed plane telling a reporter that the plane insisted on crashing itself.

"We were on autopilot and the plane suddenly decided to descend, as though we were on final approach. I switched to manual and took us back up to altitude, but the plane forced us down again, and from there I was fighting it the whole way. It took everything I had to keep us level as we descended—the plane would have had us go down nose first—and when I realized there was no keeping us in the air, I put down the flaps and landing gear and configured us for landing. It was rough going once we touched down, but everyone would have been fine if we hadn't been rear-ended by a line of cars and trucks."

The pilot's tale doesn't surprise him. Boeing had had catastrophic experiences with a new model airplane a decade earlier, and every year or two since, he would see news reports of some sort of trouble, or outright disasters, resulting from software malfunctions.

The pilot pauses, scratches his head, and looks at the reporter. "It was just the strangest thing. If I didn't know better, I'd swear that fucking plane was trying to kill itself." The pilot sighs deeply, then turns away from the reporter and sinks into his thoughts.

He helps as many people as he can, then walks back to his car. It's after 8:00 p.m. when he reaches the Jag and it takes another three hours before traffic begins to move. He decides to get a room but finds nothing available at the nearby Budget Inn, or the Super 8. The Quality Inn, Days Inn, Motel 6, and Comfort Inn are all likewise full, so he decides to sleep in the car.

* * *

He wakes before sunrise to find Kimmie Cappuccino cuddled up next to him in bed. He has a pounding headache and it takes him a few minutes to orient himself, figure out what happened. When he remembers, he's not happy with himself.

It was a night when he wasn't working the bar. Making his way around the house, he noticed Kimmie by herself, looking ever more miserable as the evening wore on. Eventually, he had enough and took Kimmie to the only quiet place in the house—his room.

"Sit." He pointed toward the bed then opened a bureau drawer and lifted out a tin box containing some rolled joints. He lit one and shared it with her.

"It seems like you're not having a good time tonight," he said. "I'm fine."

"You're not fine." And he knew why. They were well into the second semester and Kimmie had been going to his parties regularly. But she was still painfully shy and only seemed to open up when she was working the bar with him or when he had her over to watch TV with him and his roommates.

"You need to break out of your shell," he told her. "A lot of guys at the parties come up to you—I've seen it. But you shut them down. They try to talk to you, but you look away from them."

"You know what they're after."

"Not all of them," he answered. Then he reconsidered. "Okay, you're right about what they want. But that doesn't mean you can't talk to them. You might like one of them and then you'll want to . . . be close to them."

She looked away.

"I mean, I'm not trying to rush you into something. Hell, I adopted you as my little sister. I just want to see you happy."

She stared at him with her big brown eyes. "Are *you* happy, Jackson?"

He didn't answer.

"I mean, you're the life of the party. The center of attention. All the girls like you and you get enough of them. But . . . how much of it is you having fun and how much is a cover for something else?"

He didn't like where this was headed.

"I'm sorry," Kimmie said.

"No, it's okay. I just don't talk about how I feel much. Ever, actually."

"It's okay to talk about things. It's more than okay. It's important."

"Yeah? Who do you talk to?"

She shrugged. "I've tried to talk to my roommate. But she's, I don't know. She's a physics major, her brain's not wired like mine. The only reason we're roommates is we both come from Latrobe. Plus we're both neat freaks." She paused as he lit another joint. "I call my mom sometimes," she said. "She's a good listener. But she's my mom, so there are things I can't tell her. Not that she would want to hear them."

They sat quietly on the bed for a while, then he wrapped his arm around her shoulder. "Well, little sister, I have a proposition for you. How about from here on out we talk to each other? I mean, really talk." Then he removed his arm and held out his hand and they shook on it.

Then he pulled out a bottle of wine and they drank.

And now they're both lying in his bed, buck naked. He looks down at Kimmie and finds her staring up at him with a smile on her face.

"You really opened up to me last night." She nuzzles closer to him.

"Seems like we both opened up."

* * *

The sunlight hits his eyelids and he wakes up in the Jaguar. Instead of a guilty conscience, though, he wakes with a stiff back. Pushing open the door, he climbs out of the car, walks into a fallow field, and relieves himself. Then he drives to the Village Inn for breakfast.

Eating slowly, sullenly, he mulls his memory of the night before. That night with Kimmie changed their relationship. She became his confidante. And he became hers. He opened up to

Kimmie about things he'd never told anyone. He told Kimmie he felt there was something wrong with him, that there always had been, but he kept it secret, held it down.

Amazingly, she didn't judge him. Kimmie told him she expected that a lot of men who turned out great probably had the same issues. Restlessness. Aggression. Even when he admitted that he was afraid what would happen if he ever lost control of his anger, Kimmie looked at him with those doe eyes and he felt better about himself.

He pays for breakfast, uses the restroom, and exits the door of the restaurant. That's when he sees it: the dark gray Chrysler 300, pulling away. He runs toward the car, shouting, but the Chrysler is out of the parking lot before he gets close to it.

"Son-of-a-bitch."

He stares at the car until it disappears.

Stop, he tells himself. *Think*. The gray car's just a car and he's a guy with too much pent-up energy. He tells himself to forget about the Chrysler and focus on finding Jackie and Penny, saving them if they need saving. Confront his father, get answers, and maybe bring justice for Helen.

Wearily, he climbs into the car, puts it into gear, and peels out of the lot. The speedometer passes eighty before he knows it. Then, as it edges up to ninety, the engine starts wheezing. After a few minutes, the wheezing devolves into coughing and hacking, and the car starts to shake. He curses and pulls to the side of the road.

Lifting the hood, he sees that a hose has been cut and parts of the engine are dented, as though someone took a hammer to them. His mind flashes to the gray Chrysler pulling out of the restaurant parking lot, and he decides that whoever was driving that car sabotaged his Jaguar.

He curses again, then pulls out his cellphone, asks Siri to connect him to the nearest garage. An hour later, the Jaguar is being offloaded from a tow truck at a repair shop just off the interstate. The owner tells him they don't have replacement parts for a 1974 E-Type XKE and will have to get them from Denver, which will take a full day to get there, assuming his supplier in Denver even has the parts.

"That's no good," he says. "I was hoping to be in Nevada by tonight. I'm on my way to Vegas and I'm in a hurry."

"Isn't everyone in a hurry to get rich?"

He hears the voice over his shoulder and turns to see an older man dressed in loose-fitting jeans, a blue work shirt, sleeves rolled up. His chin is covered in stubble. His cheek is fat with chew, which he promptly spits on the ground.

"I apologize," the man says. "I was waiting to talk to Earl here and I couldn't help but overhear. If you're interested, I'm driving to Sin City myself. I've been on the road awhile, though, so I won't be able to push through without stopping."

He considers the offer. He hates the idea of leaving his car behind, but realizes it's actually the smart thing to do in case Donny Franco has somehow found out he's driving the Jaguar and has put out an APB on it. He doesn't think it likely, but you never know.

"I'd be happy to take you up on your offer. But I'll insist on paying for gas."

The man laughs. "Now that's an offer I'll gladly take you up on." He nods toward a 16-wheeler on the other side of the lot. "Betsy's a bit of a hog."

CHAPTER TWENTY-FOUR

THE TRUCKER HAS the stale smell of sweat and musk and dust that builds up on a man who spends hour after hour sitting behind the wheel. Every now and then he leans over and spits into a plastic cup in the console between them.

They are ten miles down the road before either of them speaks.

"So," the truck driver says, "are you running to, or running from?"

He turns to the man. "What makes you think I'm running at all?"

"You have the look."

A few miles later, the driver glances at him. "Not much of a talker, eh?"

"I have a lot on my mind."

The driver nods slowly. "Well, we have a long drive ahead of us. And I have two good ears."

He studies the man. "I never asked your name."

"I'll tell you," the driver says, "but you won't believe me."

"Sure I will."

"My parents named me Driver. Driver Carello."

"You're kidding me."

Driver shakes his head. "Nope. So, you can see why I ended up with this job. It doesn't upset me though; they could have named me *Cocksucker*."

They both laugh.

"So, what do you go by?" Driver asks.

"Jackson," he answers. "J.R. Bob. Take your pick."

"A man with aliases, eh?"

They continue down the road and he spends the time staring at the sky. It's hot and stale in the truck and he opens his window. But the air outside is hotter and staler, so he closes the window again.

"I used to have someone I could talk to," he says, thinking of Kimmie.

"What happened to her?"

"How do you know it was a her?"

"Usually the way it is, in my experience."

"I don't know what happened to her."

Driver looks over. "How's that?"

"I just don't remember. I have . . . gaps in my memory." He doesn't know why he's telling the driver about his amnesia. He hasn't told anyone else other than Owen. Maybe it's easier to confide certain things in strangers.

The trucker laughs. "I'm old enough there's lots I don't remember. And things I *wish* I didn't."

"Joking aside," he says. "When you look back, are there holes, big holes, about important things?"

Driver considers this. "I suppose so. I remember growing up, for example, but only bits and pieces. Is that what you mean?"

He shakes his head. "I can't remember my father. He lived with us for ten years before he took off, but I can't recall anything about him other than that he used to drive my brother and me to a park, where we played with a girl who turned out to be our half-sister. I also know that I fell down a dark hole after college but have no idea why."

He pauses, reaches for the bottle of water the trucker placed in a cupholder for him. "This is going to sound crazy, but a month ago, I woke up in a bar and I couldn't remember a damn thing about myself. Not even my name. It wasn't until people came up to me and started talking that anything came back to me."

"Tabula rasa."

"What?"

"It's Latin. It means blank slate. The idea being that each of us is born without anything at all in our minds and that all knowledge comes from experience, perception."

"Except I wasn't born that day. I was forty-one years old."

Driver glances over at him. "Good point. Well, you got me there. I can't explain your amnesia."

He doesn't talk for a while, trying to decide what more to tell the stranger. From time to time, he looks over at the older man. Finally, he makes his decision.

"I did have my head bashed in."

This seems to startle the driver. "Come again?"

"Just before I woke up in the bar, someone attacked me, smashed my head against a brick wall."

"So, now we're getting closer to solving the mystery of your memory loss." The trucker nods. Then, after a while, turns to him. "You look like a tough guy."

"I can hold my own."

"Any formal training?"

"I can box. Kickbox, too. So I think so."

"You think? Don't you know? Ah, the memory thing . . ."

He nods.

Driver spits some chew into his cup. "We could work through it, try to figure it out."

"How is that?"

"I could ask you questions, see if they shake loose some memories. For example, when is the first time you remember using your skills as a kickboxer?"

He thinks on this. "Right after we moved to Kansas from Philadelphia. My mother, brother, and me. Some kid in school tried to bully me, and I put him on his ass."

"How old were you?"

"Tenth grade, so, fifteen."

"Were you from a tough neighborhood in Philly?"

"No. Chestnut Hill. It was fairly affluent." An image of his house appears in his mind. It was a stone colonial with a center hall on half an acre.

"So, no reason to seek out training in self-defense."

He shakes his head, then remembers what Jimmy said to him about the Klein brothers. "Wait a minute. My brother and I were in grade school and there was a pair of brothers who used to rough us up every time they saw us. One day, we both came home with black eyes. The next day our mother drove us to a gym and paid for us to take boxing lessons. I ended up learning to kickbox, too."

"Your mother? Not your father?"

He sits up. "Wait, it *was* our father. He said he wasn't going to have his sons being bullied. And he's the one who drove us to the gym."

Driver smiles. "My own father did the same thing with me. I was a sickly kid for a long time. Other kids used to pick on me. So he took me to a gym, had a guy teach me how to box. I'd come home and he'd make me show him what I'd learned. Then he would put me on my ass and tell me I needed to learn more. My old man was an SOB." He shakes his head. "Always getting into fights. Stabbed to death in a bar, in the end."

They drive on until Driver asks Jackson if he remembers anything else about his father. "What does he look like?"

"I . . . I can only see the back of his head, over the car seat. And his shoulders. He had big shoulders. And he was tall—I remember that from the memories of him in the park."

"Anything else you remember about him? What was he like as a person?"

The question causes his mood to darken and it must show on his face.

"Sore subject?" Driver asks. "I'll back off."

They continue down the road for a while.

"He left me, my brother, and mother thirty years ago, and I haven't heard from him since."

They continue down the road a few more miles. "Recently, I've found out some things . . . I think he's been keeping an eye on me the whole time. From a distance." Saying the words seems to open the floodgates and he tells the truck driver the whole story, or as much of it as he can remember. His first marriage to Pam; his toxic relationship with Vanessa; his lawlessness as a crooked cop; the murder of his second wife, Helen, disguised to look like a suicide. Finally, learning that he had a half-sister and a niece, both of whom were stolen from his half-sister's husband by his father.

"Stolen? How'd he manage that?"

He explains Penny's illness and need for medical treatment, and his father's agreement to pay for Penny's care, but only if Jackie moved with Penny to Las Vegas.

"That was after I stole a million-two from my boss for Penny's care, only to have it taken from me before I could give it to my sister and her husband."

"What convinced you to steal from your corrupt cop boss?" the driver asks.

"My father told my sister about me, said I could get the money to pay for my niece's care. My sister approached me and, when I met my niece, I was all in."

"And once you'd stolen the money, you had to leave Philadelphia, to escape your old boss?"

He nods. "I think that was my father's plan. I'd leave Philly and come to him."

"But it didn't work out that way."

"I faked my death, moved to a small town in Kansas. I fell in love and got married. Worked in a Goodyear plant. I never felt the need to reach out to my father. It never even crossed my mind. Not that I can remember, anyway."

The trucker considers this for a few minutes. "If your father is as manipulative as you suggest, I'd expect he was quite annoyed that you didn't follow your sister to Las Vegas."

"Annoyed?" He laughs bitterly. "Yeah. Enough to keep tabs on me." He pauses. "Maybe enough to have my wife killed, to send me back to him."

"Well, if that was his plan, it sounds like it worked."

*   *   *

They drive three more hours and stop for lunch. Then they punch straight through to Green River, Utah, where the trucker pulls the 16-wheeler into the parking lot of a sad-looking, one-story motel. It has a center office with two wings of six rooms each.

"I hope you don't mind," Driver says. "It's not the nicest place in the world, but it's cheap. And so am I." He laughs.

Inside the postage-stamp-sized office, they are greeted at the counter by a morbidly obese man who looks to be in his early seventies. Every move causes the man to huff and puff.

"Thirty-six dollars a night, plus three dollars for the resort fee, tax included." The owner smiles.

"Where's the resort?" Jackson asks.

"It's in the planning stage."

Driver hands him two twenties and the owner gives him a buck change.

Jackson slides a hundred across the counter.

"Why didn't you say you wanted the Presidential Suite?" The owner snatches the bill. "It's a hundred even, all in."

"That's what I figured," he says.

A few minutes later, he enters his room and looks around. When Driver said the rooms weren't much, he was being kind. The double bed sags like a sway-back mare. The painted paneling has long cracks—some extending from the brown-stained drop ceiling to the orange shag carpeting. The bathroom tile is faded, the green porcelain toilet is chipped.

He relieves himself, then washes his face in water that smells like rotten eggs. The box air-conditioner punched into the wall next to the door is coughing out particle-laden, lukewarm air, so he turns it off and steps outside. On the other side of the motel office, a harried-looking woman clumsily wheels a suitcase from a car to her room. A small dog limps behind her.

"Come on, Ike," the woman nudges the dog. She glances his way, and he smiles politely, which earns him a grimace. The woman holds the door open for the dog, then disappears into the room.

Across the lot, Driver exits his rig and walks toward him.

"There's a decent roadside restaurant half a mile down the pike if you're interested in grabbing a bite. It's not a bad night and we could walk, get some exercise after that long ride."

He says sure and they amble along the berm of the road, passing a Holiday Inn Express and a Super 8, both of which look a lot nicer than the hovel Driver took them to.

As they make their way toward the restaurant, he takes note of how the truck driver walks. Hands in his front pockets, shoulders rolled forward, eyes down toward the ground. Humble.

The restaurant is only a little nicer than the motel, but the food's not bad. He has meatloaf and Driver shovels down a fat steak. They're both hungry and neither man talks until well into their meals.

Driver is the first to speak. "So, you think your father may be misusing your sister and your niece. And you even suspect he may have been involved with the murder of your wife."

Jackson leans back. "That about sums it up."

The older man takes a deep breath. "What if you meet up with your sister and your niece and they're fine? What if you find your father and he says he didn't have anything to do with your wife's death, and it turns out she—"

"Helen did *not* kill herself!" The plates and silverware jump as his fist strikes the table. He looks away, sees some of the waitstaff eyeing him across the counter, customers turned around in their seats.

The trucker puts up his hands. "Hey, I'm sorry."

With effort, Jackson lowers his voice. "My wife was *pregnant*. The day she died, she planned to surprise me with the news." He can feel the heat in his face, the tightness in his lips, as Driver studies him.

"I'm gonna use the restroom," he says. He stands, throws his napkin onto the table. He doesn't have to relieve himself, but he knows he has to walk away from the man who generously offered him a ride. The heat is still rising inside him and who knows what he might end up saying. He turns on the cold water, splashes his face a few times, takes deep breaths. *Inhale, hold for ten, exhale. Inhale, hold for ten, exhale.*

When he returns to the main room, Driver is standing by the cash register.

"I paid the bill," Driver says. "Left the tip."

He reaches for his wallet. "What do I owe you?"

"It's on me. I insist. I said some things that upset you. I had no right."

On the walk back to the motel, Driver lights up a cigar.

They walk on some more and Driver turns to him. "You know, you never answered my question when we first started out."

"What question?"

"Whether you're running to or running from."

"Like I said, I'm going to my father. To find out if he was involved in my wife's death. And to see if my sister and niece need saving from him. So, I'm running to." He turns to the older man, sees that Driver is staring at him, studying him as they walk.

"Yeah, I heard you," the trucker says.

"You don't believe me?"

"I didn't say that."

He considers this. "You think there's more to it."

Driver chuckles. "There's always more."

When they arrive at the motel, Driver holds out a fresh cigar. "You're allowed to smoke in your room here."

"I've never been much for cigars. But thank you."

"Probably for the best," Driver says. "This place looks like a tinder box."

Having spent the previous night in his car, he's exhausted and falls asleep as soon as he hits the bed. He awakens to feel something in the bed with him. He turns and opens his eyes to find the dark-haired girl he brought up from the party at his college condo. *Donna*. He can smell the shampoo and smoke in her hair from the cigarettes and weed. And from something else, wafting through the window.

He sits up, and as he does, he hears sirens. Donna sits up, too.

"Something's on fire," she says.

The sirens get louder.

"Come on," he says. His place is in a neighborhood of row homes and if one catches fire, they're all in danger. He and Donna throw on their clothes and make their way to the living room. His roommate Jonah is already there, as is his other roommate Tony and a girl Tony had in his room. Mike, it turns out, left to walk someone home.

"Those sirens sound really close," Tony's girl says. She has a worried look on her face.

"I'm going to find out where the fire is," he says.

*   *   *

He opens the door and almost chokes on the smoke, which is pouring in from the rooms on the other side of the motel lobby. The woman he saw earlier with the little dog stumbles out of her room, shouting.

"Ike! Someone help me! My dog's afraid and he won't leave the room!"

A patrol car rolls into the lot and a sheriff's deputy jumps out. The woman races up to the deputy, screams about her dog.

"You have to get him out!"

"It's too dangerous," the deputy says, and just then the window to the room next to the woman's breaks apart and flames shoot out. The deputy grabs hold of the woman and drags her away from the building.

"You, too," the deputy shouts to him. "Away from the building."

The motel owner appears and tells the deputy that he and the woman are the only two guests at the hotel.

"Don't forget the guy in the truck," Jackson says, pointing to the far side of the lot.

The rig is gone.

"What truck?" the deputy asks. Then he looks back toward the building and points. "Is that your car?"

He follows the deputy's hand to the back of the parking lot and spots his Jaguar.

What the hell?

"You need to move that before the fire trucks arrive," the deputy tells him.

From a distance, he hears sirens. The firefighters are on the way but they'll be too late to save the motel. The woman screams again about her dog and before he can think, his legs are carrying him toward her room.

"Hey! Get back here!"

He ignores the deputy, pushes open the woman's door, and drops to his hands and knees. "Here, boy; here, boy," he calls to the dog as he crawls along the floor. The air is thick with smoke, and very hot, and any second the fire will break through the wall. He calls out for the dog again and hears whimpering coming from under the bed. He lifts the dust ruffle and sees the dog. He stretches his arms, reaches the dog, pulls it out, and cradles it under his arm as he crawls toward the door.

"Ike!" The woman opens her arms.

He lets the dog go and it follows his owner's cry to the other side of the lot.

His knees are hurting something fierce. He limps to his car, clueless how it got to the motel. He climbs inside the Jag, spots the key on the dashboard, and drives off the property, parking the car on the berm of the road.

*   *   *

Sirens screaming, firetrucks pass him as he turns the corner. Jonah's right behind him.

"This is Kimmie's street!" he shouts to Jonah. "Her house is at the end . . ." His eyes search past the police cars and fire trucks and the swarm of first responders racing around. Flames shoot from the windows of the top two floors of Kimmie's building.

"Her apartment's on the third floor!" He takes off down the street, Jonah shouting behind him to stop. He gets halfway down the block before two giant Philly cops tackle him to the ground. He struggles fiercely and they cuff him, drag him back down the block, throw him into the rear seat of a patrol car. The next hours are a blur. He remembers seeing Kimmie at the party, recalls that she was in a huff about something and left before midnight. Then he remembers her sitting on her stoop months ago, telling him she only smokes when she's upset.

Is that what happened? he wonders in the squad car. Kimmie got upset at the party, went home, smoked in bed?

"No, no, no." *That can't be right. She's not at home. She's somewhere else. She's safe.*

The firefighters work valiantly through the night and are able to contain the fire to Kimmie's building and the one next to it.

*   *   *

He's asleep in the car by the time the sun rises. Someone knocks on the window and wakes him. He rolls down the window, sees a deputy standing next to the Jaguar.

"That was really stupid to go in after the dog," the deputy says. Then, he reaches in, clasps Jackson's shoulder. "Good man."

The deputy walks away and he gets out of the car and follows him back to the motel, what's left of it. The fire trucks are still there. The firemen are wrapping their hoses, cleaning up. The woman and her dog are gone, probably moved to another hotel nearby. He glances at the far side of the lot, where Driver parked his rig. He remembers Driver's cigar and his comment about the motel being a tinder box.

Did Driver do this? Did he start the fire, then drive away?

The owner of the motel is standing by one of the fire trucks, talking to the fire chief. He walks up to them.

"Did you see what time he left? The trucker I came in with?" he asks the owner.

"It must've been when I was asleep," the owner says.

"What about my car?" He points to the Jaguar, now on the road. "Did you see who drove it here?"

The owner shakes his head.

He feels dizzy, nauseated, and it must show.

The fire chief says, "They tell me you went into one of the rooms to save a dog. You probably inhaled a lot of smoke, and it's affecting your brain. You should get yourself checked out. Do you want some oxygen? I can hook you up to a tank."

He declines the oxygen and stares at the remains of the motel. A collapsed roof, charred beams, blackened cinderblock. Which means that his clothes, his bags, the money are all gone. Unless . . .

He walks out of the lot to his car, opens the trunk. It's all there. *How?* Then he remembers how the kid working the desk at the other motel was able to come into his room while he slept, steal a brick of hundreds. Someone obviously did the same thing to him here, only this time, they took everything and put it all into the trunk of the Jaguar. The Jag he'd left at a service station hundreds of miles behind him.

Son-of-a-bitch. I've been set up.

Someone fucked up his car so that he'd have to leave it behind.

But what did they want with the car? Not to resell it, obviously, because they returned it to him. He turns the question over in his mind and reaches the only conclusion he thinks is reasonable. They wanted the car in order to bug it, so they'd know—so *his father* would know—exactly where he was. But that doesn't make sense because his father already knew his location. How else could he have sabotaged the car? Or brought it here?

His mind starts to spin, until he stops himself, and sets about searching for GPS trackers. He spends an hour scouring every nook and cranny of the car, but finds nothing that looks like it might be a tracking device.

"I'm going crazy," he says. Sitting in the driver's seat, he closes his eyes and takes deep breaths. He relaxes and his mind takes him back to the terrible night Kimmie perished in the fire and the night the following year when he almost died of a drug over-dose. And it hits him that guilt over Kimmie's death was the reason his life crashed down around him after college. It's why he fell into drugs, lost his job. Why he almost died—would have died—had Jimmy not found him and called 911. And it was the real reason he left the corporate world to become a cop. He'd wanted to do good. Be a hero.

But why the guilt? What did he do?

More questions. Always more questions.

CHAPTER TWENTY-FIVE

IT'S 7:00 A.M. He could make Vegas by early afternoon if he hit the road now and drove straight through. But he's too tired to drive. So he takes the car to the Super 8 and checks in. He sets his phone alarm for 12:15. Five and a half hours of sleep. It's six hours to Vegas, so if he takes thirty minutes to shower before hitting the road and another half hour to eat, he can still make Vegas by 7:30 tonight.

He tosses and turns in the motel bed, trying to figure out why he feels guilty over Kimmie Cappuccino's death and struggling anew with Helen's confession that she'd been cheating on him with her *seducer*. Finally, his exhaustion overpowers him and he slips into blackness.

He floats in darkness for a long time, and when he opens his eyes, he finds himself standing in the garage in front of Helen's car, looking through the windshield. Helen is behind the wheel and he's in the passenger seat. He can't hear what Helen is telling Bob, but knows that this is the morning of Helen's confession. He knows what's coming and so can read Helen's lips when she says, "My seducer."

He sees Bob recoil, his jaw falling open, eyes widening in shock. Bob clenches his hands to his head and begins talking animatedly as Helen continues to stare ahead. Finally, Helen reaches to the pocket in the driver's-side door and pulls out some sort of book, opens it to a certain page, hands it to Bob. Through the windshield, he sees Bob open the book. It seems to take him a long minute to comprehend what he's reading, but when he does, his understanding appears to hit him like a gut punch. Bob turns to Helen, asks her something, and she turns to him and answers. From outside the car, he can't hear Bob's question or Helen's answer, but whatever she tells him must be awful, because he throws open the door, stumbles out of the car, out of the garage.

Back in his pickup, Bob sits still, the look on his face, his grip on the wheel, conveying that, inside, every nerve is firing. After some time, Helen—her head lowered, her eyes downcast—leaves the garage, passes the truck on the passenger side without looking at Bob, and enters the house.

As Helen closes the front door behind her, he watches Bob stare after her for a long time. Then Bob takes the key from the dash, starts the truck, and drives away. On the passenger seat, Jackson watches Bob drive, studies his face for signs of what he's thinking. Anger, certainly, if not rage. But that's not what Jackson finds. Instead, he sees Bob's face painted with fear. Helen has followed up her confession about her seducer with something else, something Bob can't handle, something that terrifies him.

Did she tell Bob that her seducer was more than just a lover? That the man was her one true love and that she was leaving him?

"Come on," he urges himself. "Talk out loud, or let me inside."

But Bob continues to stare through the windshield, knuckles white on the wheel, eyes wide with worry. A bead of sweat slides down the side of his face.

Bob makes his way north on 99, exits west to I-70. After thirty minutes or so, he stops at a roadside restaurant. He pauses in the doorway, takes the place in, then makes his way to a booth in the back, a four-seater next to the window. Bob slides in and Jackson sits across from him, still looking for clues as to what Bob's thinking. What Helen told him.

"Coffee," Bob tells the waitress without looking up. She extends the menu then pulls it back, walks away. Bob turns to the window, his unblinking eyes filled with pain and fear and other more nuanced emotions that Jackson can't read from across the table. He watches Bob drinking the coffee black, something Jackson can't ever remember doing.

When the mug is empty, the waitress returns and Bob orders a second cup. "And a shot of Jack Daniel's," he adds. When the coffee and liquor arrive, Bob lifts the shot glass, holds it over the coffee, seeming to struggle with whether to pour the booze in. Eventually, he does, then takes a long draft of the hot black brew. And then another.

The waitress returns and he orders another round. When Bob's finished, he calls her over. "Food," he says. "Steak and eggs. Hash browns. Toast. Potatoes." The waitress turns away and when Jackson looks into Bob's eyes, he sees that something has changed. The fear has been replaced by something else—something hard and dark.

The food arrives and Bob shovels it in, chased by more coffee and Jack. When he's done, he lifts the check and stands, tosses a fiver on the table for the tip. At the register, Bob pays the bill.

"There a bar around here?" Bob asks the waitress.

The waitress's eyes flatten. It's only noon. "Ten minutes west. First exit. On the edge of town."

Jackson watches the waitress follow Bob with her eyes as he leaves.

In the bar, he sees Bob take a seat at the end, order more whiskey. The bartender tries to strike up a conversation, but Bob waves him away. He's here to stew, figure things out. Wallow alone in his misery. But that's not how things are going to work out—Jackson knows this even before it happens. His miserly memory gives him that, at least.

After an hour or so, it happens. A woman enters the room, looks around, and sits at the bar two stools over, orders a rum and Coke. What type of woman walks into a bar alone at midday? Only one kind, Jackson knows. Studying her, he finds what he expects—a dark energy. An edge—something hungry and angry. And, behind it all, pain, telling him that she knows what she is and doesn't like herself much.

The woman takes a few sips of her drink, glances Bob's way a couple times. Then she lights up a cigarette, takes a deep drag, tilts her head back, exhales slowly. Without looking over, she says, "You want one?"

Staring ahead, Bob says sure and she slides him the pack and her lighter.

Bob lights up, takes a long drag. "Thanks," he says, sliding the pack and lighter back to the woman. When the bartender arrives, Bob tells the man to bring the lady another round, and it's her turn to thank him.

After a minute, she turns to Bob and they lock eyes.

"So . . ." the woman says.

Bob waits a beat. "I'm thinking that if I asked you what you're looking for, what you want more than anything, you'd say . . . *more*."

The woman smiles and something wicked flashes in her eyes. "My name's Carol," she says. "If you're interested."

Jackson watches his former self struggling with how to answer. Bob is at a crossroads and he's fighting with himself over which path to take. Finally, he decides.

"The name's Jackson," Bob says.

Jackson opens his eyes and finds himself twisted in the sheets of the motel bed. So that was what made him betray his wife—Helen's confession that she'd taken a lover of her own. Her confession, and whatever else she'd told him in the car—the thing that had terrified him. When exactly in their marriage had that happened? And how did they deal with each other afterward? Was their marriage a fragile truce? Pain layered over a resilient love? Or was it a complete farce?

He forces himself to get off the bed and glances at the alarm clock.

"What the hell?" The clock reads 4:00 p.m. He slept for nine hours! He checks the clock app on his cellphone and sees that he set the alarm for 12:15 a.m., not p.m. He gets out of bed, rubs his hands through his hair. *Damn.* He's lost an entire day. Still, he can make it to Las Vegas by midnight.

He heads for the bathroom, takes a hot shower, washes off the road dirt and the sweat and the smoke from the motel fire. And it's only then that he remembers the dream of him and Helen in the car. But, again, not a dream . . . a memory of something that actually happened. His brain smacked him with the first part of the scene as he stood before the *Welcome to Kournfield* sign. While he slept, it dished out a second serving. He stands in the shower trying to figure out the second scene until the water goes cold.

Finally, he gives up, dries off, dresses, and leaves for his car.

He drives for an hour, coming to the realization that he might never learn what happened with his wife. She's not around to tell him, and his fickle memory may choose to keep it hidden from him forever. But Kimmie is a different story. There is one person who may have some answers . . . He decides to make a call. His stomach is growling like crazy and he has to stop to get something to eat anyway, so he finds a greasy-spoon place south of Richfield, just off the interstate, adjacent to Fishlake National Forest. It's a small log-and-stone structure with a sign whose neon lettering doesn't illuminate. He's not even sure it's open until he pulls into the small parking lot and sees someone moving inside.

He turns off the car, lifts his cellphone. His college roommate Jonah Zahn gave him his business card the night they ran into each other in Missouri, before things went bad between them. He pulls the card from his wallet, dials Jonah's number.

"It's Jackson," he says.

Silence on the other end.

"I wouldn't blame you if you hung up on me right now, but I'm asking you not to. Please."

He hears Jonah sigh. "All right. What do you want?"

"I apologize for coming at you, but you're right that I'm still not over what happened to Kimmie, even after all this time. I feel responsible, but the thing is, I can't remember why. I thought I did right by Kimmie. I told her she was my little sister. I looked out for her. I wasn't even there when the fire started. I had no chance to save her. Right?"

Silence on the other end.

"Jonah?"

"Are you sure you want to dredge this up?"

"Dredge *what* up? Why would I feel guilty about what happened to Kimmie?"

"You really don't remember? What you did to that girl?"

"What I *did*? I looked out for her. I protected her. I even helped her get a boyfriend."

"You mean Mason Gardiner?"

"Yes. He was a good guy. I introduced Kimmie to him, played matchmaker."

"The guy was a fucking psycho!"

"*What?*"

"What do you mean 'what'? The guy was a serial rapist. A monster. No one is sure, but we thought Kimmie must have figured out what he was doing. What he *was*. That night she died, she spent the whole time at the party trying to get you to talk to her. But you were too busy hunting after that hot Italian girl. You brushed Kimmie off, like, five times. I tried to talk to her myself, so did Mike, but you know you were the only one she opened up to. I thought—we all thought—she was in love with you, even after she started dating Mason."

He closes his eyes. It's coming back to him now. Kimmie approaching him, something not right with her. "Can we talk, Jackson?" Then, "I need to talk," then, "I really need to talk." And him: "Sure, in a few minutes," and, "No problem, a little later," and walking away, hot on the scent of the Italian girl. Donna.

"Eventually, she gave up, and left," Jonah says.

And crawled into bed, crying, and lit a cigarette because Kimmie smoked when she was upset.

He remembers waking up in the back of the police car, seeing two EMTs wheeling a cart toward an ambulance. On the cart is a gray zippered body bag. And he knows what's inside it, *who's* inside it. Little Kimmie Cappuccino, with the doe eyes. The girl whose love he'd won with his million-dollar smile, whose trust he earned with promises of talking and sharing their innermost secrets. The girl who always sat quietly and listened as he unloaded his pent-up emotions, his dark side, never judging him. The girl he promised to protect from the predators, but ended up feeding to the ultimate predator.

"Are you listening?" Jonah asks.

He thinks back to the night he introduced Kimmie to Mason Gardiner. It was at one of his parties, of course. Kimmie was moping around and he took her by the hand, walked her up to Mason, a guy from one of his classes, a guy he played basketball with every now and them. Good-looking with an easy way about him. Friendly. He stood with them, facilitated the conversation until it seemed Kimmie and Mason were comfortable with each other. The next thing he knew they were going steady. And now Jonah's telling him . . .

"Mason—" He whispers the name, lets it hang in the air.

"Was arrested a month after Kimmie died," Jonah says. "Some freshman he assaulted called the police and the newspapers. She made a big deal about it, and when word got out, a bunch of other girls came forward."

"There was a trial," he remembers now.

"Eventually, but it was Mason's preliminary hearing we all went to—you, me, Mike, and Tony. Don't you remember what happened? You lost it. You ran toward that glass wall that separates the front of the courtroom from the spectator's benches, started smashing your fists against the glass, screaming. The deputies had to subdue you, drag you out. You lost it, man."

Jonah pauses. "You weren't the same after what happened to Kimmie. I mean, all of us were really upset by it—we didn't have any more parties. But it really fucked you up, which I guess . . . well, never mind."

"I was the one most affected because I was the one to blame," he says.

A pause at the other end, then, "Mason Gardiner was the one to blame."

"Where is he now?"

"Sick fuck. He spent some time in jail, then got caught again. Went to prison, and he must've said the wrong thing to the wrong person. Or someone found out why he was inside. They found him in his cell, dead, with a broomstick up his ass."

That Mason got what he deserved doesn't make him feel any better. "I remember now, all of it. It was awful, what I did. It's killing me."

"No, Jackson. It's hurting you. Kimmie's the one it killed."

"Oh, God . . ."

"I apologize for saying that. I've been carrying around feelings about Kimmie's death, too."

"I am so fucking sorry," he says through tears streaming down his face. He struggles to keep control.

"You take care, Jackson."

The line goes dead.

He drops the cell into the seat next to him and sits numbly in the car. At some point, he senses movement beside him and looks up to see a woman standing next to his car.

"Are you alright?"

"Huh?"

"You've been sitting out here for almost an hour," the woman says. "I saw you through the windows. You haven't moved a muscle."

He stares at her.

"Come inside, get something to eat."

He follows the woman, who turns out to be a waitress working at the restaurant. She leads him to a small booth, brings him some water and a menu. He asks for coffee while he decides what to order. When she returns, he asks what the chef's special is and she tells him it's a stew.

"Sounds good." He sighs.

The restaurant is empty—he's the only customer—and his food arrives quickly. The stew has an earthy smell—meat and dirt and the aroma of dark green vegetables. He dips in his soup spoon and experiences a cacophony of competing flavors vying for the attention of his palate. There are multiple meats, but he can't tell what they are. Doesn't recognize the vegetables, either, or the stock. He slides the mix down his throat and is left with a foul aftertaste. He feels his face cringe, but at the same time finds himself craving more. He lifts another heaping spoon of the stew and shovels it into his mouth.

"What is this?" he asks the waitress when she arrives to refill his coffee.

"Chef's special," she says again.

"What's in it?"

She chuckles. "What isn't?"

He holds her eyes. "Seriously."

The waitress shrugs. "Chef likes to mix it up. Could be rabbit, fish from the lake. Deer. Maybe some snake." She winks. "Maybe some mushrooms. Cactus."

"Mushrooms? Cactus?" He remembers getting high off 'shrooms in college. And he's heard peyote comes from some sort of cactus.

The waitress laughs. "I know what you're thinking, but you don't have to worry. We're not some far-out hippy place."

He gobbles down the stew, pays the bill, and heads for his car, anxious to get to Las Vegas. Ten minutes down the road, his stomach seizes up. He tries to will the cramps away, but they only worsen, and he feels bubbling in his intestines, nausea in his stomach. He turns off I-70 onto Clear Creek Canyon Road, stops the Jag on a wide section of berm, hops the guardrail, and runs down an embankment into the trees. He lowers his pants, kneels with his back against a tree, doubles over forward, and lets loose from both ends.

His misery makes time compress and expand at once and he has no idea how long he spends expurgating the poison from his system. Even after the purging is done, his torment continues. He finds himself sitting against another tree, soaking wet and shivering. His throat is parched and raw and filled with the sour taste of vomit. His head pounds. His bones ache from the inside.

What in hell was in *that stew?*

He tilts back his head, finds an odd star poking here and there through the tree cover and swiftly moving clouds. Every now and then, a large enough hole breaks open in the clouds to reveal the full moon, a bare bulb illuminating a bleak world.

He takes a few deep breaths to still himself, clear the fog and pain from his head. He's about to close his eyes when he spots something against a tree a few yards away from him. A shadow, but with substance. Something darker than the night air. It seems to be sitting against the tree behind it, just as he is. He stares at the shadow, but it is as motionless as he is. For a long time, he watches the thing, until he realizes it is watching him back.

"You're me," he says aloud.

But which *me?*

Is it Bob, looking at Jackson, sickened by what Bob has become?

Or is it Jackson, the crooked cop who terrorized a city as *JR*, looking at what he is now: a man trying to save his niece and sister while hunting down his father for answers . . . and maybe for vengeance?

A man . . . half good, half bad.

"Which is it?" he asks.

But the other only stares at him, judging him.

His mind drifts and he realizes that he would have died if Jimmy and Pam hadn't stepped in. Jimmy saved him from the overdose and Pam became his emotional pillar. Somewhere along the way, he decided he loved Pam, that he would cherish her and by doing so he would make up for what he did to Kimmie. He doubts he viewed it that way at the time, but looking back on it now, it's obvious. He would be a hero husband just as he would be a hero cop.

But was that all of it? He thinks back to Jimmy's question: Why did he take Pam, knowing that Jimmy loved her?

His thoughts suddenly skip back to the two women his mother had over to their house, one of them saying he wasn't the "good" one. Growing up, Jimmy was always the good half, the better half.

Was part of the answer to Jimmy's question—resentment? Did he take Pam so that, for once, he could be the good guy with the good wife and be more like his brother? Was that part of it? Along with guilt over Kimmie?

By the time Vanessa appeared in her parents' living room, he was beyond restless in his marriage and primed to spring from his cage. And spring he did.

It only got crazier from there. By the time he was committing crimes for Donny Franco, he was eating himself alive. Still, he stayed in the life until Owen showed up and told him about his sister, Jackie and his niece, little Penny, sick and needing money, *big money*, for treatment.

So, he decided to save Penny and leave behind the whole fucked-up mess—his wrecked marriage, his broken brother, his twisted lover, his outlaw career. But he didn't save Penny any more than he did right by Kimmie or Pam. He got rolled and lost the money he stole from Donny, an act of insanity that put a target on his head and required him to flee Philadelphia.

And flee he did, to the Middle of Nowhere, where he could disguise himself as Bob, mild-mannered captain-of-the-baseball-team Bob. And Bob met Helen and made her his wife, took care of her when she was down. Protected her.

But even that couldn't last. A few towns down the pike from Kournfield, he leased a trailer and started up again with the fighting and drugging and screwing. Is that why Helen took a lover of her own?

And what happened between them from that time to Helen's murder?

He sighs and, in that moment, realizes that the truck driver was right: he wasn't just running *to* something, but running *away* as well.

"Well, at least I know what I'm running from," he says.

Looking up, he sees his shadow lean forward from the tree, hears it ask, *Do you?*

CHAPTER TWENTY-SIX

HE WAKES WITH the sunrise. Getting to his feet takes all his strength. If anything, he feels worse than he did the night before. His head is still throbbing, his throat is sore and tastes of bile. His muscles and bones ache. But he forces himself to make the walk to the car. He has to find a motel, to hydrate and shower.

Half an hour after he starts out, he checks into a Best Western off I-15 in Beaver, Utah. There are two bottles of water in the room and he drains them the minute he walks in. He refills one of the bottles from the sink, and drinks that, too. Then he stands in the shower for a long time, lets the steaming water relax his muscles, take some of the ache out of them. He's wary about putting anything in his stomach, but knows he needs the energy, so he forces himself to eat a bland breakfast in the hotel restaurant.

It's just before ten when he leaves the hotel. Las Vegas is a little over three hours down I-15. He keeps the radio loud to drown out his thoughts. He has the Jag's roof down and it's a hundred degrees outside, but he feels like he's riding a bike in a cold rain shower. He shivers.

When he finally reaches Las Vegas, he decides to luxuriate in a high-rise casino, so he checks into the Bellagio. He splurges on a Penthouse Fountain View Suite on the 27th floor. The floor-to-ceiling windows offer a sweeping view past the fountains to the Paris Las Vegas Hotel with its giant reproduction of the Eiffel Tower. Champagne is waiting for him in the ice bucket atop the console in the living room, but he opts instead for a bottle of cold water.

It's 1:00 p.m. and he debates whether to order lunch. He stands for a minute in the middle of the living room and decides to skip it, change into his workout clothes, and head for the fitness center. He hasn't done anything physically healthy since he last left Kournfield. Maybe a good workout will help his body and his mind. The hotel's fitness center, a large space with windows overlooking a fountain, has TV screens, free weights, and every type of cardio machine. One thing it doesn't have, though, are heavy and speed bags, and he decides he needs some physical contact to work out his stress. So, he returns to his suite, puts on some sweats, grabs his wallet, then takes the elevator to the first floor and asks the concierge for a good boxing gym nearby. She recommends a place and he cabs there. The place is a little yuppy for his tastes, but it has everything he needs. He starts his workout with squats, lunges, jumping squats, double lunges, push-ups, and ab work. He jumps rope for fifteen minutes, then starts in on his bag work. He pummels the speed bag until he gets bored with it, then turns his attention to the heavy bag, where he spends thirty minutes doing combos with kick finishes—jab cross/hook kick, jab cross/switch kick—always changing the elevations of his kicks. Finally, he finishes with power, driving through individual kicks and punches until his arms and legs are rubber.

His workout attracts some attention and one of the guys who works there asks him if he wants to spar a few rounds. His first instinct is to say yes—hell, yes—but he stops himself. The guy looks street tough, MMA tough, even, but that's not why he says no. He declines because he wants to step back from hurting people. Maybe he's fooling himself by ignoring his essential nature, but for now, he doesn't feel the urge to inflict pain.

Is he really changing? Or just dehydrated and underfed? *Whatever.*

"Thanks, but no thanks," he tells the guy.

Back at the hotel, he spends an hour at the pool, doing laps, then lounging with a bottle of Nevada Pale Ale. A woman in a skimpy bikini two lounge chairs over gives him the eye. He smiles politely but doesn't accept her invitation and she eventually leaves.

At 8:30, he orders room service, flops down on the bed. Then he watches TV until the waiter rolls in the cart thirty minutes later. He has the waiter place everything on the coffee table in the living room, sends the waiter on his way, and digs in to a 14 oz. dry-aged prime rib eye. He's feeling much stronger now and he can't believe that only twenty-four hours earlier, he'd been lying on the hard ground in the forest, sick as a dog. Amazing how things can change so fast.

He finishes the meal, loads the plates, glasses, and tableware onto the cart, rolls it into the hallway, and goes to bed with plans for an early start on his quest to find his father, sister, and niece.

But sleep will not come. He twists and turns, rolls over and over. Eventually, after an hour or so, he opens his eyes, stares at the ceiling. The casino is twenty-seven floors below him, but in his mind, he can hear the jingling and jangling of the slot machines, the clickety-clack of the roulette wheel, the dealers

shouting "red nineteen" and "black six." The casino is calling—
he feels it. But he resists.

Until he doesn't.

"Shit." He sits up on the bed, sighs, looks at the clock. It's only
midnight. He could play for an hour, be back at 1:00 a.m., get
eight hours of sleep and wake up at 9:00.

He throws on his jeans and a button-down blue shirt, leaves
the suite, takes an elevator. The casino is bright and loud and
heavily oxygenated, and he feels wide awake the instant he enters. He walks around a few minutes to get the lay of the land,
then heads to the blackjack tables. At one of the tables, a man
sits by himself, protected by two large men standing behind
him. The man looks to be in his early thirties, with fashionably
conservative hair. He has manicured nails and is dressed in a suit
that looks like it cost more than most people's cars. There is a
small mole an inch below his left eye.

Every now and then someone approaches the table to play.
The man glances at the would-be player, takes his measure and
subtly shakes his head "no," and the beefy thugs tell the guy to
get lost.

He moves toward the table until he's close enough to watch
the man play. The man knows what he's doing, when to hit,
when to stand, when to split pairs, double down. He doesn't
make mistakes and his pile of chips—at least $200K—gets big-
ger with every hand.

"I'd like to play," he says to the man's thugs.

The man signals the dealer to hit him, then turns around.
They lock eyes. After a minute, the man nods and one of the
bodyguards pulls out a chair and he takes it.

He lays a brick of hundreds on the table. The dealer accepts
the cash, slides him ten yellow $1,000 chips.

"The minimum bet at this table is one thousand dollars," the dealer says.

He nods, slides forward two chips.

He and the well-dressed man play for a while, then he says, "I saw you turn away some guys before me. Why'd you give me the nod?"

Not taking his eyes off the cards, the man replies, "You look like a man who knows how to play."

Over the course of the next hour both men rack up big winnings. Neither talks until he says to the man, "So, this is how you earn a living? Going to casinos, playing blackjack?"

"Not really." The man shrugs. "But he wants me to go to a casino, I go to a casino. He wants me to play blackjack . . ."

"He? He who?"

For the first time since they started playing, the man turns to face him. "You know who I'm talking about."

He jerks up in his seat, stares at the man, recalling his mother's words about his father being one of a small group of men who control Vegas from the shadows. The man at the table is obviously tied in with that group.

"My father sent you here to meet me?" This whole experience suddenly feels surreal.

"You don't look well, Jackson," the man says. He turns to the waitress. "Bring my friend here some water."

He watches the waitress leave, then turns back to the man. A hundred questions swirl in his mind. He asks the most obvious one first. "What kind of car have you been driving?"

The man chuckles to himself. "I think you know the answer to that."

He feels his blood start to warm but forces himself to stay calm.

"Why have you been tailing me, asking questions about me?" He stares at the man. "What does my father want from me?"

"The question, Jackson, is what do you want?"

"Why is that important?"

The man leans back. "It's everything. Nothing starts until you make a choice. You have to choose."

"Choose? Between what?"

"Gentlemen?" It's the dealer. She's been waiting.

They finish the hand and continue playing. His conversation with the man has unnerved him and he starts making mistakes. Yet he continues to win.

"You're getting good cards," the man says.

"And the dealer isn't standing at eighteen." He glances at the dealer. She winks at him.

"Is *this* what you want?" The man nods toward the stacks of chips. "Money? Wealth?"

His mind skips back to a time when he was still in the life, working for Donny Franco. He and Vanessa went to New York City with a wad of cash. The MoMA was reopening after an expansion and they stayed across the street at the Baccarat Hotel. They spent most of the day at the museum, leisurely taking in the modern art. Then they returned to their suite at the luxury hotel, ate caviar, drank expensive champagne, the hotel employees all assuming he was some bigwig with money to burn, rather than just a crooked cop blowing through his share of a haul.

It felt good, but it didn't feel great. He hadn't come by the money in any way that instilled him with pride. He feels the same way about the chips on the table. They represent a lot of money, but money isn't what he really wants. So what does he want? Justice for Helen's murder, for sure. The chance to help

Jackie and Penny, if they need help. But first, he wants to confront his father, take his measure of the man.

"How can I find my father?"

"You don't find him. He finds you," the man says. "When he's ready."

He stares at the man sitting next to him. He wants to grab the man by the lapels of his jacket, shake him, smack his face until he begs for the privilege of telling him where his father is.

The man reads his face. "I'd like to see you try. Those two behind me would be all over you the minute you made your move."

"And one minute after that, they'd both be on the floor."

The man chuckles, looks up toward the surveillance cameras directly above them, sending Jackson the message that he's way outnumbered.

Frustrated, he stands and lifts $10,000 in chips, the amount he came in with. "I'd say it's been real. But I'm not sure how much of it was."

"What about the rest of your chips?" the man asks. "You've left all your winnings on the table."

"I don't care. Take 'em to the roulette wheel and bet everything on . . . red seven."

CHAPTER TWENTY-SEVEN

THE NEXT MORNING, he wakes at eight. He opens the curtains, then does some stretching exercises because his muscles are starting to tighten from the workout the day before. He walks to the bathroom, shaves, takes a hot shower, puts on fresh clothes. He's about to leave his suite when he notices the message-waiting light flashing on the hotel phone. He picks it up and the operator informs him there's a package waiting for him at the front desk. He says he'll be down in a minute, then picks up his car keys and walks to the door.

He decides to grab a quick breakfast in one of the hotel restaurants, work out a plan to find his father. The waitress brings him coffee and takes his order. He watches her walk away, lowers his gaze to the clouds swirling in his coffee.

After a minute, he lifts his eyes, reaches across the table, and takes Helen's hands in his own. "I just have to say that you look truly lovely tonight."

Helen smiles, blushes.

They're sharing a meal at a romantic restaurant in Topeka, in celebration of their sixth wedding anniversary. The restaurant is more expensive than the places they usually go, with white linen service, real silverware, and petite portions arranged like art-work on their plates.

Across the table, Helen carefully cuts her food, lifts the tiny morsels to her mouth. Everything about his wife is delicate, thoughtful. Self protective. He knows all about Helen's past. Juke told him early on that Helen had always been emotionally fragile—painfully shy as a child, always having her heart broken when she got older. Helen went to college for her teaching de-gree, then returned home after graduation and married her high-school sweetheart. But he turned out to be an asshole. He cheated on her, even struck her. It took Helen two years to re-cover after their divorce. Then her parents were both killed in a car accident.

"It upended her whole world," Juke told him. "I didn't think she was going to climb out of the dark place she fell into. That's when her depressions started."

Helen herself told him once that she didn't know where her depression came from, that she'd been a melancholy child as far back as she could remember. Part of it was that she'd always felt like she was at risk.

"I feel like I live along a fault line, that the ground could fall out from under my feet at any moment." She paused for a min-ute, then looked deeply into his eyes. "Now you're here, and in some ways, I feel very protected. But you seem dangerous at the same time. I mean, you're sweet to me, courteous, kind. But you have such a tough look to you. And, honestly, with your shirt off—all those scars—you look like a thug."

He has admitted to violence in his past, even owned up to having been an alcoholic. But he's hidden the darkest parts from her. He told her he'd gotten his skull-and-crossbones tattoo when he was in college, that he faced violence as a cop, but never that he was the cause of most of it. He's confessed to having a problem with alcohol but never told Helen about the drug use, or his insane relationship with Vanessa. Holding all this back has caused him no small amount of guilt, but he smoothed his conscience by promising himself he would make up for it by giving Helen the life she deserved. By recasting himself into a loving husband and making Helen feel protected.

Across the table at their anniversary dinner, Helen looks at him for a long moment, and he can tell she's trying to formulate what she's going to say.

"I don't know what I'd do without you," she tells him. "You're the one solid thing, the one sane thing, in my life. I love you, Bob."

They leave the restaurant arm in arm and pause on the doorstep. It's a beautiful night. There's a mild breeze and, though there is no moon, the stars twinkle brightly in the sky.

"A lovely end to a special evening," Helen says, following his gaze.

Back at the restaurant at the Bellagio, his mind fixes on Helen's telling him he was the one solid, sane thing in her life. Visions of Walt's gym and the trailer and the woman named Carol flash through his mind. *Solid*, she called him—a dagger through his heart. *Sane*, she said—a sword.

Get out. Run. Break free.

"Are you all right, sir?"

He looks up, sees the waitress standing over him. "What?"

"You haven't moved in almost an hour."

He looks down at the plate of cold eggs, cold potatoes, cold bacon.

"Would you like me to warm that up for you?" The waitress pretends she's not worried, that all that's needed to bring the scene back to normalcy is that his breakfast be reheated.

"Sure," he says. But once she's gone with his plate, he tosses a hundred onto the table and leaves the restaurant. In the men's room, the memory of their anniversary has hit him with the force of a train. Only a year later—the seventh year of their marriage, two years before Helen's death—he rents the trailer from Walt . . .

God, was he *ever* content being Goodyear Bob? Or was it a constant struggle? Was he merely a restless guy who needed to work out his fidgets every couple of weeks? Or was he an addict aching for his next fix?

Leaning over the sink, he stares into his dark eyes, but doesn't find an answer. But the words pound in his ears.

Get out. Run. Break free.

CHAPTER TWENTY-EIGHT

HE WALKS TOWARD the front doors to the hotel, then remembers the message on his hotel phone and turns around. At the front desk, he gives his name and room number to a smiling young woman and tells her he has a package. She excuses herself and returns with a large leather valise and shining eyes. Cautiously he accepts the valise and opens it. The bag is stuffed with hundred-dollar bills.

"There was a note, too," the woman says, handing him an envelope.

He opens the envelope and pulls out a piece of white stationery.

> You said to put it all on Red 7.
> I did and look what happened!
>
> The one you need to meet will be at
> 700 East Naples Drive. 12:30.
>
> -M

He folds the note, slides it into the envelope, places it into the satchel. He doesn't have to count the money to know how much is there—$1.2 million. The same amount he stole from Donny Franco. The same amount that was stolen from him. Which means his father is sending him a message—admitting he was behind the theft. Now he's paying him back. But why? Why send the message? Why repay the money?

He thanks the desk clerk, leaves the hotel. The valet has the Jaguar waiting for him. He climbs into the car, his whole body a raw nerve, a violin string vibrating to the music of pain.

He plugs the address into his cellphone, puts the car in gear, and accelerates. From Bellagio Drive, he takes a left onto Las Vegas Boulevard and sees Paris Las Vegas on his right. He turns onto East Flamingo Road, passes Bally's, then the Westin. A short drive on Paradise Road takes him to East Naples Drive, then Swenson with its scattering of sickly palm trees and cacti in white stone gardens, then back onto East Naples. Except for the big entertainment complexes and condo towers, all the buildings are squat one and two-story commercial structures, allowing the brilliant blue sky to descend almost to ground level.

He isn't sure what he expected to find at 700 East Naples Drive, but it sure wasn't a small strip mall with a 7-Eleven, a tattoo parlor, a retail spa, and a vegan restaurant. What in the world would his father be doing here?

As he gets out of the car, a blue and silver Prius pulls into a space facing East Naples across the lot from the vegan restaurant, and three gangly girls get out. He figures they are college students, and it hits him then that he's not here to meet his father. He strides quickly toward the three girls and they stop in place, alarm on their faces when they see him. He picks her out from the others right away. She's taller now, of course, and hippier, with long gangly legs and full breasts—a budding young woman. Her blond hair is a longer version of how it looked when she was a kid. But she has the same blue eyes. He reads concern in them, and confusion. Then, suddenly, they are ablaze with ten thousand watts.

"Oh my God!"

Penny opens her arms and races for him. He takes her in, hugs her, lifts her off her feet, swirls her around.

"Uncle Jackson! It's you! I can't believe it!"

He sees her friends frozen in place and wonders whether Penny ever mentioned him to them. To anyone.

Penny hugs him again, then pulls him by the arm to meet her friends. The two other girls smile and warily accept his hand. She explains that he's her uncle and this seems to allay their fears, but only somewhat. He's a hard-looking man, he knows. Relative or not, he could still be dangerous.

Penny tells her friends it's okay. Tells them to go on and eat without her. "My uncle and I have a lot of catching up to do."

She turns to him again but her eyes lock on something behind him. "The car! You still have it!" She races by him and jumps over the front passenger door into the shotgun seat. "You have to take me for a drive, Uncle Jackson! You have to!"

He laughs and leaps into the car beside her. "Where to, Robin?" he asks, remembering it was something he did when she was little. Him being Batman and she his sidekick.

Penny directs him to another vegan restaurant, Violette's Vegan Organic Café & Juice Bar, about ten miles away on East Desert Inn Road. Penny orders for both of them—a "Philly Cheesesteak" for him, the Hippie Chick Burger for her.

"I take it there's no steak in the cheesesteak." He smiles.

"Of course not." Penny launches into a spiel about how animal agriculture is a catastrophic contributor to global warming. "It's responsible for almost a fifth of global greenhouse gases. It's the reason behind most of the massive Amazonian deforestation. And it sucks up ten percent of the earth's freshwater footprint. And then there's the fact that our consumption of meat necessitates the genocide of two hundred million animals *a day*. Think about that, Uncle Jackson. Humans kill seventy billion living beings a year just so we can treat ourselves to filet mignon and Chicken McNuggets."

He doesn't know how to respond to what she's telling him. Then again, he's not really focusing on her words, but dealing with the emotions swirling inside him at seeing her, the foremost among them being concern for her safety, seeing as how her mother—his half-sister, Jackie—was extorted by their father to come to Vegas and bring Penny with her. He lets Penny talk some more—at a hundred miles an hour—then reaches across the table and places his hand over her forearm, to stop her.

"Penny. Forget about the cows for a minute. Are you alright? Are you safe?"

Her eyes instantly harden and that tells him she knows exactly what—who—he's talking about.

She looks around, leans toward him, lowers her voice. "I'm okay for now."

"And your mother?"

"She's different now."

He remembers his own mother warning him how his father changes people. That he might not recognize Jackie and Penny. "Has he changed you?"

She shakes her head vigorously. "I won't let him near me."

He stares at her. "I only recently found out that you'd moved here. That your mother brought you here ten years ago because my father said it was the only way he'd pay for your medical care. I learned it from your dad."

At his mention of her father, Penny's eyes grow sad. She lowers her head.

"He's worried sick over you and your mom. It broke his heart when you disappeared."

Penny's eyes fill with worry. "You can't tell him where we are. It would put him in a lot of danger." Then, as though something dawns on her, "How did you know we were in Las Vegas? And how did you know to find me at this exact spot today?"

"My mother knew my dad was here, though she didn't know his address or even what name he was going by. As for you being at this address, this morning, I was given a note by the desk clerk at my hotel. I believe it was given to her by a man I met in the casino last night. A man who I'm sure works for my father. Your grandfather." He pauses. "He had a mole under his left eye."

She purses her lips. "Miles. He's not a good guy. Stay away from him."

"Do you have any idea why my father would want me to meet with you?"

"No, but whatever it is, it can't be good."

He nods. "Tell me about my father. How often does he come around?"

"He's always around. In one form or another. But almost no one gets to see him. My mother does. I could if I wanted to, but . . ."

"You don't like him."

"I hate him. What he stands for."

He's about to ask what she means when the waitress arrives with their food. Penny digs into her plant-burger right away and he gets the sense she's done talking about his father and her mother, for now at least, and he decides not to press her. The "cheesesteak" is awful but he shovels it into his mouth as though it's the best thing he's ever eaten.

An hour later, he's sitting next to Penny in a hydrological sciences class, part of her Water Resources Management major. About forty students are arranged in four curved tiers of desks. Every student has their own laptop or iPad. In the front of the classroom is the professor, a rail-thin young man with a straggly beard and thick black glasses. A large screen behind him displays a world map with various regions of Earth drawn in different colors, depicting their relative direness with respect to water. The map shows that many of the coastal areas will soon be flooded with seawater while vast swaths of the earth will dry up.

The professor lays out programs being explored to combat the water crises, and the students peck away on their keyboards. Every few minutes, someone asks a question, and more than a few debates break out. Watching them, Bob has the urge to stand and applaud. He spent his own college years partying. He got As and Bs, not because he learned anything, but because he was good at memorizing and regurgitating. Penny and her classmates, on the other hand, are really trying to figure things out. Probably because they feel they have no choice; the generations before them have brought the world to the brink of destruction, so it's up to them to walk it back.

*   *   *

Penny's class finishes at five and she wants to stay behind for a few minutes to talk to her professor. He says he'll wait for her in the parking lot. When he gets to his car, he pulls his cellphone and dials.

"It's me," he says when Richie answers. "Any blowback from my dustup with Donny and his boys?"

"Blowback? More like a nuclear explosion. You left one cop dead, two shot, including a chief inspector. Donny came up with some bullshit story about taking his crew to the tracks on a tip about a big drug deal and wound up being ambushed. No one believes him, but the chief doesn't want controversy. He's hiding behind the same story Donny is. Word on the street, though, is that Donny's washed up on the force. The commissioner is making him resign, effective the first of the year. Meanwhile, Donny has his goons combing the streets on the down-low, putting out the word he wants you dead or alive."

"Have his boys paid you a visit?"

"No, and that has me worried. They busted me up pretty good when you left town ten years ago because they thought I might have the inside line on you, being your ex-partner. This time, though, I haven't heard a peep. It doesn't make sense."

"Well, be careful. Just because they haven't come for you yet doesn't mean they're not going to." He pauses. "Have you heard from Owen?"

"Are you kidding? He's been calling me every day, asking have I heard from you in Vegas yet. We've even had lunch at the diner a couple times. I told him I hadn't heard from you and I'll keep on telling him that if you want me to."

"No. You can tell him I called you. I'm going to get ahold of him myself today or tomorrow. I found his daughter—my niece—and I'm hoping she'll put me in touch with her mother. I'll tell him everything I find out."

"This is really fucked up, Jackson. You probably shoulda taken care of Donny when you had the chance, because I guarantee, he'll take care of you if he finds you."

He shakes his head. "No. I'm done killing. I can't go back to that . . . I just can't."

They hang up and he calls his brother, asks whether Donny's boys have shown up. Jimmy tells him no and, like Richie, he's surprised. He tells Jimmy to be careful, suggests he take Pam and their son out of town for a while. Jimmy says he's thinking about it. They hang up as Penny arrives at the car.

She's about to say something to him when he hears a car door slam nearby. He turns to spot a man walking toward them. It's the man he gambled with at the Bellagio. The one with the mole below his left eye. *Miles*. Behind him sits a gray Chrysler 300.

"Hello, Penny. Jackson."

"What do you want?" Penny snarls.

"A nice day to you. Your grandfather asked me to fetch you for him."

"How many times do I have to repeat that I'm not going anywhere near him?"

Miles turns to Jackson. "He wants to see you, too, and he was thinking that since you're with Penny, you could come together."

"If he wants to see me, why isn't he here with you?" he asks.

"Better that you come to him."

"Why is that?"

Miles shrugs. "Just the way it works."

Jackson glances at Penny then back at Miles. "I do intend to meet him. He owes me some explanations. But right now, I'm spending some time with my niece and she doesn't want to see him. Tell him that. And tell him I'm staying at the Bellagio. I have a lovely suite on the 27th floor. He's welcome to join me there."

Miles chuckles. "Right . . . that's very helpful." He pauses, looks at Penny. "You sure I can't change your mind?"

Penny crosses her arms. "You couldn't change my *tires*, Miles."

Anger flashes in Miles's eyes, but he smiles. "See you both later."

He watches Miles return to the Chrysler and drive out of the lot. When he's gone, he turns to see Penny staring at him.

"I'm glad you're here, Uncle Jackson. But if you know what's good for you, you'll hop in this car and drive until you reach an ocean."

"I'm not going anywhere until I put some hard questions to your grandfather. Until I'm sure you and your mom are both safe."

A sad look crosses Penny's face, and he can tell she wants to say something. But she forces herself to smile and hops over the door into the passenger seat.

"I hate the Bellagio," she says. "All those casinos. Let's just pick up your stuff and go to my place. I have a roommate, but she moved in with her boyfriend two weeks ago, so her room's empty."

At the Bellagio, he is walking Penny to the elevators when a uniformed bellman approaches him in the lobby, calls out his name. He turns and asks the man what he wants.

"Uh, you were moved to a different suite while you were out," the bellman answers. He's young, awkward, obviously not used to approaching guests like this.

"I don't like this," Penny says.

"Oh, but it's an upgrade!" The bellman beams.

"Now I really don't like it." Penny crosses her arms.

"Where are my belongings?" he asks the bellman.

"They're in the new suite."

"All right. Take us there."

When the elevator opens, the bellman leads them into the Chairman's Suite. "It's four thousand square feet," the bellman says. "It has two bedrooms, a living room, formal dining room, solarium, and a sunken bar. Would you like a tour?"

"Leave us," he says.

When the bellman is gone, he turns to Penny and follows her eyes to the dining room table. In the center of the table is a large glass bowl filled with neatly wrapped bricks of hundred-dollar bills.

"What's *that*?" Penny asks.

"If I'm right, that's your grandfather paying me back the $1.2 million he stole from me ten years ago. The money that was supposed to go to your medical care." He pauses, then decides to give her the full explanation. "As far as I can tell, he extorted your mother to bring you here with promises to pay for your medical care—after he robbed me of the money I'd taken from my boss. He knew that once I'd stolen from my boss, I'd have to leave Philadelphia and he expected me to join your mother and you out here. Only it didn't work out that way; I faked my death and never found out that you and your mom left Philly until much later."

They stare at each other and Penny says, "I was serious when I said you should leave this place right now."

He looks around. "You don't like this, do you? Not just this suite and what it means between me and my father, but the whole town."

She walks to the window overlooking the Bellagio's iconic fountains. "This town . . . they don't make anything here. They don't produce or invent. Don't cure any diseases." She pauses. "Do you know why people gamble? What they get out of it?" she asks. "Gambling releases dopamine into your brain, the same way drugs do. It makes your brain feel good. Like having a mini orgasm in your head." She turns to face him squarely. "This whole city is just one gigantic jerkoff."

He blinks. "Then why haven't you left?"

She looks away and starts walking toward the foyer. "I'll wait for you by the door."

In the bedroom, he finds his few clothes unpacked and placed into the drawers. He repacks them, along with his toiletries, and joins Penny.

"You're leaving the money?" she asks.

"It's dirty," he says.

She smiles. "Good for you, Uncle Jackson."

CHAPTER TWENTY-NINE

PENNY'S APARTMENT BUILDING on Flamingo Road is just half a mile from UNLV's campus and looks like a three-story motel. The apartment itself is a compact two-bedroom, two-bath. In the small living room, a sectional leather couch sits on a psychedelic area rug covering gray laminate flooring. Behind the couch is a large window overlooking the courtyard. The kitchen has a pass-through window with a bar top and a pair of bar stools. A two-person table is flanked by plastic chairs. The bedrooms are small, enough room for a desk and a twin bed mattress—no box spring—on an elevated metal frame. Penny's bedroom floor is stacked with folded clothing. The surfaces of the living room and kitchen area are covered with books.

He feels Penny's eyes on him as she takes him on the tour.

"It's cheap," she says. "And I pay for it on my own."

He takes the last part to mean that Penny accepts no money from her grandfather or her mother.

Penny has him put his bags into her roommate's bedroom. "I'm going to rest for an hour, then make us something to eat. Then we're going out. I'm taking you to a music bar I like. It's a great venue for up-and-coming artists. You don't have to dress up. It's not one of those places in the casinos. It's low-key." She pauses. "Actually, it's a dive."

While Penny rests, he considers his next move. He's decided he wants to learn as much as he can about his father from Penny, and then from Jackie. He wants to understand how dangerous his father is to his sister and niece. He's also looking for clues about what his father wants from him.

He enters the living room, flops on the couch, and lifts the remote to the television. It's tuned to CNN, which is playing a story about wildfires burning out of control around Los Angeles. His mind skips back to a night he was sitting on the sofa, watching a story about the looting and violence springing up in the wake of the wildfires. In one segment, a shop owner was shown being arrested after he'd been caught beating a would-be robber to death inside the remains of his store. He turns off the TV and walks to the bedroom. It's early, the sun still up, but the room is dark because the blinds are down and curtains drawn. Helen is sitting in her chair, staring at the corner. He moves his own chair up behind her and talks quietly into her ear.

"I just watched the sweetest story on one of those nature channels," he tells her. "A herd of elephants was traveling across a river and a baby elephant started to wash downstream. Some of the adults rushed after it, used themselves as shields against the current, and saved the little one. Isn't that wonderful?"

When he's finished, he rests his hand on Helen's shoulder. He tells her it's a beautiful day, asks if maybe she'd like to go out on the lake. But Helen doesn't respond, and he knows she's deep in one of her depressive cycles. Still, he sits behind her, whispering something into her ear every now and then.

Looking back on it now on Penny's sofa, he can't help contrasting Helen's dark mood that day with the joy he'd seen on

her face only a month later when Helen learned she was pregnant and was excited about it, planning on sharing the news
with him over a special dinner. He hadn't known why she looked
so happy, and she never got the chance to tell him.

What did that mean? What did it signify? He's been so busy
trying to figure out the mysteries surrounding Helen's death and
dealing with his own disturbing past that he hasn't taken the
time to think about this. He does now, and the answer comes
quickly. Helen's emotional sea change upon learning she was
pregnant arose from hope. That's what children signify—*hope*.
Hope for the world, hope for their parents. Somewhere deep
inside her, Helen believed that by bringing a child into the
world, she might change it. Alter its course. Save it.

When Helen's murderer forced her to take those pills, he
wasn't taking the life of a woman sliding down a path toward
ever-deepening depression. He was killing a woman who'd
crossed the river of darkness into the light of optimism.

A wave of despair washes over him. It's followed by rage. He
stands and paces the tiny apartment, which suddenly feels claustrophobic. He forces himself to sit on the couch again, close his
eyes, do his breathing exercises.

Where did I learn to do this?

The question takes him back to Owen and Jackie's house in
Philadelphia. It's a decent-sized Tudor in a nice neighborhood.
Well-kept lawns, mature trees. Owen does okay as an accountant, and Jackie makes a good living as a nurse. They'd told him,
though, that they'd exhausted the equity in the home to pay for
Penny's medical care, and likely would soon have to sell it and
buy something with a smaller mortgage.

In the finished basement, he and ten-year-old Penny are resting
on yoga mats on the carpeted floor. They sit cross-legged with
their hands on their knees—what she calls the *Zen position*.

"Breathing is very important," Penny tells him. "You have to learn to control it if you ever want to stop being so jumpy all the time." She tells him she learned to control her breathing because some of her medicines make her jittery. Penny closes her eyes. "Now, do what I do. Take a deep breath, inhale, through your nose. Hold it for ten seconds, then exhale slowly, through your mouth. Then repeat."

Reliving it now on the couch in Penny's apartment, he practices. *Inhale. Hold for ten. Exhale. Inhale. Hold for ten. Exhale.*

He hears Penny laughing, and opens his eyes.

"You're still doing it," Penny says, smiling.

"It helps."

A short time later, they are sitting at the small round table near the kitchen pass-through, drinking amber ales from Sin City Brewing Company and chowing down on vegan burgers.

"Yummy," he says. "Whoever thought pea protein and beet juice could taste so good? Or that I could help save the world in the city where sin never sleeps."

Penny rolls her eyes. "You're a laugh a minute. I'm sure you'd clean up at the Mirage."

They eat for a while, then he decides it's time to get serious.

"Penny, I'm going to ask you a question, and I want you to be honest with me." He pauses. "Did your mother and father ever tell you about me? Who I really was? What I was?"

She takes a deep breath, looks away, which tells him all he needs to know. His heart sinks.

She reaches over to him, takes one of his hands in her own. "To me, you were, you are, you will always be, the man who tried to save me."

His eyes fill and his throat tightens, and he can't believe he's getting this emotional.

"Uncle Jackson?"

"Yeah," the only word he can choke out.

"Don't puss out on me."

They both laugh.

He fetches more beer from the refrigerator and they move to the sofa, where he spends the next half hour telling his niece everything about how he came to be here—Helen's murder, returning to Philadelphia to find her killer, crossing paths with his ex-lover, the violent run-in with Donny Franco, finding out his father might be behind everything. Penny takes it all in, nodding every now and then, reaching out for him when he tells her about Helen.

"Before I confront my father, I need to know as much as I can about him."

"I don't know a lot of the details—my mom's kept them from me—only the broad brushstrokes, which is that he's a bad guy. This town's run like an oligarchy. Whether he's one of the very top guys, or just does things for them, I don't know. Whatever the case, he's a nasty piece of work."

"My mother told me he was a con artist back in Philly."

She nods. "I can see that. He's very smooth. Charming. Like any good sociopath, I suppose." She takes a long swallow of her beer. "He's put a lot of pressure on me to come into *the business*. Like my mother did. He offered to pay for my college. Even buy me my own condo."

"In return for what?"

"Well, that's where he's slick. He said he wouldn't ask much. Carry something somewhere for him. Get information on someone. Little things. Legal things. That's what he did with Mom. But over time, he asked her to get closer and closer to the line. Then over the line. Way over."

He waits for her to explain, but she doesn't, and he can see she's uncomfortable talking about her mother.

"What's his hold over you? Over your mother?"

She takes a deep breath but doesn't answer. She doesn't have to: the question answers itself.

"He's using each of you as leverage over the other, isn't he?"

She looks at him coldly. "And now you're here, and that gives him more leverage."

He gives her a hard look back. "Don't be so sure."

*   *   *

The Bunkhouse Saloon is on South 11th Street, in Downtown Las Vegas, about four miles from Penny's apartment. They park the Jag between 9th and 10th, on Fremont, then walk the short distance to the bar, which turns out to be housed in a one-story pink stucco building. It's a small place inside, with a stage in the corner, exposed ductwork overhead. When he and Penny enter, a young man sitting at a table stands and waves them over.

Penny introduces the guy, Adam, as a friend. Tall and gangly, Adam shyly shakes his hand and they all sit. There's already a pitcher on the table and two empty mugs, which Penny fills with beer. The band is between sets so they have some time to talk. Penny explains that, like her, Adam majors in Water Resources Management; Adam says that, after he graduates, he's moving to India or Australia, wherever the water crisis is most pronounced.

"One of the biggest challenges the world is going to face in the coming years," Penny says, "will be to access and transport potable water to the people who need it."

He listens as Adam and Penny talk about different programs and experts, and, after a while, he leans toward them. "What do you two think is happening? What do you think is going to happen in the next decade?"

"What's happening is that the bill's coming due," Adam says. "We're starting to pay the price of our environmental sins."

"What's going to happen," Penny says, her voice flat, "is that large numbers of people are going to die. They'll starve to death. Thirst. Diseases from the lack of sanitation will play a big part. There will be massive civil unrest, brutal crackdowns. And, of course, there will be war. Probably on a scale we haven't seen before, which is saying something. But the human species will survive. And we'll be smarter. Stronger. And we will care a whole lot more about the earth we live on, and the other species we share it with."

He sits back in his seat, looks from Penny to Adam. He is stunned by their remarkable combination of practicality and optimism, driven by anger. He tries to put into words what he's feeling, but before he's able, the band starts playing and the bar reverberates with music. The band has three young men and a woman. The drummer and two guitarists are men, the woman is the lead vocal. Their songs mirror the sentiments expressed to him by Penny and Adam: passionate rage fueling a forward-looking determination to save the world.

So, this is the younger generation, he thinks. So different from him and his peers at their age—confidently looking forward to comfortable lives built around high-paying jobs, big houses, nice cars, expensive vacations, pills for everything, two-month vacations. The Cloud. The Grid. Artificial Intelligence. Drones. Robots. Netflix. Self-driving cars. Planes and trains that don't need pilots or engineers. Factories that don't need workers. All theirs because they were entitled to it.

Adam fetches another pitcher of beer and they listen to the band for two sets before Penny announces it's time to leave. In the parking lot, Penny and Adam act a little awkward, as if they don't know what to do with each other, and Jackson expects that if he weren't here one of them would have ended up at the other's apartment. They are about to separate when three men emerge from the shadows.

"In town for only one day and already slumming it. Your father would be so disappointed."

"Miles." Penny spits out the name.

"And this time I brought friends."

Miles's friends are large men with dead eyes. Jackson knows the type. "You should leave while you still can," he warns the thugs, who glance at each other and chuckle. He tells Penny and Adam to get behind him, then advances on Miles and his henchmen. Miles turns as though to get out of the way, then pivots around again and, this time, he has something in his hand. Two wires shoot from the object and implant themselves into his chest, delivering fifty thousand volts of electricity.

The next few minutes are a blur of grunts and curses, shuffling feet, cracking bone and smacked flesh. He tries to force himself to his feet, but he can't seem to get off the ground. Finally, the noise stops and he hears Penny telling Adam to help her get him into the Jag. Penny and Adam are all over him and the thing that strikes him is the confusion and fear he sees in Adam's eyes as Adam glances at Penny. Then he slips back into darkness.

His first sensation is the sound of wind rushing past him. Wind and speed. He forces open his eyes and finds himself crumpled in the passenger seat of the Jaguar. He sits up and looks across to the driver's seat. Penny's hands are on the wheel and she's dancing in her seat to the sound of music he cannot hear. Hear face is painted with a beatific smile.

He calls her name and she turns to him with wildness in her eyes. He feels something inside her connect with something inside him.

Oh, no.

Penny zooms them around for another hour, finally pulling into her building's parking lot. He's a little unsteady on his feet, and she helps him out of the car and into her apartment. He lowers himself onto the couch and Penny brings him a glass of water. She sits at the other end of the sofa, but jumps up after only a minute. She disappears into her bedroom, then re-emerges wearing pajamas. She moves quickly around the apartment, cleaning up, moving things around, asking him how he feels. Does he need anything? She can't seem to still herself and he recognizes the dark energy that has overtaken her.

"Your boyfriend was afraid of you."

She stops, stares at him.

"I saw it in his eyes when he looked at you, when you were loading me into the car."

This seems to quiet her a bit. "Adam . . . hasn't seen me like that."

"You took care of Miles and his guys."

"Miles bailed. But, yeah, I dealt with the other two." She pauses. "It doesn't make sense that Miles would come at me like that. He knows what I can do."

Worry rises in his chest. "You've done this before?"

He watches her take a deep breath, force herself onto the couch. "My mother made me take up martial arts almost as soon as we got out here ten years ago. Karate. Tae Kwon Do. Jiu

Jitsu. For some reason, I really took to it." She shrugs. "I'm pretty good.

"When I turned eighteen, my grandfather held a big party at a house out in the desert. Some guy kept making advances on me. I refused him and he got rude. Very rude. I went after him, hard. I disabled him but . . . I couldn't stop myself and had to be pulled off of him. I've never forgotten the look on my grandfather's face. Like some mad scientist who just discovered how to make an atom bomb."

The worry in his chest mushrooms into fear. "I'm going to tell you something about myself," he says. "Something that I've only ever told one other person. Ever since I was very small, I've always felt like there is something inside me, pacing around. Something very dark, very angry. Furious. It's always looking for a way out, and when it gets out, it goes berserk." He pauses, locks eyes with Penny. "Is there something like that inside you, Penny?"

She blinks, looks away, then back at him. "Yeah. I suppose. I mean, I always feel restless," she says. "Edgy." She pauses. "And when I'm attacked, or see someone else attacked . . ." She looks away.

"Do you enjoy the violence of it? When you hurt someone?"

"I enjoy the *justice* of it. When I see someone victimizing someone else, I want to hurt them. Bad."

Penny's words take him back to a time when he took the ten-year-old version of her to a neighborhood park. She's playing on a jungle gym with some other kids when his cellphone rings. He walks away to take the call, and when he turns back, he sees Penny assaulting two boys with a tree branch. He runs to her, grabs her up before the boys decide they'd had enough and go after her.

"What was that?" he asks angrily as he carries her away.

"Those boys were bullying another boy who was smaller than them. It wasn't right."

"You could've put someone's eye out with that stick."

"It wasn't right," she repeats.

His mind jumps again to another memory. He's in his football uniform, staring down at an opposing player who's on his back on the ground. Jimmy pulls him away and they make their way to the huddle for the next play.

"Good block," Jimmy says. "You nailed that guy."

Back on the sofa now with Penny, he remembers that he didn't do all that blocking for Jimmy because he was being a good brother, being generous, letting Jimmy grab the glory. He did it because he *liked hitting* guys. He enjoyed hearing them grunt from the impact, liked watching them fall, hit the ground. He enjoyed the anger on their faces. The hitting, the hurting... that's why he made sure to join in any fight involving his brother. Sure, he wanted to stand up for Jimmy, but there was also the fact that it gave him the excuse to fight. Christ.

Has he ever done anything good for anyone in his whole life?

CHAPTER THIRTY

THEY SIT QUIETLY on the couch for a while.

"Oh." Penny grimaces, places her hand over her stomach.

"What's the matter?" he asks.

"Do you remember when you took care of me when I was a kid?"

"Sure." Recollections of looking after Penny when she was ten years old are among the few clear memories he has.

"It's just as bad now. Even worse, seeing as I'm an adult." She looks at him. "I get so dizzy I can't stand up, can't walk. My muscles seize. My bones hurt. I get violently ill."

This surprises him. "I thought your grandfather paid for you to get medical care, to cure you. That was the whole reason your mother agreed to bring you here."

"I had medical care out the wazoo. Here, and in clinics around the world. For years. But it didn't do me a damned bit of good."

"Jesus. I'm sorry."

She shakes her head. Sits up. "I'm not. Not anymore."

Before he can ask why, she tells him.

"You know who Helen Keller was, right? Deaf and blind as an infant, but learned to talk and read and write and became an inspiration?"

"Of course."

"Well, she was born in 1880 in Tuscumbia, Alabama."

"Okay."

"Name the three other newborns with her in the nursery." She waits. "Okay. Name me just one of them." She waits again. "You can't. Because those kids all grew up to live normal, healthy lives. They lived, they ate, they shat, and they died, and everyone has forgotten all about them. But the whole world remembers Helen Keller."

"You think your condition makes you exceptional?"

"No. My illness provides a platform for me to make myself exceptional." She shrugs. "Everything I overcome makes me stronger, more determined to survive, than other people have to be."

He shakes his head. "Penny, the things you're telling me, the things I've seen—I don't know whether to be afraid of you, or in awe."

He laughs, and she joins him.

Then, "Oh no." She throws her hand over her mouth, races for the bathroom. He follows, waits outside the door, listening to her puke her guts out.

*   *   *

The next thirty-six hours are hell on earth for Penny. Pain racks her joints and muscles. Her intestines turn to fire. She passes in and out of fever and is too fatigued to stand or even to talk. She cries while awake, moans in her sleep.

At 6:00 p.m., eighteen hours into the ordeal, Penny's cellphone rings. He hesitates but picks it up.

"Hello, Jackson."

It's a voice from the dim recesses of his mind, but he remembers it. "Jackie?"

"How is she?"

"Bad." He skips a beat. "You called Penny, but you knew it would be me who answered the phone."

"I heard you were in town, that you and Penny went out last night. You weren't at your hotel afterward, so I put two and two together, figured Penny crashed and you were taking care of her."

He takes a deep breath. "I saw Owen," he says. "In Philadelphia. He helped me with some things."

A long silence at the other end. "Are you planning on seeing me while you're in town?"

He says of course. Then, "Jackie—"

"You have questions, I know. But let's wait until we can talk face-to-face. I'll call you tomorrow."

They hang up and he goes to Penny. She's lying in her bed, her face and hair soaked with sweat. Her eyes are shut and she's grimacing.

"Dizzy spell?"

She nods. "I know I'm flat on my back, but I feel like I'm gonna fall over."

He takes her hand. "Just hold on tight."

He squeezes Penny's hand for a long time. Eventually, she slides into a fitful sleep. He watches her breathe until he's certain she won't awaken, then he takes his cellphone to the living room. Penny warned him that telling Owen where to find them would place him in danger. But a man has the right to know what's happening with his family and certainly Owen is entitled to know that his daughter and wife are alive, and where they are.

"It's Jackson," he says when the call is picked up. "I've made contact with Jackie and Penny. I'm at Penny's place right now, and I'm going to see Jackie tomorrow."

He hears Owen break down on the other end of the line. It takes a few minutes until he can pull himself together.

"Where are they? Are they okay? Are they safe?"

"Penny's in college here. UNLV. And I have to tell you, Owen, she's a force to be reckoned with."

"So, she's healthy now? Her illness has been cured? Jackson?"

"It's complicated." He explains Penny's physical condition, including the Helen Keller story. "Her attitude is amazing."

Owen is quiet for a while. "And Jackie?"

"Apparently, she works for our father. Doing what, I don't know. She didn't want to tell me any details about her life until we meet in person."

"I'm coming out there." There's steel in Owen's voice.

He considers telling Owen to stay put, but decides otherwise. Owen has the right to see his wife and daughter with his own eyes. Hug them, help them if they need it. "I'm staying with Penny. But I have a suite at the Bellagio. Meet me there when you get into town. I'll tell the hotel to expect you and give you a key."

Owen's voice chokes again as he thanks him, then they hang up.

He hears Penny calling out for him, so he races to her room, finds that she's vomited on herself. He races to the bathroom and runs some water in the tub.

"Come on," he says back in the bedroom as he lifts her off the bed. "Let's get you cleaned up."

Penny assures him she's okay to undress herself and soak in the tub, so he leaves and closes the door. After a while, she calls for him and he opens the door to find her wobbling by the tub in a terry cloth robe. He steadies her while she walks back to the bed.

"I'd like to try some soup and crackers," she says.

He helps her into the bed and goes to the kitchen, roots around, and finds some Italian wedding soup in a plastic container. He nukes a bowl of it and returns to the bedroom.

Penny's eyes and fists are clenched shut, and he can tell she's having another vicious attack of vertigo. He sets the soup down and holds her hand. After a while, he closes his eyes.

*   *   *

He finds himself on the back porch of Owen and Jackie's house. Tomorrow night it's going to happen. He and some other of Donny's boys are going to commandeer a big shipment of cocaine being brought into Philly by a gangbanger who double-crossed Donny. They'll take the coke to a rival gang, sell it for over a million bucks. Then, he's going to double-cross Donny and turn the money over to Owen and Jackie for Penny's medical care. After that, he will fake his death and disappear to Kournfield, Kansas, the Middle of Nowhere.

It's been a full week since he's taken any drugs, had any booze. A week since he's seen Vanessa. He engineered a huge fight with her. Pushed all her buttons, then pushed again. He knew she'd come at him in full fury, but she was worse than he'd expected, charging him with a carving knife. She cut him deep, once up and down, once side to side, just below his chest. The cuts were so deep, he needed stiches. The site is still bandaged, and he knows the cuts will leave scars. Vanessa has been calling him since he stormed out of her row house, but he hasn't answered.

He's nervous now. His confidence wavers. Is it the right move? Leaving Vanessa behind? Leaving everything behind? The questions play over and over, but he always comes to the same answer: He has no choice. His life is a train wreck. He betrayed his wife, betrayed his badge. Fell into a life of frank criminality. His health is failing. With each passing day, it seems, he loses more weight. His skin is sallow. His face is hollow. Some days, he barely recognizes himself. He knows that if he stays in Philly, he will die.

"Uncle Jackson?"

He opens his eyes. His ten-year-old niece is standing next to him, on the porch, dressed in pink pajamas.

"It's late," he says. "You should be in bed, like everyone else."

"I can't sleep. And *you're* not in bed."

He reaches over for her. "Come here, pumpkin." He lifts her onto the porch swing next to him. Penny leans into him, and they sit quietly.

The fat full moon is brilliant white. The stars twinkle. The crisp fall air is filled with the music of cicadas, crickets. He smells burning wood from someone's fireplace.

"Mom says you're going to save me."

He ruffles her hair. "That's funny. I was just thinking how you're the one who's saving *me*."

Penny appears to think on this. "Well, then, we'll just have to save each other."

He wraps his arm around her shoulders, pulls her closer. "I think you're right." That's exactly what's about to happen. He and Penny are spiraling downward—her because of her illness, him because of his bad choices. He knows he will never be able to make up for what he's done, what he's become. But he's convinced he can change himself, alter his course, lift himself from

the darkness. He read somewhere that all it takes to set a man on
the right path is to do one good thing. One truly selfless act
performed for the betterment of another person. One good
thing. And then one more.

Tomorrow, he will undertake a single bold act that will save
the one person in his life he hasn't harmed, hasn't betrayed.

*   *   *

The next morning, at six a.m., he wakes in an overstuffed chair
in Penny's bedroom. When he stands, all his joints are stiff, so he
shakes his legs, wiggles his arms to loosen up. Penny is out of bed
and he finds her in the kitchen, cooking breakfast and dancing
to Prince's *1999.*

She turns when she hears him and laughs. "Rise and shine. We
have a world to conquer!"

"Quite a transformation," he says.

She looks him up and down. "You look like hell."

They sit down to a full breakfast of eggs, pancakes, English
muffins, hash browns, orange juice, and coffee.

"This is some spread," he says.

"I have a full day of classes ahead of me," Penny says. "I need
energy."

"I'm going to see your mother today. She called while you
were ill, told me she'd phone me today."

Penny lays down her fork. "You remember I told you she's not
the same, right?"

"Yeah, but what does that mean?"

She looks away. "She made compromises. She told me she
had to."

"You sound hesitant about her."

"I have mixed feelings. She had to go along with him, to a certain extent. I get that. But . . ."

"But what?"

"But a person has to draw a line somewhere. And I don't think she did."

"Some people aren't as strong," he says.

She looks at him now, her eyes cold. "That's the problem with the whole world, isn't it? Everyone knew for years, for decades, that we were on a collision course with nature. But no one was strong enough to make the hard choices necessary to stop it."

"We're talking about your mom, now. Not global warming."

Penny looks to the ceiling. "It's all the same. Weakness. Not fighting for what's right. Everyone sliding down the slippery slope. Giving in. People like my grandfather exploit their weakness, and . . ." She trails off, then stands and angrily clears the table.

As Penny loads the dishes into the dishwasher, he raises the volume on the small TV she has in her kitchen. A news anchor is explaining that half a million Monarch butterflies—on their annual migration from Canada—fell dead from the sky onto Ziacuaro, Mexico.

"First the bees start dying, then the frogs. And now, the butterflies. The *dodo list* gets longer every day," Penny says, referring to the list of species whose extinction is being blamed on global warming. Her blue eyes are ice. Behind them he spots a swirling cloud. Fury.

"When you think of the older generations, my generation, and what we've done to the planet, to the other species who share it with us . . ." He lets the words hang as he keeps his eyes locked on Penny. Her rage is palpable, and he realizes now that she and others like her will be the avenging angels of their generation. They will bring the world back from the precipice, save what can be saved. But when they're done, they'll make sure a price is paid, by the survivors of his generation.

It makes him shudder.

CHAPTER THIRTY-ONE

PENNY LEAVES FOR a class just before ten. He expects Jackie will call him sometime this morning and they'll make arrangements to meet. What he does after that depends on what he learns from his sister. If she tells him where to find his father, he'll go there. If she can't or won't, he'll return to Penny's apartment and take it from there. Either way, he knows he's reaching the end. Sooner or later, he'll confront his father, get the answers he seeks. Or not. Either his father will turn out to be the villain behind Helen's death and he will exact some form of justice, or his father will be blameless, in which case he has no idea what he'll do to solve his wife's killing.

He shakes his head then rises from the kitchen table, where he's been sitting since Penny left for class. His coffee is cold and he takes the mug to the sink, empties it, and places it into the dishwasher. He takes a shower and, when he's done, stands before the bathroom mirror, staring into the dark eyes looking back at him. His thoughts turn to what lies ahead, and he doesn't know which he fears more—having to punish his father, or remaining in the dark as to who murdered his wife. One thing he is sure of, though, is that he will find Helen's killer and he will have vengeance.

The thought causes fear to wash through him.

Glancing at his cellphone, he sees that's it's after noon and he's surprised he hasn't heard from Jackie yet. Using the remote control, he turns on the TV in the living room and lowers himself onto the sofa. He's tired from the long night watching over Penny and he closes his eyes.

After some time, he wakes to find himself standing. The space around him feels like it stretches forever. It is night, but there is no moonlight or starlight. Just total blackness. Beneath his feet, the ground is soft. He bends down and lifts what feels like ash. He can't see what color it is, but he knows nonetheless that it is black ash, volcanic ash. He lets it spill through his fingers and starts walking. The air is hot and thin. It feels like it does when his head is under the covers and he's breathing in his own stale breath.

For a long time—hours, days? he doesn't know—he moves forward. Is he walking in a straight line? In a big circle? He can't tell; there's nothing in the void against which to measure his movement. Still, he presses on, until he sees, far in the distance, a tiny white light, a pinhole in the blackness. He realizes that the answers he seeks are in the light, and he picks up his pace, walking faster and faster, then running. The light grows, then it changes color, from white to red. Suddenly, the air reverberates with a single beat of a large drum.

He stops, but the light continues to grow in size and brightness. Now the light is moving, too, toward *him*.

Another beat of the drum, then a third beat, and the light begins to pulse in sync.

He watches the light grow in size as the drumbeat speeds up and he realizes that the light isn't just moving toward him, it's coming for him.

Terror surges through him and he turns and runs. But the drum beats faster, and the light grows brighter, and he feels heat on his back. The black void glows red now, in all directions. His back starts to burn.

He feels the hand on his shoulder, clamping down, shaking him.

"No! No!"

"Uncle Jackson!"

He opens his eyes.

His niece is standing over him.

"Hey. You were having a nightmare."

He doubles over on the sofa, gasps for breath.

"My god, you're drenched."

He wraps his arms around his chest and looks up at her. Penny is right; he's soaked in sweat. He's shaking, too. And freezing cold.

Penny brings him a blanket and a glass of water. She covers him and makes him drink, then sits next to him on the sofa. "What were you dreaming? It must've been awful."

How can he answer that? He takes a minute to gather his thoughts. "I dreamt that I was looking for answers. And . . . I found them."

*   *   *

It takes a good hour for him to fully recover. Penny spends the time reading from one of her textbooks, glancing at him every now and then. She brings him several glasses of water, which he gulps down in giant swallows. Finally, once he feels himself again, he stands and walks to the bathroom, where he splashes water on his face, combs his hair. When he's finished, he joins

Penny in the living room. As he sits down next to her, his cell-phone rings. The screen says unknown caller, but he answers it anyway.

"Jackson? How is Penny doing? A tough couple of days, eh?"

He vaguely recognizes the voice but he's not sure from where.

"It's me. Miles."

He doesn't respond.

"You're not still sore about that taser thing, I hope. Damned thing went off on its own. I have a good mind to submit a warranty claim."

In his mind's eye, he can see Miles smiling. He's going to wipe the grin right off that little shit's face the next time he sees him.

"Who is it?" Penny asks.

He presses the button for speakerphone and lays his phone on the table.

"Penny? Are you there? I hope you're feeling better."

She glares at the phone. "Did you like what I did to your two goons? Before you ran off?"

"You're a special gal, Penny. What your grandfather always says."

"Cut to the chase," he tells Miles. "What do you want?"

"It's not what I want. It's what your father wants. Which is to see you and Penny."

"Forget it," Penny says.

"Your mother's with him," Miles says. "Though she's not very happy about it."

Penny's eyes widen with concern. "What does that mean—that she's not happy?"

"Oh, you know your mother. She can be moody."

Jackson leans over the phone. "Tell my father I'll come to him. But there's no need for him to see Penny."

"No. I'm going, too." Penny is standing now.

He shakes his head at her as Miles responds.

"You and Penny will have to let me drive you," Miles says. "You'd never find the place."

Jackson glances at Penny, who shakes her own head "no."

"There's not a chance I'm letting you drive us anywhere," he says. "Penny and I will take my car. We'll follow you."

A pause at the other end. "Sounds like a plan. I'm already outside the apartment."

He hangs up on Miles, turns to Penny. "I don't like this. It feels like a setup."

"Of course it's a setup," she says. "But it was bound to go down this way. There was always going to be a showdown between him and me. And once you showed up, you had to be part of it."

He stands. "I know why I want to confront my father. But I don't know what he wants from me."

"Whatever it is, it'll be more than you want to give him."

While Penny uses the bathroom, he stands by his bed, staring down at the open suitcase, the two guns lying inside. One is the automatic he found between the mattress and box spring at his house in Kournfield. The other is the .38 that was in the lockbox he'd hidden in the attic. Looking at the guns, the suitcase, the clothes, thinking about the house he shared with Helen, brings him back to the reason he began this odyssey less than a month ago. Someone killed his sweet wife. Stole her life just as she finally found a reason to live. If, as he now suspects, his father was involved, so be it.

Still . . . He reaches down, closes the suitcase over the guns. No more killing.

A few minutes later, they exit Penny's building. The gray Chrysler is parked just across the street. He hands Penny the key to the Jaguar, tells her to get it from the parking lot. Then he crosses the street.

Miles lowers the driver's-side window. "I hope you appreciate how hard this has been on me," he says. "Chasing you all over the country in this car. Asking around about you, sending reports back to your father. Planting seeds."

"I saw you pull out of a restaurant parking lot a few days back, just before my engine was sabotaged. You want to tell me why you fucked with my car if you were just going to return it to me a couple days later?"

Miles's face betrays confusion, but he catches himself and smiles. "You're being paranoid. Then again, even paranoid people have enem—"

Miles's nose collapses under Jackson's fist.

"*What the fuck?*"

Jackson smiles. "Now, now . . . don't question why."

"You broke my nose!" Miles's eyes spit fury. His hands cover his nose, as blood drips onto his crisp white shirt and tan blazer.

Penny pulls the Jag up beside him. "Let's go, Batman," she says. But there is no mirth in her voice.

He hops in. "Easy on the clutch this time. And the accelerator."

They follow the Chrysler out of town, north on I-15. Miles speeds up and slows down, darts between cars, cuts people off.

Penny shakes her head. "He's driving angry."

They follow the interstate for about twenty miles, get off Exit 64, onto 93 North. It's a flat, two-lane road, separated by a double yellow line. Beside it, the desert stretches to the hills, sprinkled with palm trees and cacti. They're on 93 North for quite a while before Miles pulls off onto a smaller road leading toward the hills. So far, he and Penny haven't spoken a word, keeping their thoughts to themselves. But he turns to her now.

"When we get there, I don't want you taking any chances. Just hang back, let me deal with my father."

She rolls her eyes. "In case you haven't figured it out yet, this isn't just about you. It's coming to a head for me, too. I'll be graduating in another year and I'm going to move forward with my life. He needs to get out of my way. If he doesn't, I plan to go *through* him."

He purses his lips. Penny's bravado seems foolhardy. She knows her grandfather is a bad guy, but she obviously hasn't witnessed his evil firsthand. She's been sheltered. A captive of sorts. She's never been in the thick of it, and his niece isn't as hard as she thinks she is.

"I mean it," he says.

She doesn't respond and they drive on.

The Chrysler leads them onto an unmarked road a person wouldn't know was there unless they knew to look for it. The road leads them around a wide hill. Hidden behind it is a sprawling concrete and glass structure that looks like it could have been designed by I.M. Pei. A short distance from the house is a helipad on which sits a gleaming black chopper. At first he's surprised there is no fence, no gate, but then he realizes his father doesn't need one for a house no one knows is here.

He jumps out of the car as soon as it comes to a stop and, as he does, he sees a man descending the front steps. The man is medium height, fit, with strong shoulders over a narrow waist. He walks erect, proud, and sports an Italian suit cut closely to his thin figure, over Italian loafers. His eyes are obscured behind sunglasses. He removes the glasses and smiles.

Jackson glares, trying to figure out where to start with his father. Before he has a chance to decide, his father turns to Penny. "Granddaughter! It's good to see you. We have some things to discuss."

"That's a fact." Penny's face is rigid with anger. She clearly wants nothing more than to get in the man's face and have it out with him.

Jackson extends an arm to block her path.

His father tells them to follow him inside, then turns and walks back up the steps. He and Penny follow, Miles trailing behind them, holding a handkerchief to his nose. The space inside is vast: a thirty-foot ceiling overlooking a great room that opens to a dining area, kitchen, and bar. The floor is polished stone, the interior walls rough stone with metal architectural inserts. A space-age fireplace seems to float in front of the far wall. The exterior walls are floor-to-ceiling windows. Outside one is a large infinity pool. The helicopter's visible through the other.

Jackie is waiting for them inside. Although she, like Jackson, is forty-one, ten years older than when they last saw each other, she looks younger. Her olive skin is smoother, her lips fuller. Behind the surgically sculpted beauty, though, he sees something rotting inside.

She approaches him, gives him a cursory hug and plants herself next to him and Penny. His father watches silently, then seems to notice Miles for the first time.

"What happened to your nose?" his father asks his henchman. Then, as though a light bulb went off over his head: "Penny?"

Jackson raises a hand to stop Penny from answering. "Your boy here can't handle his toys."

"The taser again?" his father asks.

"Plus, he has a sharp tongue."

His father looks at Miles. "For crying out loud, you're dripping blood on the floor. Go into one of the bathrooms and clean yourself up."

Miles glowers before turning away and disappearing behind one of the stone walls.

Jackson turns to his father. "What was the point of having Miles follow me around the country once I was already on my way? Why have him sabotage my car when you were just going to give it back to me? And why did you have that truck driver burn down that hotel? Someone could have been killed."

It seems obvious to Jackson that the truck driver, who just happened to show up at the garage his Jaguar had been towed to, was another of his father's henchmen. But as happened when Jackson brought up sabotaging the car to Miles, Jackson's accusations seem to take his father aback, and Jackson wonders whether the monster before him isn't the only one who's been playing him.

Jackson's father brushes aside the allegations and turns to Jackie. "I'm sure you and your brother have a lot to catch up on. Why don't you spend some time getting reacquainted? Penny, how about you join me in the library?"

"She stays with me," Jackson says.

"It's okay," Penny tells him. "I can put up with him for a few minutes while you talk with my mom." She turns away before he can stop her and follows his father out of the room.

Jackie exhales and drops onto one of three leather sofas arranged in front of the fireplace. Jackson sits down beside her, takes her hand. The memory returns of him sitting next to her on Penny's bed, Jackie saying how worried she is, him resolving to find a way to help his niece.

"So long ago," Jackie says, as though reading his thoughts.

"A lifetime," he answers.

Looking in the direction where Penny disappeared with her grandfather, Jackie says, "You tried to help her once. *He* made sure it didn't work."

*   *   *

His mind drags him back to the night he failed Penny. He's carrying two suitcases filled with money and is walking in the parking
garage toward his car. Then the world goes black. He wakes up on
the cement floor of the garage with a pounding headache and a
knot on the back of his head. He climbs unsteadily to his feet,
looks around for the money, but it's gone. He shouts and rages
and pounds his fists against his car. He wants to find whoever
rolled him, get the money back, and beat them senseless. But who
can he turn to for help? Not Donny Franco. He was supposed to
meet Donny an hour ago, hand over the money. By now, Donny's
figured out he's been cheated and is looking for him.

The weight of his crushing failure is unbearable. But he drives
to his sister's house to tell her and Owen what happened. They
have the right to know. When he gets there, it's a terrible scene.
Jackie erupts in tears. Owen's face turns scarlet red and he makes
him retell the story over and over, obviously looking for holes,
not believing that he "lost" the money. The three of them go
round and round until they hear Penny's pipsqueak voice
through the railing on the second-floor landing. She's been sitting there the whole time, watching them. Listening.

He looks up, spots Penny's face peeking through the bannis-
ter. "What did you ask, sweetheart?"

"I asked, why is Mommy crying? Didn't you save me, Uncle
Jackson?"

What can he say to her? How can he explain what happened,
other than to admit he failed? He stares up at her, and Penny
must be able to see behind his eyes, because her own eyes fill
with tears. Then she stands and quietly retreats into her room.

After Miami came the long ride to Kansas. His plan had been to arrive in Kournfield as a man already on the road to redemption. But he blew his chance to do the one good thing. Penny's parents will lack the money they need to cure her, and he remains utterly unredeemed. And, it seems likely, unredeemable.

*   *   *

On the sofa next to him, Jackie continues. "He admitted it a few years after I brought Penny out here. He told me that without the money you took, I'd have no choice but to bring Penny here. And he figured that you would eventually join us, once you left Philly to escape the wrath of Donny Franco. But you'd already gone your own way by the time he told me this."

Anger rises within him. "So, he's been shadowing me all along. Interfering with my life. Almost ruining Penny's life. Certainly, ruining Owen's. Doing you no good."

*   *   *

Another memory surfaces, one that he hasn't recalled until now. He and Jimmy are sitting next to each other on the sofa. Their mother, Evelyn, is crying, yelling. Their father is carrying his suitcases down the steps.

"Why are you leaving? Where are you going?" Evelyn cries out.

"It's safer for everyone if you don't know."

They argue back and forth. Finally, as his father is walking out the door, his mother cries, "If you leave us now, don't you *ever* come back here. And don't even *think* about getting the boys back!"

His father turns around. "The boys are *mine*. Blood of my blood." With that, his father turns and walks out the door. He and Jimmy run to the window, tears spilling from their eyes. They watch him get into the car and drive away.

*   *   *

"Yeah," Jackie says. "He's interfered with all of our lives."

He takes a deep breath. "I think he had my wife murdered. That's why I'm here."

Jackie looks away. She seems torn, wanting to tell him something but unable to bring herself to say it.

CHAPTER THIRTY-TWO

BEFORE HE HAS the chance to urge Jackie to open up to him, Miles reenters the room and takes a seat on one of the other sofas. He's wearing a fresh suit, fresh shirt, and seems to have regained some of his composure. He's brought a bottle of San Pellegrino with him and he unscrews the cap, takes a sip.

"Don't let me interrupt," he tells them.

Feeling the sudden urge to break the rest of the man's face into pieces, Jackson stands and takes a step toward Miles.

Miles pulls a gun from his jacket and Jackie jumps to her feet. "For God's sake, put that away! If you so much as scratch one of us . . ."

Miles sneers but puts away the gun. He stands, glares again, then leaves the room.

"This is not good, Jackson," his sister says. "None of it."

He turns to his sister. "I need to understand what's going on. Why does my father want me, after all these years? I mean, why now? And what does he want with Penny?"

Jackie smiles bitterly. "There's one answer to both questions. Your father is in big trouble. Ten years ago, when he brought me and Penny here, he was buying up a lot of real estate. For reasons he never explained to me, he wanted to keep a lot of it off his own balance sheet, so he quietly set up a trust and put all of it under Penny's name. After a few years, though, he needed a bunch of properties as security for huge loans he took out to buy shares in a couple casinos. So he lied about the properties in Penny's trust, claimed they were in his name. The problem is, he overextended himself. Now, he needs to sell the trust properties to pay off the principal and the accumulated interest."

"Accumulated interest?"

Jackie pauses. "Some of his loans were with banks. Others were . . . well, not with banks."

"He's in debt to the mob," Jackson says, realizing that his father has made the same mistake in Vegas that he made back in Philadelphia. Christ, the man can't help himself.

"He's desperate," Jackie says.

"And he has no other source to pay off the loans?"

She shakes her head. "He's already sold off most of the properties he kept in his own name. But it was nowhere near enough. Not even with the key man life insurance policy proceeds he received after his partner died in an auto accident."

"Was it an accident?"

Jackie takes a deep breath and her eyes go black. "Like I said, he's desperate."

"So, he needs Penny to sign the papers and relinquish the trust properties back to him."

"She doesn't know anything about the trust. But she hates her grandfather and hates Vegas. When she finds out how much property is under her name, she's more likely to sell it all off and donate the proceeds to charity than turn it over to her grandfather."

"And when does Penny find out, about the trust?"

"When she turns twenty-one. Two months from now. Which is why you're here."

"He wants me to join up with him, then persuade Penny to return all the properties to him."

Jackie nods.

They sit quietly for a few minutes, then he switches gears. "Penny beat up a couple guys. I didn't see it because Miles tasered me. But I saw the aftermath. I saw what was in her eyes. Have you ever seen that side of her?"

Jackie closes her eyes for a moment. "Once. Once." She sits and he follows her. "And I have to tell you, it frightened me. When it happened, I thought . . . forgive me for this, Jackson, but it reminded me of the things I heard about you back in Philadelphia. All that graffiti about you."

"JRgonegetU," he says.

She nods. Then something seems to snap inside her and she begins to weep. "You can't let him get his hands on her. He'll twist her. Just like he did to me. Only with Penny it will be a lot worse. The wildness in her . . . The violence." She bends over, buries her face in her hands.

He reaches around her shoulders, hugs her. "I won't let him have her."

As if on cue, Penny reenters the room, her grandfather behind her.

Jackson unwraps his arm from his sister and stands.

"Well, it looks like you'll have to be the one to talk some sense into her," his father tells him.

He steps toward his father. "The only one who's going to be talking here is you. You have a lot of explaining to do. Questions to answer."

His father sighs. "You've always been so impatient. Actually, that's one of the things I like about you. You want things and you're in a hurry to get them. And you don't mind stepping on a few toes." He shakes his head. "So different from Jimmy. He's been such a disappointment."

"He's a good man. Better than I ever was."

"Every yin must have a yang, I suppose," his father says. "Though most of the time, the yin and yang struggle inside the same soul. Until one of them wins."

"I don't see you fighting too much with yourself."

His father studies him, and he can tell he's trying to figure out which tack to take. Which angle to work.

"When I first came out here all those years ago, you know what I did? I got a job at a place that helps gambling addicts. I met a nice girl, got engaged. Put money down on a small place outside of town. I was all ready to settle down." He shakes his head. "But it didn't work out. Guess why."

"How about you just lay it out for me."

"It all fell apart because *I* showed up. The real me. Or the stronger part of me." His father uncrosses his arms. "Isn't that what happened to you in Philadelphia, then in Kansas? You were settled down, with Pam, then Helen. Mr. Married Man, a police officer, then a company man leading the baseball team. Until, all of a sudden, *you* showed up."

His father's words cut him to the quick and his heart starts racing. What his father described is exactly what happened. Twice, he tried living a normal life, tried to be the good man. Vanessa might have been the trigger the first time, but with Helen, it was all him, prowling the nearby towns for violence, women, even drugs at times.

"Whatever mistakes I made have nothing to do with why I'm here." He glances at Jackie, then back at his father, who has an amused look on his face. "I want to know if you killed my wife."

His father raises his eyebrows. "Haven't you ever heard of Occam's razor?" Before Jackson can respond, his father raises a hand to stop him. "It's the principle that the simplest explanation is usually the best." His father's expression turns cold. "What I'm suggesting is that perhaps the answer lies closer to home than you'd like to think."

When he hears the words "Occam's razor," a memory surges to the surface so powerfully that it replaces all conscious thought.

*   *   *

It starts with the image of a razor blade in his own hand. Wearing only boxers, he's sitting on the ratty plaid couch, bent over the glass-topped coffee table, using the razor to straighten the lines of cocaine so that he can snort them through the straw.

"Save some for me." The skinny brunette with the mousy brown hair—Carol—enters the trailer home's ratty living room from the bedroom where they just had sex. His ears are still ringing; Carol's a screamer. She also apparently thinks it's sexy to walk around the trailer stark naked, as she does now.

He snorts one of the lines, pauses as Carol takes a seat next to him. Then he snorts a second line and hands the straw to Carol. Her eyes aren't on the straw, though; she's looking over his shoulder, toward the front door. He turns and sees a figure standing in the doorway. It's a woman.

Helen.

A terrible moan escapes Helen's mouth.

He shoots from the couch and starts toward her. But the coffee table is in the way and he stumbles over it. Carol tries to help him up, but she falls on top of him, slowing him down. He throws her off and races for the door, shouting Helen's name. By the time he reaches the porch, Helen is in her car, backing away fast. He shouts her name, waves at her, but her eyes are a million miles away. He runs after the car until he's halfway into Walt's parking lot. Then he pivots and dashes back to the trailer.

Carol, in jeans only now, is shouting, cursing, grabbing at him, demanding an explanation. He fights her off as he throws on his clothes. When he's ready to leave, he can't find his keys, and he shouts at Carol to help him look. She tells him to fuck himself and stomps out of the trailer. He looks everywhere for his keys, finally remembering he tossed them into the bathroom sink when he first came into the trailer and had to relieve himself.

Fifteen minutes behind Helen, he presses hard on the accelerator of his F-150 in hopes of catching her. His speedometer is still rising fast when he hears the siren behind him, sees the flashing lights in his rearview.

"No!" He smashes his palm against the steering wheel. "Fuck!"

An hour later, after a stop by the patrolman, he reaches his house and finds Helen on their bed, choking, gasping, dying, from the drugs she OD'd on. He finds the photograph torn in half, Helen's suicide note. Her statement to him that she hated him and was tearing herself away from him, forever.

For three weeks after Helen's funeral, he drifts through life in a daze. Numb to everything and everyone.

Then, in an instant, it all catches up to him. He's walking through the alley next to Juke's Place. The alley's narrow, and suddenly it fills with water. He tries to run, but it takes all his effort to move his legs. He forces one leg forward, then another, but the water keeps rising until the pressure on his chest makes it hard to breathe. He panics, desperate for air, and realizes then that it isn't water he's trapped in. It's *guilt*. Crushing him. Damning him.

He turns to the pitted brick wall and smashes his head against it. Again. Again.

And the world goes black.

CHAPTER THIRTY-THREE

HE COMES TO screaming.

While his father stands back with his arms crossed, Penny and Jackie are kneeling beside him, shaking him, shouting.

"Jackson! Snap out of it!"

"Wake up! Wake up!"

He flails his arms, throwing them off him, then wails until his body shakes. Finally, he covers his face with his hands, and weeps. Jackie and Penny kneel by him again, put their arms around him, and this time he lets them comfort him. He remembers now that it was a weekend, not a workday, that Helen killed herself. He told her he was going to batting practice and she said she had a big surprise for him when he got back.

He sees himself sitting in the car before leaving, staring at the cabin for several minutes.

Why?

And why did Helen follow him to the trailer that day? Had she seen him through a window, sitting in the car? Did that make her suspicious? Or had she already sensed what he was up to?

His mind drags him to the night Helen appeared to him in his dreams, telling him he needed to *get out*, hit the road, Jack. He remembers now that after the dream, he went to their home office, pulled out a small key he'd kept hidden in the back of one of the drawers. The key to the strongbox in the attic. It was *he* who laid the key on the desk, then unlocked the front door, deactivated the alarm. He was sending himself a message that Helen was right, it was time to leave Kournfield, time to begin the quest that would, eventually, bring him here, to the memory he wasn't ready to face.

Christ, how messed up am I that my mind could manipulate me like that? Make me produce the key, then scrub the memory so I'd think it was someone else and seek them out.

He feels Jackie's and Penny's arms around him. Minutes pass, until all he knows is that he is finished. Utterly spent. Empty.

"What's wrong? What happened?" Jackie asks.

He looks up at her, barely able to make out her face through the tears burning his eyes. *What happened?*

"I killed my wife."

CHAPTER THIRTY-FOUR

JACKIE AND PENNY help him stand, walk him to the sofa.

"Where did he go?" he asks. "My father?"

"He left the room," Jackie answers. "Mumbled something about it being difficult to see his son so unmanned." Jackie turns to Penny. "Can you give your uncle and me a few minutes alone?"

Penny looks at him and he nods. Penny exhales then leaves the house through the front door. At the same time, Jackie walks to the bar, pours herself a glass of whiskey—one for him, too—and returns to the sofa, sits next to him. He watches as she downs the brown fire in a single gulp. When she lays her empty glass on the coffee table, her hand is shaking. He lays down his own glass without drinking any of the whiskey. Then he waits. Finally, Jackie turns to him, her eyes filled with despair.

She opens her mouth but seemingly cannot speak. Then she takes a deep, quivering breath. "I didn't know . . . how it would turn out."

He stares at her, watches as her eyes fill with tears.

"It was just . . . a call. I knew she'd be upset. But not . . . not that . . ."

He jumps to his feet. "What the hell did you *do*?"

Jackie hunches forward. "God help me, I'm so sorry."

"You called Helen. You told her about the trailer. *That's* why she showed up."

Jackie lets out a low moan, much like the one that had escaped Helen's mouth when she stood in the doorway of the trailer— saw him with the coke on the table, the naked woman sitting beside him.

"Goddamn you to hell." It takes all his strength not to lunge at his sister, strangle her.

Jackie gives him a pleading look. "He needed you to leave Kournfield, get you here, to persuade Penny to sign everything over to him."

"So, he decided to destroy my marriage. Let Helen see me for what I truly am."

"He thought . . . *I* thought that she'd just kick you out. Then Miles would show up, lead you to us. We didn't imagine that Helen would, would . . ."

"Jesus Christ, Jackie! Helen was a depressive! She was in so much fucking pain already! How could you not have seen what she might do?"

"God forgive me."

He glares down at his sister, who looks up at him with her surgically enhanced eyes above her perfect nose, perfect lips, and perfect teeth, and it hits him that his beautiful sister has been twisted into the ugliest person he's ever seen. "I can't even imagine what you feel like inside," he says, though he knows *exactly* what she's feeling.

The front door opens, and Penny walks inside. She takes in the scene and gets a worried look on her face. At the same time, his father makes his own reappearance. Penny takes a seat at the bar while his father resumes his position by the fireplace. Jackson moves to the other side of the mantel, wondering how he'll be able to restrain himself from killing the man.

His father studies him for a long moment, then shakes his head. "If I've correctly interpreted what just happened, it seems that you've been playing a cat-and-mouse game since your wife's death, you being the cat and her killer being the mouse. Turns out, though, you're the cat *and* the mouse."

He stares at his father, not knowing where he's going with this. And not caring. He is a completely fallen man. A man with no hope of redemption.

His father takes a step toward him. "You're at a crossroads, son. You have to make a choice. Now, I can't make you into a famous blues singer like Robert Johnson, or give you a fiddle made of gold—well, actually, I could give you a gold fiddle—but that's not the point. The point is, I could offer you a place in the world that suits your nature as it suits mine."

"My nature." He spits out the words.

His father thinks for a minute, or pretends to. "I'm offering you a place by my side."

"So, what? You're Darth Vader and you want me to rule the galaxy with you?"

His father shrugs. "I'm just a businessman. I'm offering you the chance to join the family business. And once you've accepted, you can bring this one in, too," he adds, nodding at Penny. "I understand she's as taken with you as she is put off by me. Which is odd, since you're just like me, and she's like the both of us."

"*No.* She's nothing like you, or me."

"Really? You might want to think back to Sunday night."

A harsh laugh escapes his lips. "*That's* what that was about? You wanted me to see Penny defend herself? What does that prove?"

His father smiles. "I saw her *defend herself* once. I don't think I need to say anything more."

"You're not getting her. Or me, for that matter. I'm done, with all of it."

"You're gonna crawl into a hole?"

"Something like that." A hole, or a bottle, or a swimming pool full of white powder. He imagines himself sliding into oblivion and feels a dangerous warmth inside.

His father moves around the bar, lifts a bottle of scotch, and pours two fingers into a tumbler. He takes a sip. "I'm not going to give up on you so easily. Or Penny, for that matter."

"We have a visitor." It's Miles's voice, coming from behind the fireplace. "Cameras show a car approaching. Not one of ours."

He watches for his father's reaction. A flash of impatience breaks into his gaze, but is quickly painted over by the false charm he's displayed so far. "Well, let's go see who it is." His voice all chipper now.

Jackson tells Jackie to wait behind and he and Penny follow Miles and his father outside. They descend the front steps and watch as a blue Ford Taurus makes its way toward the house. When it stops, he is stunned to see Donny Franco and Owen, Owen driving. Donny opens his door and climbs out, a pistol in his hand.

To his right, he sees Miles pull his own gun from his jacket and point it at Donny, who ignores him, limps around the front of the car, grabs Owen by the collar, and drags him from behind the wheel. He feels Penny stiffen beside him; he puts an arm in front of her, whispers for her to hold still.

"You want to put that gun down?" Miles says to Donny.

"You want to fuck yourself?" Donny says back, pointing his gun at Miles. Then, shoving Owen to the ground, he focuses his attention on Jackson. "So nice to finally catch up to you."

"Would you care to explain who you are?" his father asks. "What this is all about?"

"That's Donny Franco. My old boss from Philly. And I'm thinking this is about payback."

"You're right," Donny says. "This is about payback. In more ways than one."

"*Owen?*" It's Jackie, at the front door. She runs down the steps, helps Owen up from the ground. "My God, are you all right?"

He notices now that Owen's face is bruised and swollen. Donny worked him over pretty good.

"Let me guess." Donny nods at Jackie. "You're the wife."

Penny takes a step forward. "And I'm his daughter—"

"That, I already know—"

"—and if you hurt him again, you'll pay."

Donny chuckles. "I have no doubt you'd try. I saw that little show you put on outside the bar. Taking down those two guys."

"How'd you find me?" Jackson can't help asking.

"Now, that's a story," Donny answers. "The last time you disappeared on me ten years ago, I sent some guys to work over your brother and ex-partner. That got me nowhere, so this time I played it smarter. Parabolic mics and wiretaps. I didn't learn anything from your brother, but Richie was a treasure trove. Owen here called him quite a few times, asking if he'd heard from you, talking about Vegas. The two of them got together a couple times at a diner. So, I started looking into Owen here. Learned he had a wife and daughter who disappeared on him right around the time you got lost. Jackie and Penny Brenner.

My people couldn't find Jackie, but it was easy to track down Penny Brenner, student at UNLV."

Donny shrugs. "Pretty simple from there. I hopped on a plane and tailed you and the karate kid. Then my guys back east told me they'd listened in on a conversation you had with Owen. Seemed he was flying out here himself. You told him you had a place at the Bellagio, which surprised me because I knew you were staying with Penny. I got the info on Owen's plane, made sure to be at the hotel when he arrived, and took the elevator with him. It wasn't hard to persuade him to take me into your suite. And holy shit. What did I find, but a candy dish full of hundred-dollar bills. And that's when I knew you'd used the money you stole from me to hit it big in Sin City."

"How did you find this house?" his father asks.

"The first thing I did when I saw you palling around with little missy here was put a tracking device on your car."

His father chuckles. "That's a good story. Now, how about everyone put their guns away and we all go inside and work this out."

Donny glares at him. "You're not working anything out, old man. This is between me and Jackson. He's coming with me and Owen—and now that I think about it, the wife and daughter, too. We're going to go back to that fancy hotel and have a little discussion, after which Jackson is going to go to a bank and bring me a shit-ton of cash to go with what he left me in the candy dish. We'll call it interest. In return for that, I'll let Owen and Mrs. Owen and baby-girl Owen go free." He pauses. "But you, Jackson, well, you know . . . I'm not letting you go anywhere."

He locks eyes with Donny, knowing that he'll kill Owen, Jackie, and Penny, no matter what he does.

"That's quite a plan," his father says. "But it's not what I want. Which means that it's not what my associate Miles wants, either. And, in case you haven't noticed, Miles has a gun pointed at your chest."

"And I have a gun pointed at his forehead."

His father looks from Donny to Miles, then back again. He smiles. "Well, then. It looks like we have a standoff."

Donny rolls his eyes and Miles's brains explode out of the back of his head. His body crumples to the ground.

Donny's turn to smile. "You didn't even see me pull the trigger, did you?"

"What the *hell?*" His father's face is crimson now. He narrows his eyes, curls his lips, bares his teeth. "Do you have any idea who you're fucking with?"

Donny rolls his eyes again. "Yeah. A rich asshole who has two eyes, two ears, and a tongue he'd gladly wag if the cops put enough pressure on him."

A second blast from Donny's gun. His father flies back as the bullet punches through his sternum and tears a hole in his heart. His father clutches at his chest and falls to the ground, his eyes fixed in utter surprise. His body twitches a few times on the ground, moans once, and releases his bowels and bladder.

"Come on now," Donny says, waving his gun. "Everybody in the car."

Jackson sighs. "You know I can't let you take these people."

Donny's reptilian eyes stare at him. Then, like a lizard with a good idea, he widens his mouth into an appalling grin. "Maybe you're right," Donny says. "There's just too many of us to squeeze into that rental car. So I'm thinking I should cull the herd." He waves his gun at Owen, Jackie, and Penny, now standing together. "Eeny meeny miny moe."

The instant Donny's gun stops on Penny, Jackson lunges forward. The gun fires but not before his shoulder hits Donny in the chest, sending him backward to the ground, the gun flying from his hand.

He takes a step and kicks the pistol away.

"Uncle Jackson?" It's Penny. "You're bleeding."

He looks down to see the crimson stain spreading on his white button-down. "Oh." He drops to one knee, and Penny rushes to him. "*No*," he says, nodding at Donny, who's struggling to get back on his feet. "Take care of him."

Penny's hands and feet move faster than those of any seasoned fighter he's seen. So fast that Donny goes cross-eyed as she pummels him.

"Find something to tie him up with," he tells Penny through his pain. "Before he comes to his senses again."

Penny looks around, but it's not rope she picks up. Instead, she lifts one of a group of metal chairs encircling a fire pit in front of the house and pulls off the rubber end-cap from one of the legs.

He hears Donny moan. "You fucking bitch. You broke my arms." He tries to get up, but can't and falls back on the ground, faceup. He turns his head toward Jackson and smiles. "I'm hurt bad, Jackson, but not as bad as you. That gut's gonna bleed out."

"Yeah? Well, you can read my obituary in prison."

"I don't think so. Whatever was going down here before I showed up wasn't kosher. Those two schmucks I shot had dirty money written all over them. Which means none of your friends is going to report me to the cops. In fact, they'll need me to help them think up a story, which I'll do when they drive me to the hospital. Maybe we'll come up with something where it was *you* that shot those two, and one of them who shot you."

"Won't work," he grunts through the pain. "All the bullets came from the same gun."

"We'll figure it out," Donny answers.

He glances at Penny, who's been watching the exchange.

She looks back at him. Then she walks over to Donny. "You shot my uncle," she says. Then she positions the chair leg directly above Donny's right eye and drives it straight down, shredding Donny's eyelid and eye and causing the remnants of both to disappear in a pool of blood.

Donny Franco screams.

And screams.

CHAPTER THIRTY-FIVE

DONNY FRANCO'S AGONIZING death seems to act as a wake-up call to Jackie, who pulls a handkerchief from her pocket and runs it over to Jackson. "Press this as hard as you can," she tells him. "It will slow the bleeding."

"Help me get him up!" Penny shouts at Owen. "He has to get to a hospital."

His abdomen is on fire. Breathing is agonizing, let alone walking. Still, he lets them lift him.

"The chopper!" Penny shouts. Then, to Jackie, "Get it started. Dad and I will carry him to it."

Jackson squints at Jackie, who says, "The one good thing he ever did for me was teach me to fly."

Jackie races for the helicopter and Penny and Owen try to move him toward it, but he plants his feet.

"Take me to my car."

"There may not be enough time to drive to a hospital," Owen says.

"I'm not going to a hospital."

This startles Penny and it takes her a minute to recover. "Don't be a dope," she says. "Of course you're going to a hospital."

"Get me to the Jag and give me the key, Penny."

The helicopter's blade now spinning, Jackie runs back to them. "What's going on?"

"He won't go," Penny says.

Jackie gets into his face. "That's crazy. You may or may not bleed out. But even if you don't, you'll die of sepsis if you're not treated."

He turns his face away from his sister, addresses Penny. "Sweetheart, listen to me. It's my time. I'm ready to go. And I'm *going* to go. The only question is where. And my choice" —he looks into the desert beyond— "is to go out there."

Penny shakes her head, locks her wet eyes on him. "Please don't do this."

"Help me into the car, all of you."

They get him to the Jaguar, into the driver's seat. Penny closes the door, and he reaches over, covers her hands with his free hand.

"Forget about me, Penny. Forget you know me. Forget you ever met me."

She shakes her head. "Please . . ."

He wants to say, *Listen to me. We each have something inside of us. Something that wants out. But what's in me is different from what's in you. We're both drawn to violence, but you said it's not the violence you seek, it's justice. Maybe so, but violence is the means your angel employs. Try to hold it back. The violence. Try mercy, Penny.*

But all he can manage is, "Try not to hurt too many people."

She stares at him. Then she nods, opens her fist, lets the key drop into his hand. He takes it, starts the car. He looks around Penny to Owen and Jackie. "Take care of each other," he grits out. Then, for the last time, he looks up at Penny. "Do what you're meant to do. Save the world, honey. Save the world."

He puts the car into gear. The rear tires grab hold of the ground and he races away.

His gut is burning like a furnace fire and he drives without knowing where he's going, without knowing where he is. The miles and minutes blur together as the sky darkens overhead. The full moon plays lead singer to the twinkling stars.

He lets the handkerchief fall away from his wound, which oozes dark red blood onto his shirt, pants, and car seat. The double-yellow line stretches into the dark horizon. Is he going west? South? East? He doesn't know. His brain floats in a fog of pain-numbing endorphins. He is about to slip into darkness when he feels sharp fingernails digging into his thighs. He turns and there she is: Vanessa, her green eyes blazing with mad fury and joy. "Faster," she says. "Faster!"

He hears a sound behind him and spots Donny Franco in the rearview mirror, straining against his belt, trying to reach forward and grab him around his neck. "I'm going to fucking kill you."

He turns back to Vanessa but finds his mother in the passenger seat. "I'm so disappointed in you."

More stirring in the back seat and he glances over his shoulder, sees Jimmy looking away, Pam staring at him, confused. Pam lowers her head into Jimmy's shoulder, and when she lifts it again, she's Jackie, crying in Owen's arms.

A hand covers his on the stick shift and he follows the arm up to find Penny's face. "This time, you did it, Uncle Jackson."

"Did what?"

"You saved me."

He starts to say no, but she's right. He took the bullet to save his niece. His one good deed came, finally, at the end of his life.

His eyes start to water and, when he rubs them, Kimmie sits beside him. "It was always you, Jackson."

He's crying freely now, and the urge to close his eyes, let go, is overwhelming. But there is one more person he must see. She announces herself in his ears, though, not his eyes. "I'm not in pain anymore," she says.

"I'm so sorry."

Helen smiles kindly. "You've made quite a mess of things without me, haven't you?"

"I'm glad you weren't here to see it. Wait! I didn't mean . . ."

"Hush." Helen reaches over, puts her finger to his lips. Then she leans into him. "It's not your fault," she whispers.

"Yes, it—"

"Stop. I had no idea what you were struggling with. You've been a man at war with yourself your whole life. But I had something dark inside, too. Something that had followed me since I was a kid and then, for reasons I still don't understand, reared up and tried to swallow me whole."

"Your seducer . . ."

*　　*　　*

He's back with Helen the morning after she went missing and spent the night in a hotel with someone else.

"Who?" he asks.

She turns to him. "My seducer."

He stares at her, unsure what to say, and they sit in painful silence. Then, with what seems to be great effort, she reaches into the driver's door pocket and pulls out her leather diary. She's had it for years and when he asked her once what was in it, she told him it's where she stored her private thoughts. He took her use of the word "private" as a signal he was not to look at it, and he never did. Now, she opens the diary to a specific page and hands it to him.

My Seducer
Black as squid ink, smooth as velvet,
You come to me, embrace me, kiss my throat,
Wrap yourself around me, a cozy blanket of abnegation,
Promise to replace my pain with the sweet swoon of darkness,
Seduce me with whispered promises of delicious
    self-destruction.

He reads the poem and his eyes fill with tears. "You . . . want to kill yourself?"

"So very badly," she answers. "God help me."

"But last night, you didn't."

"Nor any of the other times." Slowly, she looks up from the diary to him. "When you sat behind me in the bedroom all those times, you thought we were alone, but we weren't. *He* was there, too, trying to persuade me to give myself to him. But you saved me every time. Your words, your touch, your presence, gave me the strength to send him away. But these past few days, something broke inside me. Maybe I was just too tired to fight even one more time. So last night, I decided I wanted to hear only his voice. I wanted to give him what he wanted to take."

She pauses and he finds that he has stopped breathing. He feels his heart pounding in his chest, but he cannot force himself to take in air.

"I took my pills with me, all of them, to the hotel. I emptied the bottles on the desk and sat there in the dark. And he came. He sang to me all night long—about how sweet it would be—the end of all my pain. He said my spirit would float free, and I believed him. I reached for the pills, and there was only one more step to take—lift them to my mouth and swallow. I sat there for hours . . . I lifted the pills, then lowered them. I lifted them again, lowered them again. Every time I went to put them into my mouth, I could sense you behind me, hear your voice, feel your hand on my shoulder. Finally, the sun came up, and I put the pills back into the bottle and left the hotel and drove home."

He is shaking now. His heart pounds inside him. He can barely breathe. He raises his hands to his head and screams. Inside him, a panicked, furious voice roars, "*Get out! Run! Break free!*" He throws open his door and stumbles from the car, out of the garage, where he sinks to his knees. After a while, Helen approaches him, puts her hand on his shoulder.

"I'm so sorry," she says. "I didn't want to tell you how bad it's become. The struggle."

He stands and wraps his arms around her. "You can't leave me," he says quietly into her ear.

And if what you say is true—that you're only still alive because of me—then I can't leave you either. Ever.

"I remember now," he says aloud in the Jag, fighting through the pain of the bullet in his stomach.

He remembers it all now. The following week, he found the boxing gym, rented the trailer. Returned to the violence, the drugs, the women. Because the risk of losing Helen was more than he could bear, and he had to give into his addictions to face it. Needed his insane releases to keep him steady enough to stay with her, protect her as best he could against the dark seducer that was trying to take her from him.

"Do you remember sitting outside our cabin the day I told you I had a surprise for you?"

"Yes . . . You looked so happy. I thought maybe your darkest days were behind you. But . . ." His voice breaks. "I . . . I didn't have the strength . . ."

So he drove to the trailer. And Jackie called Helen, and Helen found him.

"And in the end . . ." He can't complete the sentence.

"In the end, you stayed with me. It was I who left you, remember?"

His eyes fill and he shakes his head. "No. It's still my fault."

Helen smiles. "If that's how you see it, then listen to me. I forgive you."

That's all he needs to hear. He closes his eyes.

"No. There's one more voice you need to hear. And listen to."

He opens his eyes and Helen is gone.

Get out.

Run.

Break free.

He pulls the wheel hard and the car veers to the right, off the road and onto the hardscrabble sand. He bounces against the seat, and the fire in his gut returns. He presses the pedal to the floor and the car accelerates. He grips the wheel with both hands to steady himself, but he collapses over onto the passenger seat. The car strikes a cactus, sideswipes a Joshua tree, and comes to rest.

Get out!

He wakes up and pushes open the door, drops to his hands and knees on the desert floor.

Run!

He pushes himself from the ground, swings one leg in front of the other, stumbles forward.

Run!

He falls again. His strength and will drain from him as he crawls on hands and knees.

Still, he presses on. He sees one hand in front of him, then the other. Both stained with dried blood. The stains seem to darken with every extension of his arms, until his arms and hands are black. A final extension and he can move forward no more. Prone, with one arm in front of him, he feels the last drops of his strength seeping into the ground. He claws at the sand, then goes motionless.

His eyes closed now, his nose sharpens and he takes in the desert smells. The musky, earthy scent of the creosote bush. The peculiar mushroom odor of the Joshua tree. His hearing, too, becomes more acute. He picks up the howl of a coyote, the feet of a curious lizard scuttling up to find out what he is.

A sharp intake of air and his lungs suddenly feel full and strong.

Run!

He opens his eyes and the darkness isn't as dark as he remembered it. He lifts his head, grabs at the sand, pulls himself up. Another deep breath and he starts forward, running, then sprinting.

His heart is strong again, and he feels it hammering inside his chest, pounding with pent-up anger. Fury.

Run!

He runs across the desert floor, muscles firing as his legs flex and extend, flex and extend, in a smooth, even rhythm.

In powerful bursts, his breath blows from his mouth, pushing out the anger, pushing out the fury. Taking in the air.

Run!

He runs and he runs and he runs.

Break free!

His feet dig into the desert floor, grabbing and releasing the rough sand, until, finally, he feels himself lifting from the ground, rising into the starry sky.

Free!

CHAPTER THIRTY-SIX

Rising higher and higher into the night sky, he glances down to see the earth shrinking below him, his past life, his failures, his guilt, getting smaller and smaller. He looks up toward the brilliant moon, takes the thick, cool air into his lungs. He is happy. He is free.

He is moving quickly, air rushing faster and faster against his face. So fast, he's forced to close his eyes against it.

A loud noise stops him, half groan, half growl. The terrible sound and rushing air fight against him, forcing him down, down, down, until he finds himself back on the hard earth, a prisoner of gravity. In pain.

"No," he cries. "No!"

In agony, he rolls onto his back and looks up. The brilliant moon is hidden behind a form towering above him. *What* are *you*?

The thing lowers itself over him, then shakes him, slaps his face.

Another creature approaches him, crouches, and jabs something sharp into his arm.

The first figure slaps his face again, hard.

"Uncle Jackson!"

He focuses on the darkened form. "Penny?"

"Sorry, Uncle Jackson, but I'm not letting you off that easy."

He gets it now. Jackie flew them all here in the helicopter, and now she's treating him. Jackie . . . his sister, pilot, nurse.

"This is a mistake," he says.

"Come on, we have to lift him, get him onto the chopper." Penny's voice again.

Owen and Penny lift him while Jackie holds the IV bag. They carry him to the helicopter and load him on, strap him down.

"Our father had me outfit this thing with all sorts of medical gear," Jackie says. "He figured sooner or later one of his friends would try to kill him, and he might need a quick airlift." She turns and heads for the cockpit, leaving him alone with Penny and Owen.

"This is a mistake," he repeats to Penny, now kneeling beside him. "You know what I am."

"You think you're the only one who's fucked things up? Who spends every day afraid they're *going* to fuck things up?" Penny shakes her head. "I have news for you. The world is full of us. The problem is, it's also full of people who really are fucking everything up but think they walk on water."

"But that's just it, Penny. You have to save the world."

She smiles at him, a tear in her eye. "I am going to save the world, Uncle Jackson. Starting with you."

She looks toward the cockpit, twirls her index finger.

And up they go.

ACKNOWLEDGMENTS

My gratitude begins, as always, with my wife, Lisa, for her support, encouragement, and honesty. We're in this together.

Many thanks to early readers Jill SHS Reiff, Alan Sandman, Rob and Andrea Sinnamon, Naumon and Lauren Amjed, and Greg and Jill Cunningham.

I am deeply grateful to my agent, Cynthia Manson, who found the perfect publisher for *Backstory*. Kudos, of course, to editor Ed Stackler.

To Pam Stack, founder of the *Authors on the Air Global Radio Network*: Pam—your enthusiasm for authors and our art is inspiring.

Special thanks to Bob and Pat Gussin and the whole team at Oceanview. You've built a great publishing house and are a pleasure to work with.

Finally, to everyone who will select and read this book. Your enjoyment is important to me, as is your feedback. I worked hard to craft you a story that would grab you on page one and not let you go until the final passage. I hope I've succeeded. Let me know.

www.williamlmyersjr.com

 @WilliamMyersJr

 WilliamLMyersJr

 @Jr.WilliamMyers